The Questors

The Novices – Book 3

the journey down an unsettled land

by
Jerre Tanner

a publication of

Editions
Aʀᴛ-ᗰusic-Poeᴛʀʏ
Honolulu, Hawai'i

626 Coral Street, Suite 2605
Honolulu, Hawaii 96813-5910
(808) 202.1503

armupo@hawaii.rr.com

CONTENTS

The Story Thus Far

Book 1 ~ the Dispossessed

In 2170, seven young Buddhist novice monks [Brothers Full-of-Life, of-the-Palace, River, Dragon, Autumn, Dutiful and Peace] are the survivors of a world devastated by violent changes in the climate and yet another marauder attack on their monastery. They collect up their dead for cremation and burial while they take stock of their situation. Out of the funeral pyre emerges an elderly lay monk [Elder Lucky] who joins them. The decision is made to abandon their now unlivable monastery and go to the far south of the country to find asylum in another monastery there. They are joined by a lay family [Elder Brother, Lucky Bird, Jade] who have volunteered to help them and by six young children [Smiley, Mischief, Charming, Little Lord, Sweetheart, Baby Helpless] and their caregiver [Sister Rose], survivors from an orphanage also attacked by marauders. On the way to the coast they learn of a possible patron, a last member of the royal family [Lord X]. He proposes they establish their new monastery in an inaccessible but beautiful valley in the northwestern mountains. The most physically fit of the group go on pilgrimage through rugged mountainous terrain to the secluded valley where they find conditions supportive of a possible religious site. There, too, they discover traditional protectors of Buddhist temples, as depicted in temple art, who are actually aliens from other planets, visitors to Earth living among humans for thousands of years. The novice monks enlist their help to save and restore Earth. They are shape-shifter dragons [the Nāga, Princess Nittaya Charoënkul], half-bird soldiers [the Garudas], human-like giants [the Nats], giant bears [the Yaksha, Manjushri the XVI], and little people with big heads [the Kubera]. Then, too, there are strange creatures of pure energy, very frightening [the Nnnnmr]. A plan is laid out to go on crusade the length of the country, carrying a message of hope to the few scattered human survivors. Plans are made to leave the valley and return to the coast.

Book 2 – the Seekers

Brother of-the-Palace has finished his report and inventory on the resources available in the Valley. A meeting of all the consulates of the Interstellar League is planned before the monastics return to Abandoned Island to report to Lord X. Nittaya, head of the Nāgaland Consulate, agrees to organize this event by creating a grand display space in a floating pavilion. The monastics flee the pavilion when it is threatened by a storm raging overhead. High winds and slashing rain bombard the Valley only dissipating the night before their departure, providing a good omen. Brother Full-of-Life shows of-the-Palace six gemstones of great value given him by HRH Manjushri XVI to finance the early stages of their quest. Presenting their reports to Lord X earns his appreciation for and blessing of their ownership of the Valley. After the New Year they move their base to the capitol city where they prepare for ordination and bring on seven lay staff [Fame, Angel, Lily, Virtue, Hero, Bright, Grace] to plan their future tours. They try out the five evenings of plays performed by the boys and Lessons delivered by Full-of-Life in the ruins of the monastery on the lake near their home. Their performances were further polished in presentations at two sites in the capitol city. As a final test, presentations are given at two monasteries outside the capitol city. All are successful. The decision is made to start the country-wide tour, the rest of the monastics going on to the Valley to establish the monastery. A rickety old bus is hired to take the performers on tour the length of the country. They start out excited at the prospect.

"I believe like a child that suffering will be healed and made up for, that all the humiliating absurdity of human contradictions will vanish like a pitiful mirage, like the despicable fabrication of the impotent and infinitely small Euclidean mind of man, that in the world's *finale*, at the moment of eternal harmony, something so precious will come to pass that it will suffice for all hearts, for the comforting of all resentments, for the atonement of all the crimes of humanity, for all the blood that they've shed; that it will make it not only possible to forgive but to justify all that has happened."

— Fyodor Dostoevsky, The Brothers Karamazov

CHAPTER 1

I'd hoped to feel we were flying into an exciting new beginning to our pilgrimage, but the reality of our plight was far different. In our rickety bus we bumped along the highway's ruts and potholes heading out of the capitol city and over the vast flatlands. Only with much tedium did we eventually arrive at our destination. Now a low mountain ridge appeared ahead. Two arms of the ridge flanked us to right and left, directing us ahead to the edge of a large lake. There we turned onto a grand avenue leading us around behind the lake into the center of this enclosed valley. We came upon a massive main gate with its five archways, too solidly built to allow much damage over time. Beyond this imposing landmark we came upon a broad parking lot lakeside and massive ruins on the other. We parked our bus and got out for a better look.

In the hour before dawn four monks approached us there beside the lake, the ominous skeleton of the first temple looming behind them. This structure had been chosen before which we were to play, but there were all kinds of problems with the location. The site originally was designed for people arriving by car, bus, boat, or plane to congregate here and board local conveyances, with knowledgeable guides, on which to be transported to places of interest around the compound.

Immediately beyond this meeting-place was a field of thirty-two pillars with sayings of the Buddha inscribed on them. They were all intact, having little damage. Life and I both thought this would be a better location for our production, with our actors wandering through the pillars as though in a forest, but were resoundingly denied access by our local hosts. Feeling conflict was not the way to begin our residence, we gave in and accepted their site decision. We walked back to the greeting pavilion, looked over the situation and decided on a bit different playing area from that chosen by our hosts. This building had a short flight of steps up to its main floor. We suggested, rather than playing at the foot of the stairs, we would play at the top of the stairs. Our hosts seemed surprised at this suggestion but agreed to it. Life and I walked up and down the length of the building looking for a suitable backdrop for our production but found nothing. All the dramatic backdrops, heaps of wanton destruction, seemed to be located deeper within the building, too far away to be practical. Well, it would just have to do. We finally chose a play area between two massive pillars still holding an equally massive beam overhead. It seemed like a proscenium, providing a frame in which we could play.

Our audience for the most part would be arriving via the lake. Only the monks themselves would come from the opposite direction, via land, their living quarters near the mountains at the far edge of this circumscribed valley. They very kindly provided us with a nice snack which they now spread out for us on the parking pavement in front of the pavilion. We all sat cross-legged nibbling on things, mostly fruits and vegetables. We carried on polite conversations as we ate. Unlike us at our monastery the older monks here survived, being the ones to hide themselves away. The young monks and novices, choosing to take up defense of the temples, were consequently all struck down. Slowly, a feeling rose in me of the character of our hosts—a quiet resignation to a dismal future and death. They all were infected with it.

And I could see how it came about they had these feelings. This place, born just before the Great Turn, was built on a monumental scale, the largest religious site in a world filled with large religious sites, with money from a government not usually supportive of religion of any kind. Here vast hoards flocked to receive spiritual blessings before three gigantic Buddhas, goldleaf covering their surfaces, goldleaf covering the pillars and walls, goldleaf everywhere! Disaster fell like vengeance upon the area—storms sweeping across the waters, fires raging through fields and forests, marauders with weapons in hand. After the grizzly task of slashing and tearing flesh, they turned their weapons to the goldleaf. Scraping away, defacing the buildings, defiling the Buddhas, they collected little gold but succeeded in vandalizing all that former glory.

And then they set the fires, cunningly placed to wreck the most havoc. In the conflagration the high wooden ceilings of the three main temples set raging into the sky. That of the great fourth temple collapsed on the Buddhas, its massive beams knocking them to the floor. The effigies, now lying on their sides, were engulfed in heat. They melted—not much, just a little—rendering their sublime faces distorted and grotesque, their exquisite hands in holy gesture, now obscene in suggestion. Thus was the spiritual defiled. And so the

Buddhas remained, and would remain unless salvaged by a returning civilization. Our new friends here had little hope for that happening in their lifetimes. My heart wept for them, but I hoped we would be the start of a change of heart for these deserving people.

By now the sun was sending its rays across the heavens, already warming the earth. We pulled down our tents from the bus and erected them in the shadow of the temple, the only shelter nearby. Our new friends helped us, as much as they could; and then we parted company for the day. Our valiant little troupe settled down on our mats, hoping for a good day's sleep. Alas, as the scorching sun advanced across the sky, we fried in our skin, not having adequate protection from the heat from the sky above amplified by the heat rising from the pavement below. We clearly must find a better place to camp than this. At last! Twilight rescued us, although the desire was to lie back on our mat to catch the sleep that had evaded us during the day. But duty summoned us, and we arose most reluctantly, especially the boys who had fussed all day against the elements. Fires were struck, using charcoal from the building beside us, and we slowly revived over our porridge and tea. Normally the boys would be restless, wanting to run off exploring, but this evening they were barely more than listless. I gathered the three of them in the first night's play, helping them to walk through the play in their minds imagining everything they would do—expression, position in the play area, gestures, *et cetera*. It was slow going. They half asleep, would they put our audience asleep, too? That would be a disaster for our first night in the series.

The time for the performance approached, and our audience came in boats from one side and in procession the monks from the other, all sitting cross-legged on the still hot pavement. The crescent moon, in its last phase, would soon sink behind the mountain setting; but the sky shone with myriad stars, the Milky Way sweeping from horizon to horizon just behind our backdrop of scorched pillars and beams. On signal, the spots came on suddenly, illuminating these scars on our proscenium, the audience making an audible gasp. Fame raised his paper megaphone and barkered into it all the audience needed to know beforehand. Then silence. Smiley and Little Lord entered, taking their place center stage—Smiley on his knees beseechingly and Little Lord standing beside him, arm raised above as though to strike. They held the pose a moment longer than usual, but here dramatic and powerful. Then Little Lord began his speech, "You are horrid ...," over-acting way beyond his usual excess. In despair, I lowered my head into my hands, expecting failure. Instead, the audience was immediately astir, muffled cries of protest emerging from them. Smiley surprisingly matched in pathos his protests of innocence for ravishing the Earth, taking the audience with him, they giving cries of commiseration to his speeches. The knot of the drama pulled tight, Smiley collapses on the floor, Little Lord's arm again raised to strike, the moment held once more a bit too long. I feared Sweetheart, as redeeming angel, had missed his cue, but then I heard the stir from the audience, with loud cries of protest. And then Sweetheart sweeps onstage, causing a surprised pause, then cheers. When calmed, Sweetheart delivers his "I believe ..." speech. As never before, this audience is completely silent throughout the monologue, only at the end declaring their approval with applause and cheers. The rest of the performance becomes anticlimactic as Little Lord begs forgiveness from the now standing Smiley and they end in an embrace of accord, Sweetheart looming over in benediction, the audience arisen themselves in cheers and noisy applause. I heave a great sigh of relief.

Now it is Life's turn. The spots come up on him standing by the lectern. He opens what appears to be a large book and begins reading. "We are living through the most terrible times ..." and on through the litany of the calamities of the last century. As he goes on, moans are heard, then cries and here and there weeping. This lesson always raises emotional reactions from audiences, but this perhaps the most. Comes now the transition, "I believe in the inherent goodness of Human Beings ..." and his call to have hope in the future. At first there are calls of protest, but as Life goes on more accord is heard until the end when the audience again rises to its feet in cheers and applause. Then Fame appears before the spots, interrupts the applause to announce the series of four more plays and lessons for the coming nights and invites the audience to return. He gets a hearty response. Then the audience comes forward in waves to greet our players and talk over the issues raised. The boys are deluged; I rush to help them. Making my way through the press, mostly of women, I come upon three beaming little boys being their charming best. So many hugs and kisses! I fear they shall be warped for life. In turn, I soon find myself encircled by monks, all asking if I, too, share the belief in the goodness of Mankind. When I answer "yes" there is considerable consternation. I say to them, "Wait! After the fifth night you will understand all." Still, there are many questions; I answer them best as I could.

After most depart, an old wizened hermetic stands solitary before me. He takes my hand in both of his saying, "My son, as one ages, the hardest belief to hold is Faith. Everything in this life seems calculated to sweep Faith away, and without Faith there is no Hope. As you age, remember this. Remember this, and fight it!" He pressed my hand tightly. Deeply touched, all I could muster was a vapid, "Oh, yes, I know," while squeezing his hand in return. So often in my life since then have I thought of his warning, seen his face, looked again into his haunted eyes.

So distracted was I by this person that I forgot to ask these monks if there were a more sheltered place during the day where we could spread our sleeping mats. Fortunately, there were cooler heads than mine, and in no time we were led off to be shown such a place. It was a good walk from the gathering pagoda to the location, but that did not concern us. We ascended flights of stairs at the edge of the compound until we were beside the second temple. There, they took us to the side of these stairs where underneath was a large storage room. We saw plenty of space for our little troupe, in company with ordered assemblies of strange and familiar tools looking like they had not been touched for eons. As our hosts turned toward the mountain to return to their haunts, we turned in the opposite direction to fetch our things from the meeting pavilion. To a person, we were all very tired, having slept only fitfully the day before. Once we returned back under the stairs we stretched out on our mats and were soon asleep even though it was still several hours before dawn.

That evening, as the sinking sun shot its rays in colors heavenward from in hiding beyond rows of craggy mountains, we rose much refreshed. I corralled the four boys of the second night play for a run-through. It was a bit rough, but I was confident they would do much better in front of the audience. We walked past the pavilion to the lakeside where we all splashed our faces in the crystalline waters, washing away the sleep from our eyes. Much refreshed, we turned our attention to the play area, correcting placement of the spots and bringing picturesque debris to arrange at its edges. Fame suggested we might turn two of the spots to shine up into the sky over the lake as a beacon to our audience arriving via the waters. What surprised us this night was the numbers arriving from the road, most walking but some in variously contrived vehicles. I helped the boys get into their tunic costumes and apply their makeup, toning down a bit their extravagant tendencies. Soon enough, we were ready for the evening's performance.

This night, Fame gave his little before-performance speech of welcome, announcing further performances the coming three nights. I did a quick assessment of the audience and was pleased to see a good seventy-five people sitting cross-legged on the pavement, many bringing mats to soften rough surfaces. Again monks were well represented.

"I'm alone. / I'm all alone." Cried out Little Lord, wringing his hands and turning his head all around. And we were off, the audience more demonstrative than the night before. I find it so curious how audiences in our time give in to their instincts to shout words of warning, advice, or encouragement to the actors. I would have sat there passively and let the drama unfold as it would, not in need of anything from me. Instead, they jump up, gesture wildly and shout at the actors. I'm told unsophisticated audiences will believe the actions onstage are 'real' as opposed to artifice, the feeling being the actors might listen to their advice and thereby avoid the obvious oncoming disaster. Our boys don't seem to mind this and go on without paying any attention to them.

After the play, with Smiley leading the other three boys off with shouts of approval from this audience, Life makes his appearance in his all-white habit and recounts the list of disasters that have befallen our Mother Earth and the life she nurtures. Then he makes the proposal for the formation of communities, and the benefits to obtain, ending with the suggestion child-rearing could begin again, with wildly divergent reactions, weeping being among the most common. It is over and the boys enter to join Life in bows, the audience rushing forward, even the world-weary monks among them. They ask, "Is it really time to do these things?" and we respond with "Yes." They seem amazed.

And so on, with the third night vows to forsake war and purge the soul of negative/destructive feeling, the audience vigorously joining in; the fourth night the announcement of the formation of our monastery and university in the Valley as catalysts of progress and change; the fifth and final night with the announcement of aliens, traditional defenders of the temples, to help in the restoration of our Earth. People always seem skeptical about the aliens but manage to accept symbolic protectors of the temple, as in sculpture and painting, now being broadened to include our establishment. I look forward to the time we will have several aliens traveling with us, revealing their presence this last night. What theatre that will make!

After the final performance we are invited to a 'banquet' hosted by our fellow monks. We walk with them to their quarters next to the mountain range and partake in their humble fare, now garnished to appear festive. I bless them for the efforts they have gone to. We monks and novices of the Valley extend invitations to these wise practitioners to visit the Valley, share their knowledge, and learn a thing or two while there. We have a good time, not forgetting to thank our hosts for permitting our performances. At the very end we accompany them to their temple of prayer, in sorry state, to join with them in devotion, signaling the unity of our professions and our brotherhood. We walk, unaccompanied, to our dormitory under-the-stairs where we spend our final day here at this place. Come evening we pack up everything, say our farewells to our brethren here, put all our things in place on the bus, and head out to our caravan *rendezvous* point going to the coast where our next performances are to take place.

CHAPTER 2

We were to have met a caravan going to our coastal city destination, but we are early at the *rendezvous* place and discover the caravan is running late. Our management come to me for a decision—should we wait here or head out on our own? I do not care for waiting, so I settle on striking out without the caravan's protection. We drive on, keeping an eye out for possible places to camp for the day. We are crossing a broad river valley floor, after all, and there seem to be no sheltering hills to protect us from the sun's harsh rays. We drive on. Then we see ahead a bridge. We stop before crossing to make sure it is passable. It is then we discover a nice piece of land under the bridge, beside the flowing river. Perfect! We park the bus and unload our gear, pitching our tents in the shade, beside the cooling waters. We have a simple meal and settle down for the approaching day.

I think I fell asleep almost immediately. But then I had an unsettling dream in which I had this feeling I was not alone. The scary thing was I've had this feeling before. Where? In the Valley. Yes, for sure. In the Valley. I awoke with a start. Yet the feeling of a presence did not leave me. I sat up, squinting in the harsh light, trying to see if anyone were actually around. I see nothing. I mean, I saw no one. I scanned the surroundings. No one. The feeling of a presence had become stronger than before. That feeling. When have I had it before? Then, in a flash, it came to me: the Nnnnmr! That morning, in my quarters, while working on the report. I remembered the light dimming, and then he appeared. Why isn't the light dimming here? Maybe it is, the light being very bright to begin with.

"I know you're here. Be polite, and show yourself," I demanded.

Expecting one figure, I was startled to see six figures emerge in the glare. Shivers ran up and down my spine.

"I am sorry to have disturbed you," said the nearest figure, apparently the leader, smiling inappropriately.

"Why are you here? Are you following me?"

"Again, I must apologize for disturbing you. That was not our intention," he said, being too ingratiating.

"Well, what was your intention?"

"You have chosen a dangerous place to sleep. We are here to protect you," his smile completely unbelievable.

"Then you have been following me. Why are you doing that?" I demanded, fighting the rise of anger within.

"No, we are not following you. I apologize for upsetting you," he said. I was not convinced.

"But you must be, otherwise how would you know where we had parked? Please give me an answer to this question," I barked, failing to keep emotions under control.

"You are a valuable person. There are other valuable persons here. Danger must not find you," his face smiling too broadly for the expression of such noble sentiments.

"Does Manjushri know you are here? Or Nittaya? I suspect not," I countered, knowing full well this was a clandestine operation.

"We are here to protect you. That is all." With that, he suddenly stopped smiling and presented a stern visage, equally disturbing.

"You must stop! Go back to the Valley, or wherever you are stationed. I don't want you here. I don't need you here. If you continue, I shall report you to the League."

"We are here to protect you. You are in danger here. You ..." He suddenly broke off. He, and the other five figures, a most curious expression on their faces, suddenly became transparent and faded rapidly away. Even the creepy feeling they gave me faded with them. And then they were gone. Completely gone. I sat there, not believing what just happened. Surely I dreamed this, it never could have happened. The implications of their presence here are vast, a major diplomatic blunder they could not, would not, have made. Therefore I must have dreamt it. But should I tell Life about it? I hate to bother him if it's just a dream.

And, so, I spent the rest of the day turning in indecision. Was it a dream? Or not.

At dusk, everyone aroused, collected for prayers and then porridge and tea. A scouting team declared the bridge passable. We were soon on our way, leaving that haunted place behind, and I still hadn't made up my mind about telling Life.

It was the middle of the night. Clouds obscured the nocturnal sky, throwing us into profound darkness. The driver and I were at that moment discussing whether the spots might be brought forward to help illuminate the road when we were hit with torrential rains. Suddenly the road was no longer visible, and we had to stop. "For sure," said the driver, "we're now going to need those spots more than ever." I sent several able hands to the back of the bus to retrieve a pair. Moments later we had them in hand, wondering how to arrange them so they would work. We couldn't mount them outside without the rain putting out their wicks. Deploying them inside the bus only produced a sheen across the glass windshield rendering it impossible to see through. The sheen disappeared if we put the spots flush on the glass, but the beams of light shot ahead some two meters above the road, being no help at all. Someone had the idea to shine the spots out of the first of the side windows on either side, pointing the beams forward onto the road. This worked only partially, a large shadow from the hood of the bus obscuring the road directly in front. Still, it was better than nothing. On we went at a much-reduced speed.

We had gone no more than ten kilometers when several people in apparent distress came into view ahead by the side of the road. They frantically waved to us to stop, which we did, of course. The driver pulled up next to them and opened the door. Three young males rushed into the bus, up the steps, and positioned themselves equidistant along the isle between the seats. They pulled dangerous looking knives from their clothing, shouting threats at us. We were all quite shocked at this sudden turn of events. We realized, then, they were ordering us to leave the bus. Panic gripped us all. Well, not all. Life rose from his seat and, with great calm, raised his hands for everyone to be quiet.

"My friends," he began, "as you can see, we have children here. It is not good for them to be out in this bad weather. Perhaps it's possible to work out a compromise. We would be happy to take you to shelter in some nearby village, or wherever you would want."

Without pause he continued, "As you can see, we are a religious order. We are on an important humanitarian mission, blessed by the highest sacred powers. Should we be delayed in our mission, bad luck would fall on those who caused the delay. You would not want that to happen. Instead, you would have our blessing if you were to join us as we travel eastward, toward the coast." It was now the three youths were thrown into confusion. Clearly, they did not want bad luck to come their way. Nor were they expecting a hospitable offer to join us.

"You do not need to threaten us with your knives," added Life disarmingly. "You can put them away," he suggested. And, sure enough, the three put their knives back in their clothes.

"Here, make room for our guests to sit down," Life said to the boys who instantly gave up their seats, finding room elsewhere in the bus. Our three new guests sat in stunned silence. "Drive on," said Life to the bus driver. The door closed in a sibilant rush as the vehicle started forward.

Life sat down next to our guests and started up a conversation. "Are you hungry? Would you like something to eat?" They nodded in assent. Life whispered an instruction to Autumn who happened to be sitting next to him. Autumn quickly moved to the back of the bus in search of something to bring them. Life continued, "How did you come by the side of the road back there? It seems an unfriendly place to be." Before they could do more than nod and grunt some kind of affirmation, Life moved on. "It looks like you've had a hard time lately. Things have not gone well for you, huh? Have you thought of joining a religious order? There will always be a place for you there. You will be able to do good works and earn many blessings on your spirit."

Then, before they had a chance to be on guard, Life changed the subject. "Someone sent you to meet us along the road, didn't they?" One of the youths nodded in the affirmative, the other two looking confused. "It was the big man in the royal palace, wasn't it?" Life pried. This time two of the youths nodded "yes."

With perfect timing, Autumn returned carrying a large food box which Life opened and offered to the youths. They reached with eager hands, soon filling mouths with Lucky Bird's finest efforts. Soon, the transformation was complete. In place of three desperate youths, there were chatty guys letting slip their secrets.

It seems, rather than the royal usurper, these three youths were under control of a local hooligan who had been tipped off by an attendee of our recent theatricals. Suspecting we were potential trouble he thought to waylay us, perhaps thereby earning rewards from higherups. The three boys sent to do the job were not equal to the task.

And here they were, having the best of times with us. We learned their names [Farmer, Loyal and Soldier] and heard their life's stories, tragic as tragic could be, well known by all members of our generation—orphaned at an early age, surviving by a miracle, desperately hanging on to whatever foundation had come their way. Clearly, they needed to be rescued.

"Come with us to the coast. I'm sure we can find a good prospect for you there. Or you could go with us on our pilgrimage down the coast if you want to look for something farther away. Maybe you would even consider becoming a novice to our order?" Life summed up, the rest of us raising eyebrows at his last suggestion. Only later did I realize Life had taken on two new roles—that of 'Savior of Lost Spirits', and that of 'Recruiter of Novices' for the monastery, both of which he was to apply with increasing fervor.

Having eaten their fill Farmer, Loyal and Soldier were soon nodding off to sleep. "Now!" Dragon whispered to Life. Let's quickly tie them up and take their knives."

"No need," whispered back Life. "They have already been disarmed and are no longer a threat to us. I ask you. I ask you all, to befriend these boys. By mischance, they have fallen in with the wrong people but now have a chance to correct that mistake. They, as all people, are worthy of being saved. Show your compassion to these unfortunates. And remember you, but for Saving Grace, could be walking in their footsteps."

The truth of Life's statement could not be defaulted by any one of us. Silence fell like a comforting embrace on us all as we thought over what he had said.

And, so, our humble vehicle lumbered on through the darkness toward our goal on the coast. Taking to heart Life's words, as our three guests awoke from their slumbers, we cheerfully went about introducing ourselves to them, offering up our friendship. We, of course, had immediate concerns for where we shall find shelter to park for the day; and they, being intimately familiar with the lay of the land hereabouts, had several suggestions.

The place all three recommended most highly was ahead a few kilometers. The area of the river valley we were passing through had been highly industrialized before the Change. They suggested we sequester ourselves away in a particular warehouse offering two solid walls and a roof as shelter against both sun and rain. No one would think to look for us there, they said. Trusting them, we went to the place and parked. It was still raining when we went to sleep. When we woke up the sun had come out making the air heavy with humidity. After evening prayer and breakfast we took our seats on the bus and headed toward the range of mountains forming the northeastern part of our country where the broad river valley came to an end.

Our next performance site was in this mountain range, about sixty kilometers from the coast. It was an important historic site, Hero and Bright told us, receiving only minor damage from fires that decimated the forests around the temples. Because the area is constantly engulfed in mists, these pine and bamboo forests have substantially grown back. It is a considerable drive from the valley floor high up the mountain side with the road nearly washed out in several places. The site is unique in that a resort in the style of a monastery was built near the ancient historic site approximately one hundred fifty years ago. The resort was abandoned at the time of the Great Change, with the monks incorporating the buildings into religious use. We are to stay at the former resort and deliver our performances inside, in one of the public rooms, since heavy mists and rain occur frequently outdoors. Our audience shall be exclusively the monks and nuns in residence, approximately twenty-five people, the site being too far and too hazardous for villagers to attend. We have been instructed to reduce the number of nights for performances from five to two. I felt this was a great hardship for our young actors and an affront; but Life felt it was an intriguing experiment, that the boys would do fine.

We were met by three monks at the resort gates and ushered to our rooms where we refreshed ourselves and then went to a temple for morning prayers and afterwards to a dining hall for a light meal prior to turning in for the day. Farmer, Loyal, and Soldier were stunned by our accommodations, never before having a room of their own. Equally intimidated by the ritual and setting for our prayers, they could do little more than gaze around open-mouthed at the splendor of the hall and the gilded Buddha sculpture before whom we prayed. Then on to supper where they were startled at the quality of the food they were given. I heard them later questioning Autumn.

"Is this the kind of food you get to eat?" and his answering back, "Yes, usually." That wasn't quite the truth, and I smiled at Autumn's exaggeration.

That evening we returned to the hall for prayers. I observed our young guests were now acclimatized enough to bow during prayers. Our breakfast of porridge and tea was also impressive to them. I asked how they slept, and they answered, "Good," with affirmative nods of the heads. I got no better answer from them than this.

After eating we were met by our three hosts who took us to the public room so that we could strategize our performance setup. At one end of the room was a large raised dais on which we could perform. The elevation of the stage would not be a problem for our little audience since they would be sitting on chairs. Portable steps were brought, allowing our actors to make entrances and exits from the sides. Three spots would be enough to illuminate this playing area. Any more would be blinding. Our performances would begin the following night doing the first three plays/lessons ending with the vow-taking, with a break between plays of at least an hour. That should provide a dramatic ending to the first night. The second night would be the two remaining plays. Our hosts then took us along the road to the site of the old monastery where we were given a tour. Again, our three young ex-thugs were much impressed with what they saw, being reduced to intimidated silence. Afterwards, I asked Loyal what he thought, his reply being, "Is this the way monks live?" to which I replied, "Yes, for the most part." He nodded, appearing thoughtful. We returned to our quarters, said morning prayers and, having eaten our little supper, settled down before dawn for the day.

That evening, rising at dusk, we participated in evening prayers again and breakfast, going to the public room to get ready to perform. Soon enough our little audience filed in and took their place on the chairs. This would be the first chance Farmer, Loyal, and Soldier would have to see our plays, and I was curious how they would react, perhaps more so than reaction of the monastics. Well, it was all very interesting. The monks and nuns responded much as our audience at the university in the capitol city—silence throughout the performance, polite applause at the end. The three youths, on the other hand, sat rapt, engrossed in the drama, wanting to react but constrained by the silence of the dominant audience. Then, after Life's declaration of faith and the first of the performances was over, they came forward. Too shy to speak to Life himself, they came over to speak with me, all declaring Life to be a great holy man. Soldier said to me, "I see now what you are doing, and there's no trouble there, not like what my boss said. Yeah, it's all good."

"I'm glad to hear you think so," I answered. "This is just the beginning. There's much more."

I checked out how Smiley, Little Lord, and Sweetheart were doing, and they did not seem the least bit fatigued. I suggested they lie down on the floor and rest before the next performance, which they did. For all of five minutes. Then they were chasing each other around the room. Our hosts were serving hot tea at the other end of the room. I collected up the boys and took them over for some, thinking this would be a way to get them to sit quietly while they drank it.

Soon enough it was time for the next play, the one on forming into communities. It ran much as the first, the monks and nuns silent with polite applause at the end of play and lesson, the three youths suppressing their reactions as best they could. Afterwards, we were served the midnight meal and then another rest period. I was certain at least a few of the monks would come over to comment on the 'communities' concept, how the monastery was a natural community, but no one did. And the mention of children … no reaction to that, either. Was this monastic community so involuted they could not be touched? Or just smugly satisfied? I was beginning to think perhaps the latter. Meanwhile, our three youths were significantly stirred and full of questions. We were a community, weren't we? Were we going to get married and have children? How could being in a community help with raising children? And so on. Good questions. But even more was coming in the next play, the taking of the vow to forbid war and negative feelings. I was curious, too, how my fellow monks and nuns would react to taking the vows. I would soon see. The third play drew the same dearth of reaction, as before, save for polite applause at the end. Then Life stepped forward to deliver the third lesson. His performance was especially dramatic, rising to a real peak as he said the vow. Then, raising his arms to the audience, and telling them to rise and say the vow with him, in an instant every single person was on their feet lustily saying the vow after him, several even holding their hands over their heart. And, at last, vigorous applause. They, too, had been touched! Now nearly everyone in the audience came forward, eager to talk.

Right away, Life was confronted. "What is the difference between rage and anger?" "Why did you leave out anger from your list?" And Life's response, "Rage is an extreme, reason not being in control. It is destructive and swift. Anger, on the other hand, can be a creative feeling when controlled. Anger comes from within, welling to the surface, always shaped by the will. With the introspective mind, anger teaches, a means to improve the spirit."

Then, "War is ingrained in Humanity. How can we, as individuals, hope to put an end to it?" Life's answer, "War begins with the individual, then becomes collective. One puts an end to warfare by declaring its obsolescence as an individual, then as a community, and finally as a nation. But it begins with you and me, my friend." Our three former warriors take this very much to heart, Soldier saying, "I see now how you are a threat to my people. Without warfare they have no function, no purpose." Life answering, "Without warfare we all have a function, a purpose—to promote peace. Peace is easier to administer by winning over the hearts of others to join with one willingly. Otherwise, there is always resistance in warfare, force being necessary to bend others to the will. Peace is the way of the future." They nod, not so much in agreement, I think, as in recognition of the logic of the statement.

The night ended, as before, with prayer and a simple meal. I was curious to see if our youthful warriors would still bend the back during prayer; and, sure enough, they did. I rejoiced just within myself. Life was right to think of saving their souls, much against the collective thinking of the rest of us, as there was obvious fertile ground here.

The following night arrived, we beginning our play later than the previous evening. I had no idea how the monastic audience would react to its message and was anticipating it with some trepidation. Sure enough, it came after Life's lesson had concluded. "Why form a new monastery. You are welcome to join us in reaching your goals. After all, there is much room for expansion here. And we are not so far from people as is your valley." They had a point, of course, except for the alien consulates being established in the Valley. That point would be revealed in the final play and lesson, being presented after our midnight meal. All I could say was, "Wait. There is a further explanation in the final play and lesson." They looked at me with raised eyebrow.

More than ever, this night, I wished for a few aliens traveling with us to come forward and reveal themselves. What could be more dramatic than having, say, a Nāga in human form, looking like any one of us, metamorphose into his natural form, all teeth and slashing tail, looking ever so much like myriad sculptures even at this holy site, to confirm the point. When Life was finished and the audience coming forward, the monastics, their faces pinched in jealousy, saying, "Why you. Here are we, centuries old, long since proven, more worthy." They had a point. I, having a narrow vision, could not give an argument to them why we were chosen. One would have to ask this of the aliens themselves. And they were not here to answer, even if they deigned. Thus did we sustain the assault, determining—us, singly, then as a group—to leave this place the following night.

On the other hand, our trio of former attackers, now more than ever won over, came up to us, eyes bulging wide, saying, "Aliens! What do they look like? Scary, eh?" We, being as direct as possible, referred them to the artwork around temples depicting the images of protectors in evidence on and before the walls. There! That is how they looked. "Wow!" they said in awe.

Later, as we carried boxes of costumes to the bus, Loyal linked his arm into mine and walked with me, silent. So I said to him, "Now you have seen all the plays, listened to all the lessons. Tell me, what do you think?"

He answered, "I think you guys are great. Thanks for taking us in." That was about all that I was going to get from him.

That day we slept well in our solitary rooms, rising in time to see the sun set, say prayers in the splendid temple, and enjoy our final meal. Having expressed our thanks to the abbot for hosting us, he being more austere than ever, we took our leave of the place and descended down out of the mountain retreat. Meeting the road at the foot of the mountain, we turned left and happily wended our way toward the sea.

With the mountains on our left and the valley of the capitol city on our right we drove through the night toward the northern gulf which our country shared with the great power to the north, still one more night away. Our ideal shelter in this area would be a cave, almost impossible to spot in the shadow of the night. Instead, we came upon the ruins of a stone homestead, holding out promise. Pulling the bus in behind the buildings, we struck our tents with enough time left over for supper and morning prayers. Much to our surprise our three new friends joined us elbow to elbow on the prayer mats, doing the sets of three deep bows but not the singing of the prayers which, of course, they did not know. That evening they joined us again for evening prayers, then porridge and tea, and out again on the road.

Our destination was the northern most port at the foot of the mountain range. In its day it was famous for commerce with the great country to the north with which we shared the vast northern gulf. Consequently, the port supported much luxury and high living. In anticipation of ocean inundation the last high rises to go up were built on stout cement pillars. People lived there for a while until the coming of the violent storms out of the east, across the water. These storms hollowed out the apartments, clearing them of furniture and people. Afterwards no one had the heart to live there. So the buildings stood like tall, lean white ghosts, awaiting their final fate—collapse into the waters below.

The port was famous for another feature. It was known as the Bay of Two Thousand Islands. With ocean inundation the number in this title was reduced by maybe a thousand, those remaining no less spectacular for the fact. Formed from limestone, they took the characteristic gumdrop shape, including near vertical sides. Where forests had grown on their summits now they are bare save for a hybrid vine that plunges over the precipitate edges, looking like long thin strands of wispy hair on an otherwise bald pate. The view took one's breath away. Without doubt, here was one of the most beautiful places on our precious Mother Earth.

The city, built on the lowlands on either side of the delta formed by our great northern river, was now mostly under water with a flat-topped ridge to the east at the very mouth of the river. Tying the two parts of the city together, west and east, was a grand bridge sporting two tall towers still raised above the tides, awakening a desire to cross it even though access on either side was under water. The ridge, the first of a legion of islands extending into the gulf, sported a giant Ferris wheel, now twisted and bent all out of shape by high winds and storms. On the opposite end of this promontory was a Christian church, safely above the waters, whose pastor strenuously lobbied Hero and Bright to be the place for our performances in the port city. It seemed a difficult location to our DPI people, nearly all our potential audience having to come by boat, plus it was not Buddhist; yet the pastor was unrelenting. At several other of our sites people have had to come by boat, so our people rationalized. And it IS a religious site. So why not! And they agreed.

Now here we were, in our bus, looking out over waters of the bay to the island where we were to perform. It seemed an impassable gulf between the two places. Then we were met by a pleasant middle-aged man who led us to boats that conveyed us to the island-ridge, practically to the front of the church. And there we were, looking westward, back at the mountain which now seemed very far away indeed. We were met by that persuasive pastor, or rather priest, who proved to be a kind and generous person making our stay there a most pleasant one. He had organized a crew of people to husband our stay. They pitched our tents for us, in a most satisfactory location, and provided for all our food needs. They even arranged for fuel for the bus which was delivered while we were at the church. A performance area was set up in front of the church, a regal façade with tall arching wooden doors in the center, circular windows above, ending with a tall steeple with cross on top. Entrances and exits would have to be through the central doors behind. We could play with movement of the spots, dramatically illuminating parts of the façade, even lighting up the tall steeple. What fun! Our gracious host was not concerned with our adhering to our Monday to Friday schedule. He said we could start any day so long as we did not perform on a Sunday – their Sabbath. We agreed to start on Tuesday and end on Saturday.

A most felicitous discovery was made. The actors' voices were magically amplified, projecting strongly to the water's edge and beyond. Consequently, people could remain on their boats if they wanted and still hear dialogue clearly. River suggested this might be the result of the broad expanse of the church wall in relation to the close body of water, which was as good an explanation for the phenomenon as anyone could hope for.

Tuesday arrived, we all prepared for the performance. Midnight rolled around, and so did our audience. I was told the majority would be Christian with a sprinkle of other denominations from the interested community. Whatever I was expecting, I was interested to look over the faces of the audience ... and discovered there the faces of my countrywomen and men. Even, here and there, a child-in-arms, looking wide-eyed. I was curious, too, how these Christians would react to our Buddhist-weighed script. I got my answer soon enough.

The high steeple was illuminated by three spots. Fame began with his opening speech about the five plays etc., inviting the audience up after performances to meet the actors. Then spots off, save for one remaining on the steeple. Then one spot up on Smiley and Little Lord. From then on the audience was like any of our audiences, indistinguishable, human. Afterwards, they rushed forward, many with tears lining their faces, moved by the strong declaration of belief.

They, too, want to believe! We tell them, "Believe!" and they look back at us, startled. But the germ of an idea is planted, most firmly planted. And they carry it off to their homes.

The second night the idea of forming into communities—the same reaction. But I see them casting furtive glances around, as though sizing up others in the audience. Afterwards, they surge forward, their faces not lined in tears now but shining, shining with new possibilities, a birth of hope. I see it in their faces. I think of that old monk who squeezed my hands and spoke of Faith. And Hope. Our pastor/host came up to us after everyone had left, his face radiating joy. "I hoped," he said. "I hoped this is what you would offer us. And you have! My deepest thanks." Looking into his face I saw he would pick up the message and carry it forward with his congregation. I went to Hero and Bright and thanked them for their wise decision. I think they were gratified, at least a bit.

The third, vow-taking, night arrived with me feeling certain how this audience would react when it came time to stand and take the vow. They would do so with considerable gusto. The boys did their part with a flair, Life coming forward and taking over. I must say, Life did not deliver the lead-up to the vow with as much high theatre delivery as he had elsewhere, but I didn't expect his delivery to have much effect on the audience. Yet, when the time came for the audience to rise and take the vow, there were a number in the audience that remained seated and did not say the vow, a look of confusion and conflict on their faces. After the performance was over several came forward to express worries. It seems, in their services they regularly declare a belief in their faith and were concerned on this occasion there might be a conflict with Life's vow. They felt, however lofty the sentiment, they would need to 'clear' the vow-taking with the priest before they would feel free to take any action. The priest, not exactly surprised at this reaction, said, "Had I known the content of the vow I would have announced my approval of it beforehand. If you would kindly give me a copy of it I will take it up with my congregation this coming Sabbath. A worthy undertaking, it has merit and presents food for thought. I foresee no problems." Most curious.

The next two nights went as expected, with the announcement of aliens among us causing an especial stir. Of course, people came forward wanting to know who among us were aliens. That did it! I went to Hero and Bright, telling them to do whatever it took to get us a couple of aliens to be on show, maybe those two Nāgas who went with our latest installment payment to Lord X. They would be perfect. For some reason Hero and Bright were reluctant to do this. So I told them if they didn't, I would write Nittaya asking her to send us several persons. They liked that idea even less. Racking my brain for ideas, I came up with a concept I thought was rather creative. Farmer and Sailor were both well-muscled young men, and with some creative makeup might be made to look like Nāganese in human form. I would school them in how to move and talk, adding the right touch of verisimilitude. Hero and Bright liked that idea much more, and so it was decided. I looked out over the accumulation of people and saw our three new friends standing near the illuminated church façade. I went directly over to them and made the proposal to Farmer and Soldier.

Loyal spoke up, "We were just now talking over an idea we had. We would like to learn the lines to the first play. You know, the one with just three characters. Just out of fun. We think we could give it a different twist. At least, we'd like to try."

Doing some quick mental gymnastics, I proposed a counter-plan. "I'd like to make you an even better offer. I'd be happy to work with you to learn the lines and set the action for onstage, if you will agree to do another kind of acting job, especially you and you," pointing to Farmer and Sailor.

"Okay. Sure. What kind of acting job is it?" They asked.

"Since you two fit the physical type, I'd like for you to dress up and act like two Nāga guards so that people will believe it's true when we talk about having aliens around. So! What do you think?"

They looked at each other, surprised. "I don't know." "Yeah, maybe." "What do we have to do?"

"Just stand there looking fierce," I said.

They looked at each other again and shrugged. "Yeah, we can do that."

"Great! Then it's decided. We'll work together on the first play and on making you two into our Nāga guards. Shake!" and we shook hands all around.

Rather than leaving the island the next evening it had been decided we would sit in on the priest's Catholic service. He had invited us to join them, and besides, it would be a good learning experience for us. For me, the most outstanding aspect of his service was the music. There were four singers, sounding well trained, singing music of a highly complex texture. If angels sang together this might be what they would sound like. His lesson, he called it a homily, was on the subject of the vow of the third evening which he read and then discussed point by point, doing a rather good job I thought. The only point on which there was any dissension was to whom the vow should be made, God the Father or Mother Earth. Interesting. We Buddhists don't have a 'God the Father,' or any being remotely like that. I guess its immaterial to whom one makes a vow, just so long as one feels bound to the core of one's being to fulfill the commitment.

After the service we said our farewells and thanks to the priest, boarded our boats and were rowed back to our bus parked by the side of the mountain. To our driver's great delight, there was a large metal barrel standing by the bus door. More fuel! But what a job it was to hustle it into the bus and down the aisle to the very back. I hadn't bothered to think about what kind of fuel our old reliable wreck ran on and used this occasion to ask our driver while we all were taking a break from loading up. He told me it was safflower oil. I was quite startled. Of course, I was familiar with safflower as a delicious tea and medicinal, but not as an oil. He said it was our great neighbor to the north that had discovered the process several thousand years ago, had salvaged the plant from modern threats, and were again manufacturing the oil from the seeds. Our close proximity here to the border insured its local availability. He also extolled the use of the oil for cooking, praising its mild flavor and healthfulness. I asked what he planned to do for fuel as we moved south. He seemed unconcerned, saying, "Oh, something always turns up. We'll manage." Somehow, I found that not very reassuring.

CHAPTER 3

By the time we got everything loaded on the bus, and got our-selves in and were traveling up the coast to our next performances, the horizon to our right, beyond the islands and gulf waters, was flushed with light. We must find shelter for the day. The whole area through which we were traveling had been heavily populated. Ruins of buildings were on every side. The culprit of their destruction was not fires, nor even marauders, but great winds at hundreds of kilome-ters blown in from off the gulf. It seemed to have a characteristic way of twisting and shredding the very materials of which these buildings were constructed. Our best opportunity for shelter, as logic would have it, would be in some relatively intact building along the highway. Our old bus rounded a corner, and logic was thrown to the wind. There ahead an overpass in good condition, shelter underneath star-ing us in the face. We pulled over and stopped under the overpass. What a perfect find! From the roadbed up to the girders of the bridge was a gentle, rounded slope ideal for spreading our mats, heads ele-vated above feet for blissful slumber. Providentially, adding to the bliss, was a gentle breeze wafting around and over us, carrying away the heat of the day.

And so we slept, we gentle spirits.

That evening after prayers and breakfast we again hit the road, heading up the coast. As the devastation of the buildings worked its power on our spirits, covering us in a moody gloom, a nearly full moon rose from a cluster of islands out in the Gulf, casting extravagant silvery wealth everywhere, raising our moods along with it. I can't remember when I had last seen a moonrise that seemed to carry such joy and promise. Soon, we were happily chatting among ourselves, telling all the things we wanted to do, places to go. Along about midnight we arrived at the village where our host monastery was located. We looked for the street sign marking the turnoff place that would lead to the monastery. We quickly discovered there were no street signs anywhere. We learned later they had all been blown down by the storm winds, breaking off at the bottom, being carried away by the wind or other events. We looked out for a local along the road who might point the way, but these days people were rarely to be seen walking along the road. A propitious turn in the road yet again revealed to our left, up mountain, the monastery, in all its glory, lying like a slumberous infant on its mother's breast. I think we nearly all gasped at the glorious vision reclining there in argent loveliness. Turning around the bus, we retraced our steps, trying to locate the turnoff. We found a road that looked promising and followed it uphill for a time, realizing it was not the one. We turned back down and, as we went, gazed upon the Bay with its many islands in moonlight, another breathless vision, feeling the wrong turn was so that we could ponder this sweeping view. We turned back on the highway, turning at the next street, toiling upward, when suddenly there we were, passing between marble struck Buddhas in benediction on either side of the street, repeated again and again as we traveled on. Next we saw on our left above us, a flight of stairs leading up to a tri-portal gate, symbolic for having no doors to close one out, with yet more flights of stairs upward to the monastic compound beyond. The road continued on around to other doors where we parked. We were met there by a bevy of young monks insistent on doing the job of unloading our conveyance. Happy were we to let them as we stood nearby and watched.

I could not help but notice how well-preserved all the buildings were and commented on it to a resident monk standing close-by. In the moonshine a bright smile lit his face.

"We here are divinely blessed," he explained, "by villagers who love this place. After big storms where buildings were damaged, they came with their tools and boards, and put everything back to rights, even when it meant completely rebuilding something. Who could be more fortunate than us." I heartily agreed. I noted, too, the more than usual exaggeration of the upturn of the buildings' eaves in the compound, a practice from ancient times for sacred buildings in our country. Here, the eves were particularly felicitous, causing the heart to dance for joy seeing them.

The bus now unloaded, our helpers carried our gear and everything to the rooms prepared for us and on to the place designated for the performances. There, in a modest square, we would perform in the round with entrances and exits through the audience. What fun! I always feel audiences are more involved in such arrangements.

With all our gear stowed in its proper place, we accompanied our diligent brothers-in-faith to their dining hall where we were given a simple but nourishing meal. Everyone was very friendly. At the table, the brother to my left and I got into a lengthy conversation. He started, "I hope you don't mind if a large number of people from the communities round about us come to your performances. There is always high interest in the things we do here."

"Of course, we would be delighted," I said. "The plays are more directed to the laity than to the religious. The more that come to witness the better, I think." Changing the subject, I asked, "I am aware you here are known as meditation monastics and wondered what that meant."

"As I mentioned, we are fortunate to have a supportive community around us," he beamed. "They are also prospering as, I understand, few communities are nowadays. We do not have to do our own farming but can follow the traditional means of gathering alms provided by the supportive people around us. That way, we have time to practice meditation, as was done in earlier times."

"Does that mean," I ask, "you go out in the evenings and collect food?"

"Yes. That is what we do," he answered.

"Oh, I have never had the opportunity to do that. May I join you tomorrow evening?"

"Yes, certainly you may. Do you have an alms bowl?"

"Yes, I was given one at my ordination, but it is many hundreds of kilometers from here."

"That's okay. We'll find you one. We collect here, just outside this building, at sunset every evening. We go barefoot. Is that going to cause you any trouble?"

"It might, come to think of it. I'll carry my sandals with me, just in case."

"Then it's agreed?"

"Agreed."

"But more than just collect alms, we also practice several kinds of meditation. For instance in early times, a Zen master came to us and taught this means of meditation. We do this, as well as several other schools of meditation."

"Really?! How might I begin one of the Zen methods?"

"After prayers, look for me and I will introduce you to our Zen master."

"Thank you. I would appreciate that." And on in like vein our conversation ran.

Then on, to their great temple, where we joined them in prayer. The temple was graced with a singularly awe-inspiring Buddha and corona, brilliantly dazzling in the light of many candles. It was hard to bow one's head in deprivation of the hallowed sight, and I struggled to tear my eyes away. Afterwards, I joined up with my brother-of-the-table, and we went on to meet the Zen master. Quite an imposing man, in top physical condition, he led me to their meditation room and began instruction. We were not alone, for I noted several individuals in common dress and full head of hair had joined our session. I wish I could say the first attempt was an amazing experience, which it was not. But the more nights I followed the discipline the better it got, to the point, when it came for us to leave the monastery, I felt much regret.

It was a full night for me. I had promised Farmer, Loyal and Soldier we would begin work on the first play, the one with only three characters. None of the three could read. I could have read the lines to them, but I thought it would be more interesting for Smiley, Little Lord and Sweetheart to join us with the boys saying the words for them. It was a definite experience for all of us, a lot of fun. And I think we all learned something from it, too. We didn't get very far, though. That night, as the boys started out the play, I was startled bold upright from my slump. Miraculously, they were saying the words with underpinnings of meaning I had not heard from them before. How interesting. Have we fallen into a new technique for theatre? How fortuitous that would be!

But I jump ahead. I have left out my experience in alms-collecting. I met up with the resident monks and was given a bowl for receiving food. It was much larger than the one I was given at ordination. After the evening's experience I came to feel my own bowl, so far away, was purely for ceremonial, symbolic use, not meant for real use. We were to pray throughout the going → collecting → coming back. Above all, we were to avoid any direct communication of any kind with the people from whom we were given alms. And that meant no smiling at, or nodding to, anyone. Instead, we would collectively pray over them. This act seemed to give them much joy, even causing them to weep. I so easily could have been right there, weeping along with them. All was explained to me later. It was understood we were grateful for the food. But we were performing a job and being paid to do so [i.e., receiving food, giving blessing]. On the other hand, they were receiving spiritual blessing for their good deed, something very important to them. I felt the truth of this and commiserated. The event had far-reaching significance for me, the whole being a positive experience. Save for my poor feet, unaccustomed to all those little pebbles that seemed to get between the road and me. I refrained from putting on my sandals until our homeward trek but paid the price for it, limping around afterwards. Still, I count this alms-gathering as one of the great experiences of my life and would have paid a higher price, if needed, for it.

As to note something of particular interest, there is a technique for preparing food for almsgiving. Rice is scooped from the rice pot directly into the alms bowl. Different dishes, on the other hand, are wrapped in some manner so as not to flow all together in a big, gooey mess in the bowl. Thus when we return home and turn in our bowls to our kitchen staff—they basically little more than dish washers—their job is to separate everything, put all the rice into a common pot, and all the other little packages into like dishes as much as they can. It makes serving up later a whole lot easier. And, the truth be known, I ate more tasty food here than anywhere else since Nittaya's table. And that's saying something.

The second night's play/lesson went well, the audience reaction being the outstanding thing here. I think this was our most involved audience ever, and one of our largest thus far. From Fame's introduction on, there was applause at individual lines and a seemingly endless commentary running along. So much crying and rending of clothes I could not believe, the mention of 'extinction' causing such a tumult I thought we were going to have to stop the performance. Then came the mention of communities and things went quickly in the other direction. "We've already done that!" and "Old news!" they shouted. When it was Life's turn he made a little speech before the lesson saying, "I am happy to hear of your accomplishments in forming communities here. These words are then not directly meant for you. Please know there are many, many people out there who still are alone and in danger. They have not been blessed, like you. Think on them as you listen to these words and know how lucky you are to have advanced so far as you have. Embrace those loving and lovely people around you. And forge ahead!" To which the cheers that rose up fairly rattled the roof tiles around us. The lesson over, the audience rushed forward *en masse* to surround Life, trying all together to tell him of their separate life's story. My, my, my. What a community! I was hugged by, and hugged back, so many people in so short a time. I think perhaps they had just realized what they had done here and saw it for the first time in relation to others. I was introduced to several of the community leaders and said to them we would like to send scholars to study what they were doing so that the knowledge could be shared with those just beginning to form their own community. "We shall welcome them with open arms," they said. I was not aware at the time, Fame telling me later, donations flowed in as never before. He had to enlist the aid of Hero and Bright to help manage it all.

I was so excited by the evening that attempts to meditate were futile. I had to give up, and go instead to collect my six would-be actors for rehearsal. All of us were on a super-high, finding hard going to settle down to mundane business. The three boys were fairly jumping up and down with excitement, the three older youths flushed with the headiness of it all, Loyal throwing an arm around me and saying how blessed he felt by our taking them in and making them a part of our journey. Silly me, I broke down in tears, all crowding round trying to cheer me up. We didn't get much done that night but, boy, did we have camaraderie.

Sleeping well, sunset seemed to come in no time. This was the night of The Vow and the full moon. There was no way of knowing how our audience here would react. I suspected the elements of the vow would be new to them, but there was no way knowing beforehand how they would react to it. I tried to put expectation out of mind as I went to breakfast, prayer and meditation. It almost worked as I kneeled before that profound Buddha, the sculpture that breathed and moved before my very eyes, blessing us in His transformative being. In His benevolent presence I was calmed. Calmness carried over into meditation class, and I did much better than the previous night.

Then came time for the play. The square seemed jammed with people, our biggest audience ever, I thought, even bigger than the ones on the plaza in the capitol city. The play came to an end with the five boys all reciting the vow. Spots off. There was such a din of shouting I couldn't understand what was being said until they picked up from someone chanting, "End war! End war!" And then it was "End hate! End hate!" Then I had a glimpse of the night we would have. Calmness flew from me. Spots up on Life. Now was the night when this lesson would have its most dramatic delivery. He began as he speaks normally, asking the audience to hear him out. Then, like a Grecian column he stood, his face more pale than I had ever seen, arms tied to his side, his skirts in fluted folds, the upward-directed spots making him tower above. The lesson commenced in sepulchral tones, raising at times to screams as he spoke to the threats we vulnerable face. Then the condemnation of War, and a flood of relief flowing from the audience. Again, the condemnation of the negative impulses and audience flowing back. Come to the vow and, at last, Life raises his hands above the shoulders, bidding the audience stand. There is a broad rumble as they come to their feet, repeating the words as fed to them, in an ominous jumble. And then the vow has been taken, such jubilation heard. I imagine nothing so much as accounts I have read of cathedral bells' change-ringing in holiday mode. They surge forward from all sides, and we are surrounded by glowing faces, all shouting something unintelligible to us. River thinks to turn on all the spots and shine them up into the night sky. Now all in the square are illuminated, their faces upturned. There is a surge of humanity toward Life, and a jolt of fear rises in me. This is Full Moon madness. They pick him up and carry him in their upturned hands, arms raised high as they will go, and run around and around the edge of the square. It does not end but seems to gather momentum. At last, seemingly out of nowhere, the elderly abbot appears at the top of a temple's stairs, raising his arms wide, embracing all. Suddenly there is silence, all movement stops. Silence holds. The Abbot speaks.

"My children! My beloved children! You have reason to be joyous. Joyful from the words of our blest visitors, for they speak much truth. Time has certainly come for War to be put aside, to be seen clearly for what it is. It is also time to look within ourselves at our baser instincts and to cut them from our beings as no longer worthy of our nature. Take these thoughts with you and return to your villages, your homes. And there think what you will do to live up to the vow you have just taken. For it begins with you. Bless you for the step you are taking. Go to your homes, my children. Go to your homes now, and think on what has happened here tonight."

In silence, Life is lowered to the ground, his costume straightened by kind hands. Turning, our audience goes silently into the night, hardly a rustle heard. Soon, very soon, we stand alone on the square. The Abbot descends the stairs and comes to meet us. We all bow to the waist in his presence. He breaks the silence. "My friends, you are very courageous. I admire your courage. I don't have that kind of courage. I could never do what you are doing. I am too timid a soul. I am glad of your courage. And bless you for it. I am glad that you have come here. I am glad for the things you are saying ..."

At this point I thought, "He is going to tell us to leave. This is all sweetness before the sour. It's coming, it's coming."

"You have two more nights, is that correct?" the Abbot asked.

Life, who had stepped up before us, answered, "Yes. There are two more nights."

The Abbot took his hand and patting it said, "Then I shall be in attendance. I pray there shall be no violence against you. I warn you, also. The things you advocate could bring down upon you the wrath of Power. Surely you know this." Life nodded. "Then be wise, my child. Have means to protect yourself." He leaned forward and placed a kiss on Life's forehead. We all were dumbfounded. We stood stock still, startled, silent, as the elderly abbot turned and walked back into the temple.

In silence, we collected up our gear and carried it back to our rooms. Silently, we all entered our individual rooms and closed the doors. Silent still, we thought over the events that had just unfolded, and thought on the abbot's words.

There was a quiet knock on my door. Lighting a candle, I opened it on Farmer, looking worried, intense. I invited him in.

"Maybe now is the time. You asked us, Soldier and me. Maybe now is the time for us to dress up like those Nāga guards you talked about. We dress up, but we really guard Brother Life. We want to do this."

I was stunned, yet again this special night.

He went on, "That is what him and I used to do. Guard. We guarded the bosses. We're good at it. Him and I."

"I believe you," I said. "I wasn't prepared to move so quickly. But I see your point."

"Can we get it done for tomorrow night?" he queried, looking nervous. "Soldier's ready to go. Can we do this?"

"Go get him and bring him here. I'll think on how we can get moving on this. Go!"

Farmer silently slipped from the room. My mind raced forward. The costumes. The uniforms. That would be the problem. None of us here can sew worth speaking about. The people that can sew are in the Valley. It will take weeks for us to get anything from there. What to do? What to do? Then my mind struck rich ground. Surely there's someone in the monastery that can sew. If not the monastery, then in the villages. The problem with a villager is … the person may talk. This must be kept secret. So, it must be a monastic. I'll go to the abbot and ask him. He was the one that warned us. He will see to it the secret is kept. Well, that's the plan. At the very moment I reached the thought there was again a quiet knock on the door.

In came Farmer and Soldier, the two of them practically filling up the tiny room. "I've got an idea how to get uniforms for the two of you. Wait here. I'll be back shortly." Off I went to track down the Abbot. I suspected where his residence might be and went directly there. I was wrong but was redirected by a kind person. Coming to the residence, I was stopped by his several monk-gatekeepers. I explained who I was and why I wanted to speak with the Abbot, that is, protecting Life. I waited a few minutes. Permission was granted. I was ushered into his presence. I explained how I was following his suggestion and our need for a good person with the needle, skirting the Nāga issue.

"We have here just the person. You can trust him. He will maintain silence," said His Holiness. Then, he placed a restraining hand on my arm, "My child," he said, gazing on me in an alarming manner, "take care for the life of your young leader. His aura … I see his aura. It shows tragedy. Tragedy! But I cannot see how, or when. You must be prepared. And watch. It is coming. It's his aura, you see," he intoned, looking downcast and worried.

I should have thought on his words, but they did not seize me. Instead, my mind was locked on the taylor and getting my would-be guards decked out. He sent me off with his attendant to the cell of the taylor. A chubby little man of unknowable age met us, smiling most kindly. He shut the door to the attendant and, just the two of us, listened to my story.

Drawing a serious face he said, "I think I can be of help."

"Come with me, then," and I practically drug him along to my room. We arrived out of breath, him especially. I opened the door and ushered him in. Had Soldier and Farmer not been sitting on the bed I doubted we all four would have fit in the room. The taylor/monk was startled at the sight of them [they are a bit rough around the edges] but warmed to them quickly. How to explain what a Nāganese is and what they look like in human form?

I put it this way: "Imagine you are looking at one of those dragon sculptures they use to guard temples."

"Yes, we have several sculptures here."

"Imagine now, that the sculpture comes to life and is standing before you."

"That's a scary thought."

"Well, imagine it is a good friend of yours, someone you like very much."

"I'm having a hard time imagining that."

"Okay. Then imagine this dragon can change itself into a human, a nice person, a friend you can talk to about anything."

"That's easy. I can imagine that," he nodded affirmatively, his portly cheeks echoing the movement.

"Good! You are asked to make a guard's uniform for this friend, which is to be his job."

"Oh, that's easy. I've got it right up here," and he tapped the side of his head.

"That's great! Now, these two young men are your friends. They need guard's uniforms. Are you willing to make the uniforms for them? It is to be kept secret."

"You say the Abbot sent you to me?" I nod 'yes.' "I will do it. When do you need the uniforms? Tonight?! I don't think there's time to have them by tonight."

"Do you have anything on hand that might work?"

"Hummm, well-l-l, I might have."

"Would you be willing to take the two guys here with you and have them try on what it is you have?"

He looked at Farmer and Soldier dubiously. "We're good people," said Soldier. "Do you think these monks would have us around if we weren't?"

"No-o-o-o, I guess they wouldn't," he said, dubiously. He looked at me. Then he looked back at the two. Breaking into a broad smile he said, "Okay. I can do it."

"Then be off," I said. "Time is flying."

Up and off the three of them went, and I was left alone with my thoughts, hoping against hope whatever this little person had in mind would fit and work. Trying to think ahead, I go two doors down to Autumn's room and ask for the makeup kit. Naturally, he was curious why I needed it and was disappointed by my lack of explanation. Then back to my room to await the three's return.

In no time at all, it seemed, I heard a rap on my door. There they stood! The three of them! The two guys in their uniform. Did it work? I couldn't have dreamed for a more perfect getup. Our little taylor/monk, now a prized friend! I rushed them in and had them sit, all three, on the edge of the bed.

"Well? What do you think?" I asked the uniformed duo.

"Hey! Couldn't get much better," Soldier said, spreading his palms waist high as if to say, "Can't you see how good I look?"

Pants and shirt were basic khaki, the pants having a green stripe running up the outer seam, from shoe to waist; the shirt with short sleeve, collar of the same green, with a green stripe up the front where are the buttonholes; all tight fitted, revealing the muscular development of the bodies underneath. All that was missing was the makeup needed on the face to suggest a Nāga dragon not perfectly shape-shifted into human, and the mannerisms of Nāganese in human form, both these missing elements my job to supply. I thank the chubby little taylor/monk, remind him to be silent regarding this affair, and send him on his way.

I start with Soldier since he is the closest. Dark brown pigment is discreetly applied to either side of the nose, accenting its sharp lines, the same applied under the cheeks to accent the bone. Then the eyes, disguising the epicanthic eye fold while keeping the basic almond shape, accenting and elongating its taper, then applying a discreet green haze between the eye and the bone of the cheek; and the disguise is complete. I step back and look at him. I'm amazed at how little it took to create the illusion. Then Farmer. I do the same thing and his transformation is even more marked. I become quite pleased with myself.

Now for Nāganese movement. I illustrate how a Nāga is not quite comfortable in human form, how he walks without his long tail, deals with a five-digit hand, how he talks—deep and resonant—and, finally, how he tries to suppress his basic arrogance. They try it out, refining as they go along. After a while they become adroit in the deception, and time to show off to Life.

Off we go to his room, knocking softly at his door. Hearing a stirring within, the door is soon opened. Life, startled, took a step back, then realized the deception and laughed. "Come in," he said. I motioned our two 'guards' to stand next to Life's lamp so he could take in our labors. "What is this all about?" he asked. "Soldier? Farmer?" Looking intently at them.

"I am following the Abbot's suggestion," I said, "and am supplying you with pseudo Nāga guards. They will be on either side of you at all times except when you are delivering your lessons."

"Oh, I don't think that's necessary," he replied.

"Well, others of us do. So you must do as we say. You have no choice."

Life smiled at this and shook his head. That was the extent of his protest.

"We must change our play area," I said. "We can't let you perform in the round this evening. We must perform against a backdrop."

"There is a small temple to the right of the square. Shall we perform there?"

"Yes. That would be good. Then it is decided."

I left the three of them and returned to my room. Day was approaching, so I turned in.

That evening directly after sunset I took River and Autumn to the square to make changes in location to the little temple on the right. Then on to breakfast where, sitting on either side of Life, Farmer and Soldier caused a bit of a stir. No one actually came out and said or did anything, just subdued whispers and stares. Again I thought, "That's good." After the meal, I collected up the boys and explained what was happening. They were much amused at the thought of Farmer and Soldier playing at being Nāga guards, amused that is until I explained to them that we could not take chances with Life's life, that the excesses of the previous night could not be repeated. They soon sobered up. Given the content of the fourth and fifth evenings, I did not expect the level of reaction to be as high as the evening of the Vow. Still, we could not take any chances. The two exotic-looking persons standing guard on either side of Life should promote an atmosphere of restraint.

And, sure enough, the two evenings witnessed calmer gatherings. Both nights our audience was larger than before, with youths, even, climbing onto the roofs in order to see. When the lessons were over and the audience surged forward, Soldier and Farmer moved close in to Life, preventing any intimate contact. Indeed, on the last night, when Life spoke of the League and its alien members, our two guards did a bit of a maneuver at the mention of Nāgas and Nāgaland, inferring the connection. That caused a bit of a sensation and afterwards people coming over to get a closer look at them. It was funny, really. I struggled to keep a straight face. I noted most favorably, Soldier and Farmer did actually possess some acting skills.

After all was over, and the audience was gone, the Abbot called for a general meeting in the dining hall. While now convinced of the genuine character of the man, I admit to being apprehensive regarding the purpose of the meeting. Once everyone was settled at tables the abbot rose from his chair. Silence fell upon us.

"My cherished brethren and honored visitors," he began, "these last several days have provided us a monumental experience, one we shall hold in memory for a considerable time. Our visitors have given us wisdom that we need take on as part of our living." He paused here as though to let the thought sink in.

Taking up a new direction, he continued, "We are among but a few monasteries closest to the Valley and share a common creed. It would be to our mutual benefit, the communities around us included, to make a formal alliance with the monastery there in order that we should all benefit." Here a general murmur arose from us at table. "Therefore, this night, I set for all time a brotherhood between our two monasteries, that we join in our good works as equals in the name of the profound beliefs that bind us." A spontaneous cheer arose from our many throats. I was dumbfounded. I did not expect this, but was very happy for it, rejoiced in it. I could not have hoped for anything better.

Afterwards, a small delegation—Life, Fame, Hero, Bright and I—met with the Abbot to create the bridges that would tie us together, including lay exchanges. I became excited at the prospect. Among the important exchanges, I thought, would be the opportunity for our novices to study for and receive their ordinations here. I'd already mentioned our scholars coming here to study the structuring of the communities round about, but also they sending their farmers to the Valley to study developments there. I felt, too, it might be worthwhile for their community leaders to come to the Valley to establish contact with the consulates of the League. Get them in direct communication, I thought.

After this most profitable meeting I noticed Life and the Abbot walking off together, the Abbot putting a paternal arm around his shoulder. I left the door to my room open to keep a watch for Life's return, but it was nearly dawn when I heard his footsteps approach. I was all ears, dying to hear what the Abbot had to say. I jumped up and ran to meet him at his door. He invited me in. We sat, looking at each other. "Well," I finally said, "what did the Abbot have to say?"

"He tested me," Life began. "He tested me, asking questions for my answer. I couldn't imagine what he was doing. At the end I finally understood." Life fell into silence at this point.

"What? He asked you questions? What kind of questions?" I asked impatiently.

"So you will understand, he offered me ordination as an abbot, tomorrow night, saying I knew more than enough to qualify. I'm afraid that means we'll have to stay here longer than planned. I hope no one will mind."

"Mind?! Why should any of us mind? We shall be joyous for the occasion. Life, this is simply wonderful news!" I enthused. "I'll even send word to our driver in the village to join us for the occasion."

"Then you think I should do it?" he asked.

"Do it?! There's no question. Yes, of course you should do it. You're already our leader. It's about time to make it official."

"Will you be by my side and assist?" he asked.

"Yes. Of course. I would be honored."

And so it was decided. I hardly slept that day in anticipation of witnessing the rarest of ceremonies. That evening, at prayers, the ceremony was announced, a fasting declared. Special prayer books were found and distributed, several sets of robes collected, gifts for placing on the altar assembled, the audience donning festive garments, our driver arriving in a flurry with friends from the village. Finally, all was ready. As the chanting of the first set of prayers began a sliver of silver appeared far out on the Gulf swelling into the moon, just past its fullest, casting its own unique light on the assembly, vying with the candle-lit gilded altar for which was more splendid. Early on, I assist stripping Life's habit from his shoulders, a simple cloth thrown over him instead. Then a period of silence for meditation, me thinking of the glory Life shall bring to our monastery. The prayers sung, prayers with which I have but the dimmest memory, singing bowls tapped for their floating resonance, causing time to become suspended, too. Vows taken, the temple bell outside droning deep-throated peals of a somber joy. More candles lit and gifts carried to the altar, there to stand in for the joy rising in all our hearts. Gentle light, all around, the final, long hymn intoned in the deepest human throat, brings a new set of robes to wrap his shoulders, tie his waist. We all bow deeply, again and again and again; we stand, we kneel, and we bow. And then, suddenly, it's over. It is over, and Life is our new abbot. Abbot Life. It will take time to get used to.

We are collected in procession, Soldier and Farmer having made their way to my side behind Life, torches struck, as we wind into the open air, pausing at the fiercest guardian images to give thanks, then on and on to the giant marble Buddha, facing eternally into the Gulf, birthplace of both moon and sun, where again, fires flaring in the night, we pray. The temple bell sends up its somber tone, up into the star-filled night, into eternity. I kneel there on stone, my heart but to burst, weeping with joy and love.

Then up we rise, wending back to the dining hall where we are served a banquet. An almost-banquet, poor things, because they tried. Seated beside the Abbot is Life, or rather the Abbot Full-of-Life, not quite smiling as much as the wizened old man on his right, bestowing blessing all around.

Now, it is all over, and we retire to our little cells, Soldier and Farmer lingering there a moment to see that I was fine. I leave the door ajar to hear Life's footsteps so that I might find if he is alright. But the old abbot has accompanied him to his door, calling him "my son." He says, "I shall not see you this evening before your departure, but I wish you good speed in your mission. Watch out! Protect yourself, and do good work." He again leans forward, placing a kiss on Life's forehead, then turns, departs. Life stands there, motionless for a moment, looking overcome with feeling. Then he spies me peeking from my room, and smiles.

"What are you doing, still up?" he asks.

"I'm waiting to see that you get home okay, that's what," I reply. "What time will we be leaving tonight?"

"As soon as we can get organized. Right after sunset if we can manage that quickly. Now, go to bed!"

"Yes, I shall now have to do everything you tell me to," I say with false meekness. I give a little wave, turn, and close the door behind me. Putting out the candle, I stretch out on the narrow bed. I swear, all day I heard nothing but singing bowls, their unguent tones droning on and on, forever and ever.

CHAPTER 4

We head out early, the western sky still rosy. We pass the rows of Buddhas in benediction, now wise to the full significance bestowed as we drove up here. Down the mountainside we slide, coming to the coastal road, us going south. Our destination is the port city where we formerly had embarked for Abandoned Island, again to await our pre-scribed caravan. I've learned my lesson: better to wait and take the 'van than fall prey to who knows what on one's own. Then it's a long trip to our next destination. We won't be idle, though. I'm sure we'll give performances along the way, like a year ago. Plus, I'll be working with Farmer, Loyal and Soldier on the first play. If they get it ready in time it might be interesting to give an experimental performance while with the 'van.

On the bus, we rehearse the play, us seven. At this point the boys have become fond of their counterparts and insist on sitting on their laps as we go through the lines: Farmer/Smiley, Soldier/Little Lord, Loyal/Sweetheart. When our former hoodlums get a scene right the boys reward them with a little peck on the cheek. They act as though it's all very funny, but I see clearly they are touched by the ges-ture, perhaps never knowing love before. And, of course, the boys completely idolize their older counterparts. I sit and watch while the drama unfolds before me, requiring no intervention on my part.

In the middle of the night, Fame came over, saying he needed to talk with me in private. I thought, Money Matters, and we isolated ourselves as best we could in such cramped corners. Whispering back and forth, Fame began, "I can't believe how much we raised in dona-tions this past week."

"Can you tell me how much?" He gave me a tally of the number of gold and silver pieces he had. The amount surpassed even the sale of one of Manjushri's gemstones.

"I don't feel comfortable carrying that amount around with us, what with ..." and he nodded in the direction of our three former hoodlums.

"Ah, now that's not fair. But I feel it's not wise to tempt anyone who knows only want."

"We need to make a shipment to Lily, in the Valley. The money will be safer there with her."

"Unfortunately, we won't be able to do that until we get to the port city. Where is the money now?"

"It's stashed way back in the corner there, in a box, behind everything else," Fame said, pointing to the back of the bus.

"Well, it should be safe there until we reach our destination. It will take a day, perhaps two, for the courier to meet us in the port city."

"Let's hope the caravan is late, as usual. That way, the courier won't have to chase us down."

"When you send the message," I cautioned, "be sure to ask for Nāga guards to ..." Then all kinds of signals lit up in my brain. "Nāga guards! Perfect! Soldier and Farmer can meet them and see the real-life article for themselves. Perfect!"

"What are you saying." Asked Fame, thoroughly puzzled.

"Sorry. You saw those two young men as Life's guards? Yes. Well, they'll be able to see the Nāganese for themselves now and refine their acting chops." Again, another brilliant flash, "Come to think of it, let's ask for the two to be hired as our security guards."

"Security guards? Do you think we need them?"

"Yes, I do; and so did the abbot back at the monastery."

"Alright, I will ask," said Fame.

I went back to my actors.

Time and kilometers pass swiftly beneath our feet and soon we are on the lookout for a place to camp for the day. No place like the overpass comes our way, so we look intently at the ruins around us, hoping for a place big enough to pull off and spread out the sleeping gear. Nothing's coming our way. It's beginning to get light. We're talking about sleeping in the bus; but, still, it will need sheltering to protect us from frying inside. We all begin to feel a tinge of desperation, when Mischief calls out, pointing just behind us. At first, I'm afraid, many of us thought it was one of his bad jokes and disbelieved him. Fortunately, the driver had stopped and backed up to where Mischief had pointed. Sure enough, there it was. We had missed it, I think, because it was mainly invisible from the approach, visible only looking back; and Mischief was the only one doing that. We got out, looked the place over and found it perfect. Not only could we park the bus inside out of sight but there were also second and third floors where we could be out of the sun and spread our mats. There was also a grand view of islands out in the bay and cooler breezes off the water. We gave Mischief a round of applause. He ate it up, milking it for all it was worth. I haven't seen him smile like that in a long time.

We said our prayers, had a bite to eat and settled down for the day. I dropped off rather quickly, I think. There I was, trying to keep out of sight. They were following me, maybe eight, maybe ten of them, carrying long knives. I practically tasted the hatred coming from them it was so invasive. What had I done to deserve this? Who knows? I couldn't think of a thing. They were approaching; I was vulnerable in this place and was forced to move. I slid along the wall, trying to make myself as invisible as possible. Ahead was a dark open doorway across an open space. If I could cross over without being seen, I could close the door, maybe lock it even, and escape on the stairs. But how to cross that space? I could just run for it, damn the noise; or I could try to slip across it, maybe even on my stomach, slithering across. Yes, that sounded like a great idea. Down on all fours, then the stomach, out in the open going for the door. Shoes! Shoes in front of my face! Shoes all around, them towering over. They kick me in the side, flip me over on my back. Then the knives! I see them flash. Then down, into my flesh! I feel the pain! I feel my dying! I sit up, covered in sweat. The sun is a glare out the windows. Everyone around sleeping in peace. I try to calm my beating heart, it wanting to tear out of my chest. What could this positively frightful dream mean? I look at the floor. No solace there. I look on the sleeping faces of my beloved wayfarers and find much solace there. My heart calms. I soon can breathe again. But no sleep for the rest of the day. I lay there, quietly, thinking if I do so I will trick sleep into returning. No way! Sleep has fled such a scene.

Dusk slowly creeps in. One by one, they open their eyes, sit up and look around. Seeing me, they smile. How lovely! After all that hatred, a smile most beautiful. Sweetheart runs to me, gives me his evening hug, never before so welcomed. How lucky I am! Was the dream so horrible I would see my real great fortune? Yes, that must be the reason. Why else? Then evening prayer, the drone of it never more consoling. Breakfast, warming the tummy; then into the bus and we are on our way, leaving those frightful bandits behind. At last, I am calm again.

My six guys call me, and rehearsal picks up where we left off. Kilometers roll underneath. Lines are said in treble, repeated in bass—said and repeated, said and repeated. We pull over and have our midnight meal, everyone more jolly than usual. I think the glow from the past week still hangs over us. How precious their jolliness is! How well they all deserve it. Then back to rehearsal—treble and bass, treble and bass. I think the play now bent for me, expecting each line repeated an octave lower. It has a kind of flow, a kind of music to it I'm finding ingratiating. Finally, the thought comes to me. The reason for the violent dream is for me to more fully appreciate the gifts I've been given. Yes, that's surely the reason. My heart warms to this, and I finally feel myself again. Curious that I now find myself sitting beside three young men who not too long ago pulled knives on me, on us. And now I love them, as my brothers, feeling I shall love them more and more as time goes on. Feeling I trust them, even now, with my life, with Life's too, with his life in their hands. I look at the three, beaming down on the little boys in their laps, and think what marvelous fathers they would make. That we should have such fathers raising broods of children. Oh! I hope they have. I hope they have. And I start to cry. Oh, fool that I am!

The six thespians break off, look at me in surprise, start patting me on arms and shoulders. I apologize, "I'm so sorry. I guess I'm feeling very emotional tonight, what with all that's happened this past week."

"Yeah, me too."

"Don't cry."

"Come on, be happy."

"Hey, big guy?"

And on.

And so, I dry my tears and be happy with them.

As day approaches, we enter the outskirts of the port city, all in ruins. Ruins, ruins all about. It seems, all of mankind's efforts now in ruins. We go to the *rendezvous* point and stop. Lots of people round about, waiting as we shall have to wait, for the caravan has not arrived.

I collar Fame. "Quickly. We must quickly send a message off to the Valley. Go. Go." And off he runs.

First, a pale flush appears over the bay, breaking up in the silhouette of the islands. It rises, defiantly. Then pale rose makes her entrance just at that magical point where sea and sky meet. She pushes up a delicate petal until, touching a cloud, it bursts into flame. The fire spreads, jumping from horizontal Sirius to sister Sirius up and up like a step ladder into the sky-dome, too fast to flee. With it, the surfaces of the waters burst in sympathetic fires, too, spreading across in sheens to the very shore. Then the fire is overhead, in far-reaching streaks, as a tip of the fiery orb emerges, scalding, from the sea. Light flashes across the landscape to touch our skin. Instantly, we all head for the hulking station to take cover in its shadows.

We each, or in groups, light our own fires to make our supper, disgruntled our caravan has not yet arrived, nor sent word. Mats now are spread out on the floor, under the high-arching roof, and tired bodies recline on them, expecting soft slumber. And so it comes, lulling first this one and that, silence slipping in after. Soon enough, all is still, in slumber's grasp. I have trouble with the slide, my soul trembling in horror at what the day may bring, what ghosts lurk in store for me. I tell it, "Be calm. Be calm." but it doesn't listen. So I lie there, listening instead to the disparate snores rising all about, envying them. Slumber finally catches me up without noticing, and I am oblivion.

We wake. Blessedly, we wake to sunset glow, from the west, over the flat river plain, nudging, "Time to go. Time to go." But there is no caravan. This is the very thing that makes me itchy about caravans. I hate to wait! Yes, I know. The courier from the Valley has not yet arrived. We don't want them having to run after us, do we? So, it's good we are waiting. Yes?

The courier arrives, and they have brought two Nāgas, fierce looking, to guard the hoard. I rush to grab Farmer and Soldier so they can see them, meet them, closely watch them. They stop dead in their tracks at the sight of the Nāgas, totally intimidated, these particular aliens being especially fearsome. Bowing first, I say to the Nāgas, "Pardon me. I've spoken about Nāgas to my two friends here, and it has been their fondest wish to make the acquaintance of someone of your noble kind. May I please introduce them to you?" They grunt approval. I bring my friends forward. "Say your name first," I instruct, "then bow deeply to the waist. If he puts out his arm, let him put his hand on your shoulder, then you put your hand on his same shoulder."

"My name is Farmer," then he bowed deeply. There seemed to be a glimmer of approval on the Nāga's face for he immediately stretched out his arm and placed his hand on Farmer's shoulder. Farmer did a tiny instinctive slump but then corrected himself and reached for the Nāga's shoulder. It was farther off than expected, and he had to maneuver to reach it. The Nāga, somehow ingratiated by the little drama, announced his name, three octaves lower than expected, causing poor Farmer to practically jump out of his skin. Then the Nāga hugged him! I'd never seen that before. Poor Farmer was then passed on to the second Nāga. This time, forewarned, Farmer was prepared. The whole introduction went more smoothly, including another hug at the end. Now it was Soldier's turn. Knowing what to expect did not help him much, he ending up in much the same state as Farmer. Still, they had enough pluck left over to ask the two Nāgas to show them their dragon form. Off they went, somewhere private. I did not think much about it until I heard two cries of alarm rise up from my friends. I smiled as I pictured what was happening. A Nāga, in his native form, is quite arresting, to say the least—teeth and tail. Back the four came, the Nāgas with an arrogant swagger, the humans holding on to each other for support. Good! Now they know.

Thinking ahead, I asked the Nāgas, "Would you consider joining us if, in the future, we needed your protection?" Both responded with an immediate, "Yes," in sepulchral tones. I confirmed, "Thank you. I will keep you in mind," bowing to them, stepping backward.

And that was that.

Once out of earshot, I asked my friends, "Well, what did you think?"

They answered, practically at once, "Wow!" And then, "I wouldn't want to be on their bad side." And, "Did you feel that shoulder? They must be something strong." And on in like vein.

"Has this helped you acting them out?" I ask, knowing full well their answer.

Again, in unison, "Yeah!"

Farmer noted, especially, "The arrogance. You have to see that arrogance to believe it."

Soldier, "Yeah. Isn't it something?"

Then Farmer, again. "You know why they hugged us? They wanted to show us in a way like everyone would accept how strong they really were."

"Yeah," said Soldier, "that was no friendly hug." Moving on to acting, they compared notes, then talked about refining their performance. I just smiled softly to myself, loving every second.

Ahead, I see coming toward us Fame with Autumn and River trailing behind pulling a low, wheeled shallow bucket, a brown box of some size in it. Knowing what's in that box, I excuse myself to Soldier and Farmer and join Fame. "Where were you? I needed your help getting the box out of the back of the bus."

"Oh, sorry," suddenly realizing how thoughtless I'd been. "They sent along two especially fierce Nāganese to guard our 'shipment'."

"You will be glad to know," he said, trying to hide his irritation, "we have permission to hire Farmer and Soldier as security."

"Wonderful! That's a relief."

"You also have several letters waiting for you back at the bus."

"Oh? Who from? Did you happen to notice?"

"It is not my position to make note of such things." Definitely irritated now.

"Sorry. Nothing was happening, then suddenly everything is happening. I think I got my priorities mixed up."

"Thank you. I appreciate that." And no more was said on the matter.

We reached the couriers. They were the ones that had met us before, in the capitol city. They knew the procedure and did their job swiftly. The two Nāgas stood to the side, looking slightly bored, I thought, as I glanced at them. The brown box was passed over to them and disappeared into an even larger box. Off they went, the four of them. I'd like to think I never imagined anything happening to our box on the way to the Valley; but in a flash a whole drama unfolded in my mind.

The box never reaches the Valley but instead falls into the hands of the leader of the marauders, there to be parceled out to various warlords who, in turn, arm their armies. The word went down. Stop those pesky monks at any cost!

That wasn't what happened at all. The money arrived in the Valley later that night. The decision would then be made to send the final payment for the Valley to Lord X the following night. In a few days more the signed papers would be received from the Lord. We now shall be owners of the Valley!

But, of course, that hadn't happened yet. Fame and I were just standing there, watching the couriers and Nāgas depart with our money. I don't know what he was thinking, but I certainly had my thoughts.

"What a relief!" he said with a deep sigh.

Forgetting totally about my mail, I thought only of telling Farmer and Soldier they were now our official Security Department. They were at the bus, Loyal with them, playing some kind of convoluted tag game with the boys. Their gales of laughter could be heard some distance away. Thinking only that the money was no longer our responsibility I tried to join in, not understanding the rules, botching up everything. Heedlessly, I joined the laughter, too. Our laughter, noisy and bothersome as it was, cleansed my soul of its darkness, and I felt almost human again. We all fell to the ground, the nine of us, only five having the right to act like children.

When we had become silent again, and were resting from the exertion, I raised up on an elbow. "Farmer. Soldier. It's official. You two are our Security Department. Congratulations!" I made an awkward bow to them.

"What?! Security Department?! Us?" and some such.

"Yes. It has been confirmed." Whispering, "What do you want for salary?" I asked, index finger at my lips.

Soldier whispered back, "We're already getting a salary—food and lodging, somebody looking after me."

"Yeah," whispered Farmer, too. "What else do I need?" shoulders in a shrug. Then in normal voice, "Why are we whispering?"

"No need," I answered, in normal voice. "We're fine." And nothing on the subject was ever mentioned again.

Fame walked over to me with letters in his hand. Still on the ground, I took them, now curious to know who they were from. Sitting cross-legged, I looked at the front of the envelopes and saw one was from Nittaya, the other from Grace. I opened Grace's first. It read—

> Dear Brother of-the-Palace,
>
> Please to know everything here is progressing well. I, like you, have fallen in love with this special place. I pinch myself daily to check that I am not dreaming being here. I am not alone in thriving here; we all are doing well. Everyone sends their love to you.
>
> Construction is going on everywhere in the Valley. Several consulates are in the midst of building new structures, all fitting in beautifully with the older buildings. A new Administration building is going up in the center of the Valley. There are four floors thus far. I think the roof is next but am not sure. The University will have its first building completed, behind the Administration building, toward the mountainside. The newest building, surpassing all others in sheer size, is the temple that is replacing the old gates. The foundation has gone in and seems enormous. I am told a large reclining Buddha has been commissioned from our greatest living artist and is to be in the likeness of the Nats ambassador. They say the Buddha will be positioned so as to be contemplating the far wall of the Valley.
>
> We all await the completion of your tour and return to the Valley. Then we can become a complete community again.
>
> With the blessing of the Buddha, I remain
>
> Your Grace

What a lovely letter. I should have replied immediately, to return with the courier. Next, I read Nittaya's letter.

> My cherished Palace,
>
> How regretful I was to have missed Life's ordination and your troupe of players' great success at the

monastery up the northern coast. You know, there are always ways to get in touch with me quickly, if needs. I had thought to send you several of my guards, but hesitated without your approval. They would have instant communication with me, you but tell them and I would know immediately. Should I do this?

You must be alerted to the doings of the Nnnnmr. They are up to something, but we have not discovered what. Please be vigilant. Report their presence to me if you discover it.

The construction of the temple at the entrance has just begun. I've commissioned the famous sculptor T[...] M[...] to create the Reclining Buddha in the Nats style. I've seen small models and expect the installed work to be arresting, touching.

I have befriended your lovely Rose. What a wonderful addition she is to our community.

Please, now, communicate with me. Keep me posted with what's happening.

Yours, P. Nittaya

With a warm glow, I put away the letters and give them little thought afterwards. Instead, we took up rehearsal on the play, our new recruits giving their first, halting run-through. They would do much better later but, still, their interpretation shone through and stirred unseen visions.

Shortly before dawn a 'van scout appeared on a two-wheeler to announce the arrival of the caravan this coming evening. We are to have our payment ready for collection beforehand and be ready to depart at a moment's notice. Yes, yes. It all seemed rush, rush. Instead, it shall be tedious beyond reckoning. If we got on the road by midnight it would be a miracle. Instead, it would be best to just say our morning prayers, eat our little supper, and settle down for the day. Unfortunately, we are at sea-level here, the temperature at its highest; no sea breezes like those wafting up the lofty northern coast. There will be a few of us whose awake-ness permits them to take in the chorus of snorers. I hear them naught, this day, for slumber catches me unawares, and I know nothing of such chorusing.

I awake in a pool of sweat, a great commotion going on over the sunset which has lighted up the entire sky. I run out to see. It is indeed magnificent, the sun, behind the horizon sending up bright rays that streak far, all the way to the other horizon. In a moment it is broken and the beams retreat after their mother who has gone to visit other nations, other continents. Night now pulls its velvet cloak across the sky, turning on the stars as it goes.

"Where do you get this nonsense," I say to myself. "Oh, it just comes to me. It's more fun to write it down than not." At least for a while it took my mind off of sweat and caravans.

We wait. No caravan. Midnight comes, but not the caravan. Alas, we'll have to spend another night here, this time with a hoard of new people coming in with the caravan. I'm not supposed to feel impatience, but here I am. Should I have spent the evening meditating? Yes, indeed I should have. But why didn't I? Because I was expecting the 'van at any moment and hate to have my meditation interrupted. I could meditate now. But the 'van could arrive at any moment, and I hate ... Yes, yes; I know. So I sit here being un-monkish, impatient.

At last! The caravan arrives! And the poor people straggle in, looking exhausted. I feel so sorry for them. Fame has gone off to pay our fee and secure a place for us in the 'van. People see that we are monks and ask us to bless them. They weep when we do so, and then they give us a little flower, or a leaf, or even a pretty stone they have picked up. It breaks my heart to take anything from them, it being their most precious treasure. Then I realize we are giving them our most precious treasure, too. So we are sharing. These people are the Walkers. They have no carts, busses, or luxury cars. They have but themselves, their feet. They are leaving some place, some untenable place, and going to a new place where hope is leading them, there to find their bliss. Alas! Some will die on the way. If their hope is unfounded they may all die after they have arrived. But aren't we all like these walkers? Leaving an untenable place, led by hope to what we have dreamed, whether it exists or not, there to live or die, as is our fate. What was it the old monk said? "Hope cannot exist without faith," or something like that. So we all have faith. That's the binder. I'm not supposed to, but I bow to them and touch their fingers, as they give me their flowers, their stones. I have the stones still. I've kept them. They are my precious treasures now.

It is too late in the morning to start out in the caravan. We shall spend another day in the station, crowds of people all around.

Instead of feeling anger or impatience I feel humble, touched by the Walkers' faith. As I lay down on my mat I think on them, and their courage, and on us, our little troupe. We are doing exactly what we should be doing, that which no one else has the courage to do, and I look forward to our performances before these people as the 'van moves down the coast.

CHAPTER 5

I speak with Fame, and Life. It is decided. We shall give our first performance this next morning, at our stopping place. No great temple as our backdrop, no educated monks of erudite temper in audience, we shall play first for the Walkers, then whomever else comes along.

The 'van is a veritable hive of noise: jerry-rigged motors coughing and sputtering, cart-people shouting cheery greetings to each other, Walkers in their quiet pain. For the privileged, the 'van is an opportunity to socialize, invitations extended back and forth. We immediately receive a handful of invitations, Fame picking them over. He selects three and passes them on to me. I look at them and find them mildly 'interesting', select one, and collar River and Autumn to go with me. We three find our host's trailer without difficulty and hail it down. They throw open the door and welcome us in.

Hosts are husband and wife, slightly past middle age, not lacking in charm. We find they are from the south, up north here on a pilgrimage visiting some of the great Buddhas, their search being limited by choice to those located on mountain tops. They are on their way home somewhat disappointed. Several of their prized locations were no longer accessible by people of their age, stairs being heavily damaged and impassible. Yet they were able to visit some, plus a few scattered monasteries not on their itinerary. They spoke of young monks, prayer, and the meditative life. We were served up tiny delicacies, tiny glasses, enticing morsels, more tormenting than satisfying. We told them of our plays we would be presenting, this falling on but half-interested ears. I did not expect them to show up. They said nothing further of prayer or meditation, so we said our thanks and departed.

Next was the trailer of a young couple, their eyes most bright and flashing, their accommodation luxuriously set out. They, too, were from the south, the great city there. They had nothing to say, nothing to talk about. The impression I had was they were traveling around, looking for something and hoping they might find it in us. We quickly proved to be very dull and were sent on our way. Autumn and River looked at me and asked, "What was that all about?" Feeling

I knew only too well what it was about, replied, "Oh, I can't possibly imagine," and let the subject drop.

The last card led us to the trailer of an elderly man, quite distinguished, a scholar, who had buried his wife and all his children. He served up an excellent tea. He was very sad, indeed, and we hurried to cheer him up. Nothing moved him so much as news of the University we were founding in the Valley, and he questioned us at great length about it. We invited him to visit, he promising he would. I never heard from him again. I presume death found him before he had a chance to return north. Yet his lifework did eventually find its way to our library.

We returned to our humble bus, sobered by our experience. I felt unsure whether we were ready for such activity, though once the plays began invitations came flooding in. Before denying all invitations I remembered this was the way Life had met Nittaya, setting in motion everything which has happened in the year since. My condemnation must not be so speedy.

We stop at a large building, like a giant inverted U, where we are to spend the day. I am told it was an "airline hangar," whatever possible use that implies. Vast doors are at either end, one end closed and the other partially open, neither working any longer. It is perfect for holding the 'van's people. Quickly, we set up next to the wall, ceiling high above, turn on our spots, Fame barkering away at his best. Soon a small crowd has assembled, and we begin. Little Lord and Smiley hardly appear before the lights when we are interrupted with a commotion in the audience. Apparently, they are reacting to the children, being close to them, their feelings complex. But the play goes on, their reaction raw and intense. Women stand and rend their clothes, their hair. Others shout threats at Little Lord, terrifying him. Fame comes forward, reminding them it is a play they are witnessing. No one is really being threatened, being injured. This mollifies them somewhat, but not entirely. Finally Sweetheart appears, the angel salvation, and all is clear. The antagonists embrace, the angel glories over, lights down, the resolution approved in salvos, still more violent than I would have liked. Life's voice resonates against the cavernous walls, ricocheting here and there, making of him a mighty force. In the end, declaring his faith in Humanity, his voice bouncing around, is joined by many until it is just a roar, nothing intelligible. In resignation, he simply stops and bows. Lights down. But he already has gained Hero-status in the minds of our Walkers, this coming night putting a lift in their stride, a backbone in their resolve.

Over the course of the next mornings I learned this was the way of the Walkers—intense, passionate. No ill would come of it, except possibly to their own being. So I came to accept it for what it was and marveled that they could feel so powerfully. I even came to envy them, their passion.

As we re-crossed the great river valley, heading westward around the great inundation of what had been the river delta, we again came upon the industrialized area where we had stayed one day, going in the opposite direction. Near daylight, we pulled up to a complex of industrial buildings where we were to stay. We made note of where the Walkers were congregating and headed into that building, setting up against a wall. This time the building was not so resonant, some tiny echo, not like the hangar. This morning's play was the call to form communities. A message for the Walkers, if for no others. The audience seemed calmer this morning, the play flowing without major interruption. The beginning of Life's lesson, on the other hand, got off to a rockier start, mentioning the ills that brought us to such a pass. But it ended most positively with, as I said, the call to form communities and start families. There was a subdued rustle at this mention, leading to a wild burst of applause at the end.

The audience rushed forward. Alert Farmer and Soldier, as Nāgas, adroitly stepped forward on Life's either side, intimidating too close an approach, too boisterous a manner. Yet still able to approach, the Walkers treated Life with proper respect. The greater stir appeared to be among themselves as they appeared to group and regroup, perhaps trying on the idea of community. A seed had been planted. That night the 'van continued west across the plain, mountains looming closer. By morning we were still some distance from them. The 'van people set up large canvases under which we were to spend the day. While these 'tents' were twice as high as the tallest person, they provided poor sites for our play. We jerry-rigged one of our tents as backdrop, but were at a loss how to elevate the boys so they could be seen more than two people deep. Someone suggested they stand on chairs. While that limited their movement, they were now visible to most of the audience. This is the vow-taking play, the turning point, and crucial that it carry to the audience. Because the children's voices did not project well without a solid backdrop or ceiling, everyone had to be absolutely still. You could hear a pin drop. Then

Life. Came time for the vow-taking, everyone stood, and Life vanished behind heads and shoulders. Life would shout a line of the vow, the first section would repeat it, the middle section would repeat after, and then the back. It had a rolling force to it that was quite dramatic. Came the last line of the vow, rolling away back, everyone waiting until those in back said it, then cheering. Of all our people, the Walkers have probably felt the force of warfare and class abuse more than any others. They needed little persuasion for its cessation. They certainly expressed themselves most lustily on the subject.

Sometime near the middle of the day we were hit with a deluge of rain. It came down with such force it collapsed the canvas in several places and flooded all the ground on which we had placed our sleeping mats. Once the rain had stopped and the canvas restored, we were still left with soggy mats, setting the conditions for a wretched afternoon. Besides, humidity and temperature soared. Sleep became impossible. I sat there, cross legged, in abject misery, thinking 'things' over. I decided I'd had enough of the plays and lessons. I'd observed enough audiences to know the range of reactions. I was no longer surprised by reactions but, worst, could predict them. Moreover, after the reactions at the mountain monastery to the north, being beyond imagining, these new audiences were ... I don't want to say 'boring' but, rather, 'expected.' I've too restless a temperament to accept 'expected.' I resolve to turn my attention to other issues and let things like 'audience reaction' take their place in the hierarchy.

First, I take on the little stack of cards/invitations that have been given me by Fame. Which of these are duds, like that young couple, or fertile ground, like the old scholar? I look at them, one by one, turning them over as I go. They tell me exactly nothing, nothing beyond names and position in the 'van. Perhaps there's something in the handwriting? I look at the scratchings and tone marks—lines ascending or descending, loops in letters open or closed. Alas! I have no idea what that means. I stare at the cards. I say, "Speak to me," and they are silent. I feel despair welling up. That's not good.

Perhaps I should think on something else. I sit there. Thinking. Dawning, slowly, is the vague feeling I'm overlooking something. Something important. But what? I wrack my brain. Nothing comes. Except that feeling. Gnawing away. Something pending? Not pending. Well, many things are pending, but nothing of a particularly pressing nature. I think on. Danger? Yes! Danger. Something of a dangerous nature. I wonder. Nittaya has offered to send Nāga guards.

Perhaps I should ask her to go ahead and send them. Better to err on the side of caution than ... Yes, I will have a letter ready to send her by the time we reach our next destination ahead, the new coastal city. Nothing beyond the writing of a letter occurs to me.

Time for quick prayers and breakfast before we're off. I'm certainly glad to see this place behind us. We travel on west, the mountains looming closer. By dawn we have reached the foothills and turn south. Again, we are to spend the day in caves—cool, cool caves. I watch them rush to set up for their performance, the last of the series. Soon, I think, Farmer and Soldier will no longer have to strut their stuff as fake Nāgas. We'll have real ones to wow the crowds. What fun! I hear voices booming away, echoes flying all around. I try not to pay attention. I've taken paper and pen—that marvelous flaxen paper from the monastery in the hidden valley north of us here—and write asking for the Nāgas to be sent. Then I take another piece of paper and answer Grace's nice letter. And then, while I'm at it, I write Rose and tell her about Life's ordination as our abbot. She probably already knows about it, but she should know of it from me, too. There. At least now I've done something. Mollified, I sit there smiling, feeling very pleased with myself.

Another night's travel, now on a coastal plain, mountains to our right, ocean to our left, the width of our country, already narrow, begins to narrow even more. The destination city, ahead, has been the transportation hub of the north for centuries; and consequently it has been the site of much warfare, being leveled more than once. In modern times it has been the site of numerous attacks from the marauders. The monastery where we shall perform has been attacked, all the monks and novices killed, the buildings reduced to ash. All that remains is the colorful gateway, three-portals with fanciful little pagodas rising on top, still with its famous yellow vertical stripes with red characters on them, speaking of joy and the words of the Buddha. Ours shall be a memorial to our brethren who have lost their lives in these halls. Villagers from around the ruins may attend. Perhaps there will be only ghosts in attendance.

We approach the city from the north. Formerly, travelers would have crossed a river into the city on one of two bridges beside a picturesque escarpment. Now, the sea has encroached far inland. Walkers are taken by small, flat-bottom boats into the devastated streets. We in vehicles must wait in line for a hulking old rig connected to corroding, saggy cables to jerk us over. We pass the still standing bridges on the way, connecting promontory to promontory, looking grand and useless. Then we are in the city. My countrymen are lovers of grand gestures and here, incarnate, are certainly grand gestures. Boulevards, broad circles with fountains and sculpture in the center, monuments to great men—kings!—of the past. How sorry it all looks now, broken and lying, mostly, on the ground, its former grandeur in tatters. No one to repair it, nor will there be for centuries, if we survive. The few citizens still alive live their days in cabins barely two meters wide, overturned crates, lean-tos, canvas. Yet they live.

The caravan proceeds on to the city's station where there is shelter enough to wait out the day. We go on to the site of the former monastery and pile out of the bus, admiring the gate in the starlight. There is a small square in front of it. It will be perfect for the performances. We run around looking for shelter for the coming day and find only a storefront whose ground floor is relatively intact. We shall have to sleep cheek to jowl, but at least we'll be in shelter. We start fires, fueled by the abundant charcoal all around, say prayers, eat a slim supper, and turn in. I thought I'd toss all day but instead slept like a baby. Twilight was soon upon us. Prayer, again, breakfast, and setup for the performance. The guys shone the spots into the sky, Fame barkered, and soon we had a little audience for our performance. Exactly sixteen people. Before the plays start I take Loyal aside to talk with him.

"Loyal," I said, "I'm sorry for not spending time with you sooner."

"That's okay," he said softly.

"No it isn't. Farmer, Soldier, and I kind of fell into doing some things that grew very quickly, faster than we expected. They ended up getting hired as our Security Department. It was like lightening."

"Yeah, I noticed that."

"See? I knew you would feel left out. I'm so sorry. I didn't mean for that to happen to you."

"I don't feel left out at all. I've actually wanted some time to think about what I've wanted to do. I haven't been sure ... Helping out with the crew for the plays has been perfect for me."

"Loyal, I've been wanting to ask you, would you like to be my assistant and help me out?"

"Your assistant? That would be great. Sure. Of course."

"Wonderful! Can you start right now?"

"Yeah, sure." A rather long pause, then, "Palace, I've been meaning to give you this." From beneath his shirt he pulled out his long knife. "Please keep it. I'm not going to have any use for it anymore," he said, looking at me, sober-faced.

Oh, stupid me! I'm suddenly fighting back the tears for the sheer joy of the moment. There I am, holding his treacherous looking knife in my hands, knowing full well the last possible thing to do is cry. I choke back the tears and the words get choked back, too. I sit there, dumbly. He looks at me, expecting me to say something. So I lower my head as though I'm examining the knife for something or other, trying to gain time.

"Palace," he asks. "Palace?"

A big gasp escapes me. I'd been holding my breath, but now the words come. "Loyal, thank you for this gift. It shall be one of my most treasured possessions." He puts his hand on top of mine and gives it a quick squeeze, quickly letting go.

"Palace," he says, "I've learned so much in the few short weeks we've been with you folks, more than in my whole past lifetime. I'm changed, a different person. I'm ashamed of that life and don't ever want to go back. I want to stay with you monks, doing good things for people, for the world. That is what I want my life here on to be."

"Does that mean you want to join the monastery?"

"I wasn't sure before this moment, but I am now. Yes. I want to join your monastery."

That did it! The floodgates broke, and out came the tears. I hate it! Every little thing, and I'm crying. It's so unmanly. I turned away, trying to hide the worst of it.

"Palace," he said, pulling at my arm. I turned back and glanced up at him. Tears were running down his cheeks, too.

"Well," I said in a shaky voice, "I guess you'll fit right in."

Together, we went to the gates, to the play area, waiting for Life to be finished with his lesson. He had long since dispensed with the big thick book but kept the lectern. Hand lightly resting on it, he delivered his "I believe" speech from memory, with great solemnity.

Loyal squeezed my arm and whispered, "See? That's it. That's what I mean. You can't listen to that and not be changed."

At the end of the speech our little audience rose, approving, all stomping and applause, a surprisingly big sound, then moving forward to speak with Life, our pseudo-Nāga guards getting there first. My countrymen are a gregarious lot, loving guileless informality. Dealing with Nāgas is out of their league. Poor things, our little audience were suddenly reduced to formal bows, a few murmured words, a hasty retreat. I'm not sure the Nāgas, real or fake, were exactly fair to them, but at least it keeps our beloved Abbot above any threat of harm.

When all had settled back down, Loyal and I go to Life with the news. "Life, Loyal has just told me he wishes to join our Monastery. Is it possible this night to formally induct him into the novitiate?" I asked.

"Congratulations! What wonderful news," he said, taking Loyal by the hand. "Now, this is what must happen: we announce your wish to join the order. Then there is a wait period, say a few days, allowing time for any objections to be voiced. After that, you can be inducted. I suggest we do this here, the same night after our last performance. Here, in front of these hallowed gates. I can't think of a finer occasion."

"Thank you. Yes," said Loyal, overcome.

"Everybody. May I have your attention?" Everyone stopped what they were doing and looked at Life. "Loyal has just asked me to induct him into the order." A whoop goes up from our two play-Nāgas. "If there is no objection, I will conduct the service after our final performance four nights from now." There are scattered cheers and clapping. "There, now, it's official," said Life, smiling, to Loyal, he looking stunned at the rapidity of events.

Soldier and Farmer now descended on him, pounding his back, giving him a good shake. "Wow!" they say. "So you're really going to do it?" and "Who woulda thought!" and even "The thug that became a holy man!" Finally, Soldier summed it up, "Hey, guy, these have been heavy days, these last few weeks. Can you believe what's happening to us? We are the luckiest guys in the world!"

"Yes, we are indeed," answered Loyal back, finally smiling again.

Our midnight meal ready, we said prayers and ate. "Loyal, can you read?" I asked.

"No," he answered, rather sheepishly.

"Do you know how to do math?"

"Math? Do you mean work with numbers? No."

"Good. Then I shall teach you," I said. "How about starting tonight? We'll start with numbers. Okay?"

"Sure. Tonight's good. I have nothing else to do."

"Very good. We have workbooks. Rose made workbooks for us. You haven't met Rose yet. You'll love her. She's in the Valley now, the acting head of the monastery while Life is here. Her workbooks take it one step at a time. Math is like another language. You have to learn it word by word, and you have to think in that language in order to 'speak' it." I rattled on terribly. Loyal looked stunned.

I wash our bowls, Loyal's and mine, dry them and put them in the proper box. Then it's to the bus to get a workbook and back by the fire where we can see clearly. We hunker down, our heads practically touching. "We'll start by learning the numbers and what they mean. Here they are." I show him in the workbook. "0, 1, 2, 3, 4, 5, 6, 7, 8, 9, 10. Like our ten fingers. Now, you know what the word "1" means. Hold up 'one' fingers." He laughs at me as he puts up an index finger. And on we go.

He's a good student, picking up ideas quickly. We breeze through the first lesson, and then the second. I leave him to do the simple addition problems of the third. I look back and see a starving mind at last eating a nourishing meal. Shortly, he waves me over to check his work. Perfect. On to the fourth lesson, then fifth and sixth and on. We stop at 10 because it's time for morning prayer, supper, and sleep. Loyal's feeling good about himself. On he and I go the next four nights, paying little heed to the performances going on over yonder, in the square. We sense the audience has grown by the commotion they make but pay no more attention to it. Loyal now adds columns of figures, five digits wide, flawlessly. Then it's on to subtraction. But we must pause.

Preparations begin for his induction. He must have habits in place of his regular rag-tag clothes. Both Autumn and River agree to give him one of their habits so that he will have a set and a spare,

Autumn also agreeing to assist Loyal in the rituals. The night of the final play, the night of induction, I bring out the razor from its box and strap it a time or two. Loyal kneels before me and is shorn of the hair on his head. Also the eyebrows and beard, part of our tradition. He is transformed! From rough warrior with ponytail topknot to contemplative recluse. He is dressed with special underclothing so that he should not be naked when shorn of his outer garments, replaced with novice habit.

The final play is over. Only a few of the audience departs, the bulk remaining, a chance to witness a rare ritual in these days. We of The Order assemble before the gates, on our knees, our portable Buddha placed in front. Our prayer books are all marked for the prayers to be sung, the singing bowl readied for measured stroke, candles scattered like stars among us. Life steps before kneeling Loyal, Nāganese Farmer and Soldier standing not far behind, lending a surreal quality to the ritual. Three long-spaced tones float from the mouth of the singing bowl, setting pace for the coming ceremony. The first prayer is intoned, verse after verse, these ancient texts more relevant now than ever, I think. From time to time we chanters bow our heads to the floor, spaced out, in a sort of grand rhythm only the angels would know. Now Loyal stands, is stripped of his old clothes, they summarily discarded, and is covered in new raiment, his habit, the spare neatly folded in narrow rectangle and placed before him. The time comes for collected gifts to be placed before the Buddha. We have but one: Loyal's shorn topknot that he wanted placed there in testament to his renouncing his former life. I'd thought of the knife, too, but we all came to feel the sight of so dangerous looking an implement might be too upsetting. On we prayed, and on more, blessing our inductee, thrice over. Come, now, the vows, nine of which he directly agrees to, ninety-nine cursorily read, representing the total two-hundred-ninety-eight. More prayers and bowing, and he at last is welcomed into our Order. All of us, even the audience, show happy smiles. Some thoughtful person has put out plates with pleasantly arranged fruits and vegetables to share. Where that came from is a mystery. With only one morsel, my refreshment came from watching our audience relish what for them was a rare treat.

"Welcome," I said to Loyal. "Welcome into our fold, our family." He beamed, beyond words.

For a time I fell to the sin of pride, congratulating myself in thinking I brought the first recruit into the fold. Later, I was humbled in discovering Life was regularly sending recruits directly to the Valley, going as far back as a student from that university in the capitol city. I was far from being the first. Oh well. I was quite amazed, on returning to the Valley nearly a year later, to be met by … Ah, well.

The following night we moved to the station, awaiting the arrival of the next caravan that would carry us on south, parallel to the coast. There was a mind-numbing repetitiveness to our travels on which I shall not dwell. I shall but briefly mention the next phase of our journey, definitely the most difficult yet. Formerly, a modern highway and rail system ran south along the coast, linking north and south of our country. The land on which these were located was of low elevation, only a few feet above sea level. Came the great inundation, the ocean advanced far inland, in many places up to the foothills. Gone was the good highway, now under as much as six meters of water. The choice of thoroughfare was secondary roads, even dirt roads, ruts and craters everywhere. Our progress, never rapid, was reduced to a snail's pace. What would have taken us six days or a week now took us twice that. The compensation for being slow was the more interesting landscape, we now traveling through mountain valleys with vistas opening up of ocean and mountain to admire. We performed our five evenings of plays/lessons and then, at popular urging, repeated them. In between we gave the first performance of the trio of adults performing the first play. It was well-accepted, I think, because the feelings portrayed aspired to a kind of high passion, nothing like the boys' performance. All in all, it was an experiment well worth doing, not alone for stroking our actors' self-esteem. The plan is for them to perform it again as opportunity presents itself.

Oh, yes, Nittaya's two Nāga guards caught up with us a few days into our southward trek. It was just in time to relieve Framer and Soldier before their performances in the play. People thought they saw familiarities between the former guards and the actors. They made enquiries. It was also in time for the real Nāgas to strut around a bit, during Life's last lesson, on mention of aliens and Nāgas in particular. Afterwards, we got many invitations specifically requesting their presence. We declined all of them.

At last, much to our relief, we saw our destination city materialize on the flatlands to our south. The monastery was on a high hill where city met river, flowing from western mountains to its mouth directly on the eastern edge of the city. The city was originally many kilometers inland from the ocean, it now a coastal city, alas, without any benefits of coastal cities—beaches, thriving port, scenic escarpments. In its place was a pathetic sight of swamped buildings, half submerged skeletons of trees, tiny islands of little rhyme or reason. The promontory on which the monastery occupied the summit, formerly covered in trees, was now a raw and jagged unsightliness, the road twisting up its side washed out, collapsed. We would have to ascend its wounded torso on foot, carrying everything up on our backs. Not a happy prospect. But what delight met us once we reached the top! Behind us stood a pagoda on a rounded summit, reaching upward ten stories. In front, a long walkway with central divide, stretching along the summit's spine, little hills causing rises and dips. At the far end a tri-portal gate, monumental even from this distance. Pointed eves were seen beyond without being clear what they were. Naturally, they were of temple buildings helping shape an inner square of sublime proportion. As we progressed along the walk pennants were hoisted above the gate, showing their colors to us. Then, as we approached nearer, conches sounded a regal blast. Finally, the monastic community arranged themselves on the steps, waving handkerchiefs. Never had we been so festively greeted! We shouted and waved back, right up to their very presence on walls above. We were taken in, sat down, and served delicious cups of tea, the most delicious not of my own making I must admit.

It seems, we are their first visitors in a generation. I mean, their first monastic visitors. They are eager to learn the news from the north. We tell them of this monastery and that, who is struggling, who prospers. They marvel at it all. They, like us, are young with one lay elder, their abbot twenty-six years old, five years the senior of Life. He's a jolly fellow, seeming to like the social life, like now with this welcoming party. We tell him of the social life on the caravans and he fairly lights up. I certainly can't fault him for that, either; I, who have a more active social life than we Buddhist monks are supposed to have. I predict this young man will be among our early visitors to the Valley and shall remain a friend for life.

The monastery escaped attack from marauders in an interesting twist of events. Once the national government fell, two rival warlords moved into the area, meaning to take it over. They battled so strongly among themselves, their ranks were seriously reduced leaving both of them too weak to make a serious inroad into controlling the area. Other powers have threatened to move in but, thankfully, none have. The city has also been the hub of east-west traffic with the four countries to the west, and I suspect there's been influence from that direction in helping to keep the independence. There is more than one monk here speaking with a heavy foreign accent I site to prove my point. Incidentally, speaking of aliens, the abbot was eager to meet our Nāga guards and made a great point of taking them to see the superb friezes of dragons here at the monastery temple. He told them of a dragon in the 15th century performing numerous deeds of valor in defense of this particular temple and his being much loved consequently. I'm sure, before we leave, he shall have persuaded them to drop their human form and show him their dragon one.

Our time of conviviality over, we were led to our cells and then given a tour of the premises for the purpose of deciding where we should like to set up our stage. Beyond the marvelous gate there is a good-sized enclosed quadrangle with the main temple opposite from the gate. The two buildings on either side, the eves we saw from a distance, were given over to specific monastery functions. The gates, being of a particularly striking character, became our choice for the performances—not the outside façade but the inside. There is a large central arching door. Rather than the two smaller outer doors being closely attached to the center, here these doors are separated by perhaps two or three meters and stand distinctly on their own. Inside the gate there is a rectangular room, open on the fourth side, supported by two well shaped pillars, looking like nothing so much as a stage. The impression is heightened by a well-proportioned terrace with a few steps leading down to the square. We could not ask for a better facility for our performances. We were curious whether we should expect many people from the surrounding communities and were told there might be a good number, especially by way of word-of-mouth as the nights progressed.

By now dawn was breaking over the eastern horizon, out over the water. We joined our hosts in morning prayer and then retired to our cells for the day. There would be one night in preparation and the following night the plays would begin.

Loyal, having mastered addition and subtraction, is currently working on multiplication. He is also learning to read. He has taken over teaching the boys, learning one day and teaching the next. He is a natural. The boys, I am sure, prefer him to me.

I was told the evening of vow-taking went well as did the final evening of extra-terrestrials, the Nāgas putting on an especially good showing. Our jolly host saw to it we had a good time while guests at his monastery. Beyond that happening, absolutely nothing of any significance took place. But one more night, happily spent in prayer and meditation in the company of our newest brethren, and we went uneventfully into town center to await the next caravan heading south.

CHAPTER 6

In practically no time at all the Walkers discovered us and asked our blessing. Of course, we gave it, unstintingly, as they later gave us their passionate reaction to our plays. Meanwhile, as we awaited the arrival of our new caravan, I was hunted down by a courier and presented a letter sent by Nittaya. It read:

My Cherished Palace,

Your letter was received as I trust you have by now received my two reliable young fellows into your midst. They have been instructed at length on the does and don'ts of frontier service and should serve you well. Should they misbehave, you have but to tell me and all will be set to rights.

Grace tells me the Valley Foundation is now the official owner of the environs. Congratulations. This is a grand achievement, one I am sure brings you feelings of relief and achievement. How exemplary are the efforts of your mighty little band!

Meanwhile, my suspicions of the Nnnnmrs increase. I again repeat to you to be vigilant, watchful of things out of the ordinary that might have our invisible friends' fingerprints. I worry that you are vulnerable, unfamiliar with their ways and means. You must promise to tell me of anything, anything, out of the ordinary. Have no concern with burdening me, for this is a burden I take up willingly. Now mind me, and do as I say.

I've been thinking about coming for a visit while you are at the city of the former royal court. It has been some time since I've been there and have a desire to retrace haunts of long ago. Would you be free to join my ramblings?

We continue here in peace and tranquility.

Yours, P. Nittaya

As I read the paragraph about the Nnnnmrs I am in shock. I completely forgot about the little event under the bridge, back there, hundreds of kilometers ago. Immediately, I take up paper—while the courier is waiting, he enjoying a cup of hot tea—and jot down the whole incident. Better, I feel, tell Nittaya than burden busy Life. Once done, I hand the envelope to the courier, carefully noting his locking it up in his pouch, knowing it shall be in the hands of the Princess before another night has passed. Feeling shamefaced with guilt, I mope around wishing already for Nittaya's instructions on how to carry on.

I come upon Loyal holding class with the five boys. I watch, 'observe' I believe it is called. As I'd hoped, they are doing better under his instruction than they were under mine. A pleasant relief.

Loyal was also put in charge of invitations while in caravan. Unlike me, he seems to have a feel for it, and I look forward to meeting some honorable people. Perhaps, since he still struggles with reading, it slows him down, letting him read between the lines.

I meander on, coming upon Farmer and Soldier now in their real face. I ask how they are doing, and they tell me of scouting around, looking for broader realms of threat than simply looking after Life. I think to tell them to be on the lookout for the Nnnnmr, but hesitate. How to tell them to be on the lookout for creatures they can't see? So I concentrate on describing the 'being watched' creepy feeling.

"Yeah, I have that feeling all the time," confessed Soldier.

"Does your skin ever tingle, too?" I ask.

"Yeah, sometimes," he replied.

"Promise me, if you have both feelings at the same time, come to me immediately," I instruct.

"I promise. Why? Does that mean something?"

"Maybe," I say.

They both look at me, questioning. I say nothing more on the subject.

Then I seek out Life. I tell him, "I've just gotten a letter from Nittaya. She wants to visit while we are in the city of the old royal court."

"Excellent," he says. "How is the princess doing?"

"Well. Apparently a bit bored. I think that's why she wants to visit."

"I think that would be a good occasion for her. It marks the end of our being in the north of the country and our entrance into the south. Perhaps she could prepare us for the transition."

Now I'm in a muddle. Should I mention anything at all about the Nnnnmrs and her warnings? Life looks completely at peace with the world, a state I feel I should not disturb with any vague fears. So I merely ask, "How are you and the Nāga guards getting along?"

"Fine. We are doing fine," he replies, giving me a reassuring grin.

"Nittaya tells me she's read them the riot act. If they misbehave she's to be told. Okay?"

"Okay." More reassuring grins.

On I walk. Now I feel as though the world is in suspension, as though something is about to happen. I tell myself how silly I am. 'Suspension' feeling, indeed. That's because you finally wrote to Nittaya and are awaiting her response. Your 'action' can't get in gear until after you have heard from Nittaya. And she hasn't even received your letter yet. That's why you feel suspended. It's because you are in suspension, dolt! All right. All right. I shall be calm and just wait.

And then it begins. I feel I'm being watched. I'm being watched and also have that 'chicken skin' feeling. I have them both at once! I'm in the presence of the Nnnnmr!

"Okay. I know you're here. Show yourself," I say in a soft voice. Nothing. I look for a nearby place where I'll be in relative privacy. I say aloud, "I know you're here. Show yourself." Nothing. This is really bad. They're not responding. "Come on. Show yourselves," I say louder, firmer. Still nothing. "I've written the Princess about that earlier incident, as you perfectly well know. This shall not pass, I assure you." I pause to see if there'll be a reaction of some sort. Again, nothing. The thought floats into my head I may be fabricating this, that there may not be any Nnnnmrs around, that I'm just talking to myself. I decide to put myself in the presence of the two Nāgas and see if the feeling goes away. I retrace my steps. There they are outside Life's door.

"Do you know about the Nnnnmr?" I ask.

"Do you mean do I know of the Nnnnmr, or know of their possible plotting?" one asks in return.

"Yes, both," I reply.

"Yes," he replies.

"Oh," I say to the abrupt answer. "Do they give you a creepy feeling when they are present but don't show themselves?"

"What do you mean?"

"Ahhh, I mean can you tell if they are nearby without actually seeing them?"

"Yes."

"Are there any nearby now?"

"No."

"Hmmm. Okay, if you do feel any of them around, or see any, come to me. Do not report this to Life."

"I cannot do that. That is not in my instructions," he said, his jaw rather firmly set.

"Oh, so you have instructions on the matter," I said, finding the knowledge of great interest.

"I am not permitted to discuss my orders," he replied in at least an octave deeper tone.

"And well I would not want you to," I answer. All very interesting. I should simply put all this out of mind until I hear back from Nittaya. She shall instruct on a course of action. I must be patient.

I thank him, turn, and return to where we are camped out, the feeling of being watched not abating one bit. Yes, I simply must put them out of mind and wait. There's Autumn and River, puttering around with preparing our midnight meal. I'll go help them. That'll be a good distraction.

And so I do just that.

Our midnight meal and then prayer. After prayer, meditation. If I get two nights' meditation in a row I feel lucky. I try not to be upset by that little fact, yet it disturbs me no end. Meditation is something you do regularly for years. Perhaps fifty years. Maybe then things will happen. But, above all, you can't skip ... like I seem to be doing.

In early morning, before dawn, the scout from our caravan arrives and announces the eminent arrival of the 'van. I'll believe it when I see it. We have but one more stop before the city of the old royal court. We shall again be traveling the old inland roads, no doubt running into impassible places which we shall have to pass. Yet another adventure with which we shall be blessed.

The 'van comes later than announced, an event with which we are familiar. We get started late. There are more delays along the way than usual. We arrive at our destination considerably later than planned. No matter! We all seem to have more time to waste than anything else.

The city rises before us to the south on a broad hill that rises out of the water with only a fringe of ruins to the east standing with their feet in the water. Surprisingly, many trails of smoke rise into the air above the city ruins, signifying the homes of city residents. But even more surprising is the Fort, our destination, its ramparts defining the shape of an island, rising even more to the east. Formerly, it had guarded the mouth of a river and a prosperous trading port, most of which is now submerged. We depart the 'van at a strategic point by the shore and await, what else to do, the arrival of a sad old barge that will take us to the Fort. Eventually, it arrives, and off we go. Centuries ago, human hands fit stone to mortared stone into a four-pointed star that prophetically now stands just above the tide, permitting even us nowadays to lord it over the sea. We were to perform at the East Gate, a wonderful edifice combining design elements from my country's traditions and those of the former European colonizer. The lower, massive part of the gate, built of stone and brick, is in the Western taste, the upper story and pagoda-like tower in our Asian taste. We were not told where exactly we were to perform, so we took it upon ourselves to make that decision. Outside the gate we had the prospect of the gate itself as backdrop with a bridge and highway approach as ample room for audience. Inside the gate we would have a more simple façade against which to play and a large courtyard for the audience. I felt the outside would be a better choice, our spots attractive against the massive walls, Life standing parapet-high, shouting his lessons down on audience heads like the ancient prophets. But none of that appealed to him, so performing inside the gate was chosen.

It was suggested we should stay in the administration building just to the right of the gate. Life, looking farther off at the next point of the massive stone star, saw the decorative eves of the former barracks buildings, thinking it would be merrier to stay there. Farmer and Soldier were sent off to investigate the barracks, returning with a report they were rotten at the core. So administration building it was. It wasn't in that decent shape either. We explored all the floors and decided on the second floor. Up a wide, grand staircase with curving balustrades, enough rooms for each of us to have our own, just high enough to catch the prevailing winds out of the northwest—dry winds, killer of humidity.

Performances would begin the following evening. We got ourselves organized, where we would eat, where say prayers and have meditation. It fell to me to see to setting up our portable Buddha in the meeting room designated for prayers. The poor old fellow has acquired a few nicks and chips on this pilgrimage but seems totally oblivious. After our slim midnight meal a group of us depart for the East Gate to reconnoiter so that a final decision can be made about location of performances. I've decided I shall not have an opinion on the subject, even if pressed.

We stroll out to the gate. It is an absolutely gorgeous night, the waning moon just nosing above water to the east, sending a sheen all the way from there to here. The gate is truly a stylistic marvel, managing to have a kind of flamboyant grace. The broad arches of the Mediterranean base seem to gestate and liberate the little pagoda-like structure on top. As one ascends the stairs on either side of the arching entrance, one can admire that charming little edifice at a closer and closer range. Then, as one achieves the parapet, the upper structure of the gate has become Asian, refined. It presents to the beholder a metaphor to enjoy at one's leisure. Incidentally, the view from the parapet is quite wonderful, looking out across water to fragments of cityscapes, the mountains not far beyond. I make a note to come out here one night and walk its entirety, a not inconsiderable undertaking.

And then I see it, where all is water, south of where I'm standing, the famous Blue Pagoda and white Buddha, their feet in the water, still sending out their benediction. They could not be more than ten or twelve blocks from the Fort. The sight in starlight sends my heart soaring then crashing at the realization the temple and monastery there are no more. Now I understand why Hero and Bright scheduled us here, at the Fort. It was as close to the old monastery as fortune would now allow. I determine to find a boat that will take me there— take us all there—before we depart this city.

And then it was time for morning prayer and sleep. We return to the administration building, and go to the room where our Buddha rests, there to pray. On, then, mounting the grand staircase to our rooms and sleeping mats, and the oblivion of the day.

Some blessed spirit thinks to sound the singing bowl to wake us for evening prayer, breakfast and the first evening's performance. Having some report or other to work on, I excuse myself from attending and bask instead in solitude. Still, sounds from the audience waft on the midnight air, interrupting, causing me to muse there must be a sizable audience, perhaps some fifty or sixty strong, from the sounds of it. Excellent! Then back to work. In practically no time sounds in sequence of wailing, shouts, applause, and stomping float to me in stillness of the night. I expect to hear soon the footfall of the returning troops from their opening campaign; and, sure enough, there it is. The boys are the first to find me out, come tripping over themselves to deliver their special kind of report. They are so very jolly and in no time I'm laughing with them, at them. Soon, Soldier and Farmer saunter into the room to ask if I want to mount the ramparts this night. Using the report as excuse, I demur. They leave me alone then, listening to stirrings all around. Sometime later intoned the singing bowl, in time for morning prayers and sleep, in sacred cycle.

Again the singing bowl, and it was evening prayer, breakfast, and midnight performance of the second night, the Calling to Communities. Work on the report ended while the play was going on. I thought to walk the parapet that night, left my room, left the administration building, mounted the steps leading to the parapet rim, and began my haunt.

Another gorgeous night, the clamorous stars greeted me as I mounted the wall and walked toward the gate. Keeping well back so that I would not be spied passing by, I nevertheless stole glances at the assembly, favorably noting its size. On I went, into the night, embracing its peace as I went. Soon the waters of the south spread out, punctured by the blue pagoda and stoic Buddha, his cupped hand at his chest, quietly waiting. For delivery from the flood? I, for one, could not say. I reached the zenith of the southeastern point of the Fort, turning back in a western direction, never turning my gaze from the two emergents. They seemed to take on a life of their own, silently wading through the waters as they shifted positions. The Buddha slid behind the pagoda, then emerged the other side, heading out on his own. Coming to the point where I should risk tripping over the edge of the parapet or turn my back on the silent figures, I made the hard choice. Now the city ruins swam before me, rising over a broad hill, vanishing in darkness. It was altogether sinister in its aspect, in stark contrast to the other benevolent view. Too much detail presented silvery jagged images swallowed in starkest void, all, like in a kaleidoscope, swirling before me in confusion. The shadows seemed to form into stealthy figures, up to no good, stealing through the night. There I was, now at the southwestern point of the star, not halfway through my sentry duty but far, far from my companions. I began to be uneasy with my deployment.

On through the night I walked as I turned now to the north. With each step I regret being alone. I should have been more prudent, bringing along at least one companion, any number of persons willing to come. To my left, black oily water with skeins of silver light breaking in glassy shards over the surface. Ahead, blackness of the void, unknown hills, and mountains with nothing to show but void. I walk and walk. To my right, far off, over there, I see the spots, sending shafts of light off into the sky. There is nothing to be heard from that distant quarter.

What is that ahead? Slithers off the parapet, into the turbid waters below. No doubt, some grotesque hybrid aquarian better not to acquaint oneself with. Waters below, now more aggressively slapping the brick and stone walls, in the distance the forlorn cry of a water bird, rustlings all around. At last! To the northwestern point of the star I come. I turn east, and now I see lights of humanity, far off still, these I now approach. Yet am I brushed by passing things, as though truant ghosts would touch me with their incorporeality, halt my forward movement. On my face! On my hand, I doubt it not. It was there. These apparitions hurry me forward, past the dilapidated barracks on my right, their doors perhaps spilling forth souls of armies past. Hardly soon enough, I reach the zenith of the northeastern point of the star, feeling safer with every step. The dark shape of the administration building looms ahead, then beside. Farther on the spots of the play, trails darting through the sky above. At last! The steps down from this cursed place. But as I descend, shame rises up, reddening my face. Wild imaginings, all those dark apparitions, for nothing could have been there, could it? In the front doors, greeted by soft light, up the ornate stairs, turn, in my room, a little breathless, my heart pounding from the exertion, of course. Foolish me, to let the mere thought of ghosts become incarnate.

From the gate, the audience astir at lesson's end, soon to send the boys running up the ornate stairs, in my door. This night, how I shall welcome their hail fellows.

Yet have I walked the parapets!

Now feeling rather pleased with myself, I can't help but smile, still work to have it appear sphinxlike to any who should observe. No need my little secrets be known by everyone. Farmer and Soldier come by and ask if I would like to walk the parapets with them this night. I say to them, "I've had second thoughts about my doing that. But you boys feel free to do so any time you would like." They reveal a bit of irritation with me in their looks. Of course, I should have waited to make the circumnavigation with them, but one doesn't always do what one should, does one? The incident reminds me of something that does need planning.

I seek out Life. We talk a bit about audience response to performances here and how he feels about that. I bridge then to my concern, "We are close upon a most holy site, now inundated in at least three meters of water. I feel we and all our brothers should go there in homage before we leave here."

"Yes, I know of the site you mean," said Life, "the Blue Pagoda, it being just over there. I've seen it, and the white Buddha, standing in the water. Can you speak with Bright about arranging boats to take us over there?"

I sought out Bright and explained the situation and asked that he arrange boats enough for us to visit the site, that we would undertake rites in memorial which would take some amount of time. "When would you like to do this," he asked.

I replied, "Whenever it could be arranged, just not in conflict with performances." He nodded. Good! That was set in motion.

Then he asked, "Did anyone tell you we will be performing at two different monasteries in the city of the old royal court?"

"I didn't know that," I answered, not liking surprises.

"The first one we'll go to is upriver and has many legends attached to it. The second is in the city and is Zen oriented. It's really old. The buildings are in good shape for both. You'll find them interesting."

He was about to launch into greater detail, but I silenced him with, "Well, now I know. Thank you," and left.

I returned to work on my report—proofing, revising.

Audiences for the five performances had been growing each night, the final evening counted at 137. Everyone was quite happy at that number. We had a little celebration afterwards at our supper. Life stood and said, "Thanks to you, my brothers, for your hard work every night. It would be impossible to present our plays and lessons without you being there, making your contributions, those invisible performances as telling in a production as the speaking rolls. I mean you, the lighting crew; you, the makeup person; you, the director; you, the costumer. Maybe you, especially the costumer, because I see you with needle and thread repairing the torn costumes when all the rest of us have put our things away and are off to play." He is interrupted with laughter. "My brothers, I thank you for your gifts to the production and especially for your support for our five young actors." He claps his hands energetically which everyone picks up.

When things have settled, Life continues. "Tomorrow evening when we depart this historic place, we will stop at a nearby place that is even more ancient and historic." A murmur spreads through the room. "Perhaps you looked south from the parapets here? If so, you would have seen a large white sculpture of the Buddha and a blue pagoda standing in the water. This is the place of an ancient monastery where resided not just monks, but nuns and children, too, like us. For seven hundred years they existed in harmony with this land. Then, about one hundred years ago, the ocean exceeded its shoreline, overflowing its banks and flooding the lowlands all around here. The ecclesiastics had to leave their beloved home and abandon it to the invading waters. Tomorrow, on our way, we will visit this site and sing hymns in honor of so hallowed a place. You will see there a bit of each of our lives, for we have all lived such disaster. But as that land was once dry land, so it will be again. The Buddha and pagoda survive in those waters for a reason. Open your hearts to the reason, my brothers, and rejoice with that effigy, that tower." There was silence as Life sat back down. I scanned the faces and saw their recognition.

Everyone having packed their things before sleep at dawn were ready to go early that evening. Boats were waiting for us at the East Gate that we loaded with production things and then ourselves. From the water we looked up again at the Fort and marveled at its sweep and grandeur. Along its east flank we floated, around the southeastern point. There, not far off, stood the two memorials for the first leg of our travels. We watched in fascination as they approached, seeming to have a life of their own. As the boats maneuvered round the Buddha, so that we would be facing him, he seemed to grow in stature compared to the nine-story pagoda, soon towering over it. We lashed our boats together so that they would not drift apart and commenced singing prayers. How beautifully the words seemed to express our thoughts and feelings in the presence of this icon. On we sang as all the stars of the heavens twinkled to life and illuminated our evening. They say we, living in the night without the glare of electric lights, see far better in the dark than our ancestors. I can't testify to the truth of that, but I felt I saw the Buddha clearly enough, and the Blue Pagoda with its filigree decoration and upturned eves. I see them still as I close my eyes and imagine. Also, I see them no longer wading in the water but standing free, on dry land, as they were and meant to be.

We hoped to enter the temple to visit the Buddha at the altar, but the great roof had collapsed inward, blocking entry, this our only real disappointment that hallowed eve. Our prayers over, our farewells said to the monuments, we unlashed our boats and rowed on to the station building where we were to *rendezvous* with our bus and meet the caravan going to the city of the old royal court.

To our great surprise and amazement the caravan had already arrived and was expecting to depart directly after the midnight meal. Because we were late, as the 'van people reckoned, we were not given an advantageous position in the lineup of vehicles. We were hard-pressed to load our bus and get in ourselves, giving up our largest meal of the night, before the 'van began moving. How curious Fate can be with certain things. We either wait and wait for the 'van or we scramble to get ready and go.

As we moved out we heaved a collective sigh of relief and broke out a food box, distributing morsels all around. Because we were so happy to have gotten a place on the 'van, and were actually launched on our way, we started singing jolly tunes at the top of our voices and laughing at ourselves.

CHAPTER 7

Our raucousness having finally died down I was sitting quietly playing string games with Sweetheart and Charming, with whom I was sharing a seat, when Farmer and Soldier came back saying they needed to talk. I shooed off the two boys and huddled with our Security staff.

Soldier began, "We were going to talk with you at the station, but there was no time."

"Did you know," continued Farmer, "the big leader of all the marauding armies has set himself up in one of the old royal palaces in the city where we're going next?"

"No," I said, suddenly alarmed. "Do you think they'll give us any trouble?"

"Maybe," answered Soldier. "Our boss, the guy that sent us out to stop you, got his orders from this big boss, the guy in the palace."

"We thought," continued Farmer, "if there was going to be any trouble, any follow-through, it would be in his city."

"Yeah," continued Soldier. "He'll likely send out a bunch of thugs to shut you down at one of the performances."

"How can they do that?" I ask, now giving them my complete attention.

"They'll probably knock you guys over the head and stick a knife between your ribs," Farmer described, graphically gesturing blow and thrust.

"Oh, no!" I exclaimed. "Is there anything we can do to stop them?"

"Yeah," said Farmer, "Any chance we could get twenty-five more of those Nāga guards?"

"Not unless there's been some changes back in the Valley," I answer. "But the Princess Nittaya, the head of the Nāganese Consulate, is planning on coming for performances in the city. Knowing her, she will travel with security, but how much, I don't know."

"Oh!" I exclaim, my brain finally kicking into gear. "I'll send her a letter explaining the situation. She'll know what to do." A further thought, "Oh, rats! I can't send her a letter until we actually get to the city." And yet another thought, "Wait a minute. I have to talk with one of the Nāga guards. Excuse me." I get up and walk up the aisle to the front where the two Nāganese guards are riding.

"Excuse me, I need to reach the Princess rather quickly," I kneel down. "Do you have a way of communicating directly with her?"

"I cannot answer that question," says one. "Yes," the other.

Turning to the one who answered in the affirmative, I ask, "If I write a letter to her now, can you send it to her from here?"

"Yes," the answer.

"Great! I'll get on to it right away," I say and turn back to my seat.

I tell Farmer and Soldier the good news, and they leave me to it. I search for my writing things in the hoard at the back of the bus and, with the help of Autumn and River, finally locate it. I sit and begin to write only to realize I can't, what with all the jiggling and bumping the bus is making. There! I've gone and ruined one of my precious sheets of flax-paper, too. I can't ask the driver to stop the bus long enough for me to write the letter, because we'll lose our place in the 'van. I can't think of a possible thing I can do until we reach our resting place five hours from now. Then the old brain goes into gear again and gives me an idea.

I go back up to the front of the bus and speak with the Nāga who gave me the earlier information. "Please excuse me for interrupting you again," I say as I try to bow deeply while holding on for dear life to the seat-back to keep my balance. "The bus is bumping around too much for me to write. Do you have some way of making a letter if I dictate what to say?"

His answer, "Yes."

I knew it. I suspected they had some really clever way of communicating. So I said, "If you would be kind and come with me to the back of the bus we can do the letter there." Miraculous! He got up and followed me to my seat. I in no way wanted him to feel trapped, so I slid into the seat first, allowing him the aisle seat. After all, I had not been this close physically to a Nāga since that time in the Valley when the head of the guard picked me up bodily and carried me to the Royal Presence, and him in his dragon form, too.

My Nāga friend, for he is proving to be a friend indeed, pulled from inside his uniform a small, flat, rectangular object made of a glass-like substance, his two appositive thumbs of each Nāga hand, attached to human-looking arms, claw-like pointy nails poised perpendicular to rectangular surface. He looked expectantly at me. I started dictating the letter, and his four digits flew into action, tippy tapping. A light went on in the little thing he held, and script leapt into existence before my very eyes. But it was not my language that appeared. It must have been … He was translating directly into Nāganese! I became so astonished I stopped speaking. He looked up at me, doing something quivery with the corners of his mouth. He was smiling at me. I'd never seen a Nāga guard smile before. Nittaya smiled all the time. She had really mastered the art of smiling and used it brilliantly to communicate whole worlds of feeling. Not so Nāga guards, usually.

Collecting my thoughts, I dictated the rest of the letter. The Nāga guard, having finished tapping the screen with his thumbs, took an index finger and made one final tap. The screen flickered, then returned to normal. He looked up at me and did that smile thing again. "Your letter has been sent," he said. I thanked him profusely. He got up and returned to the front of the bus. Farmer and Soldier, who had been watching the whole thing from several seats away, now came over.

I told them, "The letter has been sent to the Princess. We must wait for her response."

"Wow," said Soldier. "So that's how they do it, that's how they communicate with each other."

"Yes," said I, "it is remarkable." I continued, "The Princess will have some good strategies to deal with this 'big boss'. We'll await her instructions."

"Okay," said Farmer. "Let us know when you hear from her."

"Sure," I said. They went back to their seats. I waved the two boys

over intending to pick up our string game where we left off. They, on the other hand, had observed everything and were curious to know what happened.

"What was that all about?" demanded Charming.

"Did you see the Nāga guard change his hands? How did he do that?" Sweetheart wanted to know.

I explained, "The Nāga are what's called 'shape shifters.' They can make themselves look like anything they want. You see them up there? They're in their 'human' form. They're really dragons. We've told you this before. What you saw were its real dragon hands."

"But what were you doing?" demanded Charming. "What was that all about?"

"We were making plans for our next performances," I tried to explain without alarming the children.

"Okay. But something's different this time," Charming perceived.

I was stymied for a moment how to respond. Then, "The Nāga princess is planning to visit us while we are giving performances in the old royal city. We were planning for that," I said, hoping this would satisfy his curiosity. He nodded his head and then took up his loop of string. So, back to our games.

At this point along our way south the coastal plain narrows and the highway moves in close to the mountains. All the plain was now flooded, but the highway was clear for our use. That morning we stopped at the head of a small valley to the west of the highway where tarpaulins were stretched for our protection. A cooler breeze was descending from the mountainside making the place almost pleasant. We said morning prayers, collecting a small crowd of the faithful, mostly Walkers, I suspect. Even though we always attract the laity during prayers in the caravans, nevertheless each time I feel it is a wonderful thing to have happen. And usually there are a few people who come up afterwards to speak with one or more of us. I think this is pretty marvelous, too, and always enjoy speaking with them. They tell us their deepest secrets, their loves, their hope for the future. In return, I most ardently desire we help strengthen their faith. Faith—the thing that keeps us all moving toward better things.

That evening, as we again drive onto the highway, I had hoped to hear back from Nittaya, but it was well into the night before the Nāga guard, my new friend, came back to speak with me. A response from the Princess had been received. I shooed off the boys so he could sit and read it to me.

My cherished Palace,

Your news of possible trouble while at the old royal city came as no surprise. I suspected something like this was afoot. I would like to open communication between your security people and my Chief of Staff for Security and have the experts work out a strategy. Please set this up on your end. I see no reason for you or me to otherwise be concerned with the matter.

I also see no reason to change my plans in light of your news. In fact, it might be amusing to have a bit of action added to the general itinerary. It's been a while.

Yours most faithfully, P. Nittaya

I was shocked at the Princess's casualness toward the threat but also felt she was purposely being thus in order to mollify me. I felt the best thing to do was to follow her orders and have the two security staffs in communication with each other. Meanwhile, I also felt Life needed to know of the situation. He would surely have some relevant insight as to our policy toward aggression. Farmer and Soldier had been keenly watching the Nāga and me, expecting some kind of follow-up. I signaled them to join us now. The other Nāga at the front of the bus had been watching us also and now came to join in, too, the five of us all putting our heads together. Once I gave a short summing-up of what Nittaya was proposing, I thought I should remove myself and let the four of them hammer out whatever it was that needed hammering out. I, in turn, decided to follow up on bringing Life up to speed on what was happening.

I went up to him and asked if I could speak with him privately. He dismissed the two boys sitting with him and invited me to sit down beside him. "Life," I began, "I hesitate bothering you with matters that come up, but I feel you need to know about something looming ahead. It is serious enough to involve Princess Nittaya and the Nāga Consulate, so I think you should know about it, too."

"Yes," he said, "I am aware you shield me from routine problems that arise, and I appreciate that. I would expect, if something extraordinary would arise, you would choose to bring me in so that I could have some say in its outcome."

"Exactly," I replied. I then told him of the situation in the old royal city, that our security and Nāga security would be working together to form a strategy.

"Thank you for telling me this," he said. "I will speak with Farmer and Soldier after their meeting with the Nāga guard and open a path with them for us to talk. I see no reason for you to remain involved, though."

"But, Life," I hastily replied, "I'm already involved. There is no way I can remove myself from this matter."

"Yes, I see," he said. "I would not want you to unduly worry over it, however. The matter is largely out of your hands now. It would be wise on your part to put a little distance between yourself and this matter. Do you understand?"

"I understand," I replied, feeling somewhat put upon. But Life was right. I will worry and fret over this, regardless.

While my seat at the back of the bus was being occupied, Life and I talked of other, lesser things; both of us, I think, enjoying a rare opportunity to be together.

Eventually, my seat was vacated, and I was able to return to it. Charming and Sweetheart, keen observers of the latest round of 'musical chairs', were eager to know what was happening. I told them it was "just routine stuff," hoping they would be satisfied. But they weren't. They instinctively knew something significant was afoot and felt they were entitled to know what it was. Yet I ended up having to give them the talk about 'children's things' and 'grownups' things', that this was a 'grownups' thing' and they should put it out of mind. They weren't happy with this instruction but did let the matter drop when they saw they weren't going to get anything more out of me. They only halfheartedly took up their string games.

We did not actually enter the city of the old royal court but left the caravan a little before, taking a right turn heading for a bend in the river. The monastery was situated on a long, narrow hill of perhaps fifteen meters height, located at a bend in the river. Still close enough to the ocean for tides to inundate the low-lying areas, the road leading to the main entrance was now covered in water; but we could clamber up to the first exposed terrace and walk around to the entrance, a grand flight of stairs past four square pillars with inscriptions, up to the top of the hill where the entrance was to the Pagoda.

According to legend, about five and a half centuries ago an old woman was seen sitting on the rocky promontory, rubbing her cheeks. When asked about herself she was reported to have said a pagoda was going to be built on the spot. The king, hearing of her, did actually have built the pagoda that is here today. It is named after the old woman. The site is still well-maintained with a tile courtyard all around the pagoda.

Continuing on, we came to an elegant gate of three doors, arranged in classic style. Beyond the gate is a large courtyard planted with small trees in a geometrical pattern and a broad walkway leading to the main temple, called the Big House. Following on, beyond this building is an inner court with another temple, called the Small House. Directly behind that is the Mid House and beyond a grove of trees is the ethereal Inner Pagoda, smaller than the one on the crest of the hill, but in the same style. It is set on a square terrace with railings, four steps higher than the surroundings. Miraculously, most of the trees are still alive making the environs beautiful beyond imagining. I was told the reason why the monastery is in such good shape is the current usurper of the throne, in residence in the city, comes here on retreat.

We were met by our hosts at the elegant three-portal gate. It was they who gave us a tour of the temple buildings and Inner Pagoda. They then took us to the west side of the hill where the monks' quarters are located. They showed our bus driver how to bring the bus around to the side of the hill here to get as close as possible to where we would be staying. Off he went on a run to bring the bus from where he had parked it by the river.

I must admit I was skeptical about having to do performances at two sites in this city, but once here I was thoroughly delighted with the prospect. We would be performing mostly for the monks, but there was a sizable community surrounding the hill and an invitation to them had gone out.

The front pagoda was truly the most beautiful one I'd ever seen, and I spent as much time as I could just sitting in the tiled terrace admiring it, letting my eye play over the detail, following the rhythm of the architectural patterns as they repeated—vertical line, horizontal line, circle. I also delighted in discovering herbals in the undergrowth below the trees. I took arms-full to the cooks and was greatly embarrassed when they showed me on their shelves cannisters of the very herbs. So I decided to find a way to take the herbs with us on the bus.

Performances were to begin the next night starting at midnight. It was hoped Nittaya would arrive early enough to see the fourth and fifth plays at this site, but that was uncertain. We knew for sure she would be attending at the monastery in the city. There were vague rumors her family had something to do with that place, but I couldn't remember details. I would, of course, ask her to refresh my memory.

The main temple, or Big House as it was called, here at the crook in the river, where we prayed, appealed greatly to me. Goldleaf was held to a minimum, mostly for the images of the Buddha. Here, the dominant color eschewed gold, was instead a deep, rich brown of rubbed and stained wood. Wood was the chief building material of the temple—of the walls, of the ceiling, of the pillars that held up the roof. It lent a grave and quiet dignity to the hall. It made the little gold that was present appear that much richer, burnished. It calmed the eye, slowed its darting movement, directed to rest where it best aught, on the images of the Buddha to whom our attention should focus. Even the three Buddhas at the central altar were modest in size and each of the two side alters, recessed some small distance back, modest, too. They did not have to overpower, for the wood as wood was retiring, sought not the glory. Then the chanting. The sound of the chanting seemed to take on the dark richness of the woods, reverberating off the flat surfaces, off the convex. Thus did the woods here dominate; and thus do I feel the elders of the past knew far more in their poverty than the later ones in their prosperity.

The abbot here seemed imbued with the spirit of the Wood. He was silent, wizened, and dark, his eyes the gold in his face. And what little he said was also gold. Under his gaze, we visitors felt ourselves slowing, deepening, in his brown-rich house. Yet I wondered how the Lord of the warlords, reportedly violently vicious, cruel, could ever feel comfortable here. How could this abbot ever come to welcome such a spirit into this sacred sanctuary. I would find myself returning time and time again to this contradiction. I found no ready answer.

The side buildings, the quarters of the monks, I found spacious and airy, amply fit for the tranquil life. The real gem of these buildings was the library, home of much wisdom, my immediate delight. Many ancient volumes were to be found here. This was, yet again, another model on which to construct our library. On subsequent nights, as the plays/lessons were given, I would steal in here and peruse the works in store. There is a tactile quality to books, the feel of the animal skins used for parchment, for binding, the reedy feel of the paper. There is an olfactory quality, too, in the subtle aromas that arise as one turns the pages, a subliminal tale to the text. No wonder I should be so fascinated.

After the excitement of the Vow-taking of the third night, excitement was intensified with the announcement of the imminent arrival that night of Nittaya's circulary. Not having seen my enchanting friend for nearly half a year, and in the gathering circumstances, I was beside myself with anticipation. A shout went out announcing her arrival. We ran down to the open field at the foot of the monastery hill to meet the vehicle, and were much startled to see three circularies coming in for a landing. I suspected the Princess would be traveling here with a large entourage, but I never expected so many. The circulary closest to us was the first to open. I was expecting ... I don't know, gentlemen of the court, first, then the ladies? Instead, there were uniformed armed military, rushing out, doing elaborate maneuvers, pointing their weapons in every direction. Yes, it would be wise for security to debark first. Then the second circulary door opened. By now, I didn't bother to imagine what might be on-board. Well that I saved my energy, for a ramp was lowered and several vehicles of remarkably divergent shape, size and – yes – function emerged. Startling that they should all fit in that particular circulary. I gazed intently at the door to the third circulary, expecting courtiers to emerge from it. Instead, all that happened was strangely shaped objects poking out from the top. I never saw anything emerge from it.

On we waited. Soon we saw, off in the sky, approaching lights—from two more circularies, it appeared. They landed, filling the field. The door of the first of these opened, emitting a procession of liveried personnel in double rank. A long pause here. At last! The door of the fifth circulary opened to courtiers, and then, and then The Princess, Herself! What was I expecting? Tiara and gown? Instead, she was dressed in modestly comfortable travel clothes, perhaps but one notch above her usual attire in the Valley. Elegant, of course! The courtiers clustered around, helping her descend, walk across the grassy field, coming directly toward us. I suddenly became acutely aware of my own dress—a rumpled gray habit, not the freshest, bare feet. Life and the boys still in makeup and costume. A wave of shame flooded over me. It had clearly been too long since I was in Nittaya's company. She was not in the least dismayed at our appearance. Instead, she was delighted to see us in the middle of doing our work, as she would have imagined back in the Valley.

Life, looking much like a ghostly apparition, took Nittaya's hand and led her to meet the abbot and his people. I'd never seen Nittaya bow so deeply before as she to this old cleric. Holding back the sleeve of his habit with one hand, he took her hand in his other, inclining his head to her. In the glaring light of the field they vanished into elegant silhouette, holding the pose for eternity. Softly, they melted back into dimension as the abbot introduced her down the line to his staff. They led her off to the suite of rooms they have prepared for her.

There was no way the monastery could host all the people that came with Nittaya. I found out later they were housed and fed in the circularies themselves. How they managed to do that I can't even begin to imagine. The working out of security deployment was also complex. Aside from a few close personages, there to assist Nittaya with her personal needs, everyone else were actually security. That goes for most of the courtiers, I found out. If she had twenty courtiers around her eighteen of them were security. Those eighteen were dressed as and acted like courtiers. I was completely fooled, and I was familiar with the Nāganese. I was totally convinced any thug or marauder would not be able to tell the difference. I chuckled, imagining the surprise they were going to have.

Nittaya and her entourage reappeared from the cluster of buildings on the west. She walked directly up to Life and me and, taking both of us by the arms, led us off saying, "There is something I want to show you before the sun comes up." She led us out the gate, past the pagoda to the railing overlooking the river, beside the front flight of steps. There, she pointed to the west. And there, before us, under the lucent starry sky, stretched a grand land- and seascape leading up to the foothills, looming darkly. I gasped to see beyond them, the ghostly outline of the high mountain that forms the natural barrier between us and our neighboring country. I had not noticed it before nor how high the range was compared to the foothills.

She said softly, "I wanted to be sure the two of you took in this view." We uttered our thanks. "I also wanted an opportunity to tell you, outside the earshot of anyone else, I've brought with me 125 of my top military assembled here on Earth. Be confident we shall deal with whatever the usurper may do."

Life responded, quietly, "I have one or two requests to make should contingencies allow. How do I go about communicating these?"

"Thank you for asking," replied the princess. "Do so through the channel you have already set up."

"And thank you," said Life, doing a slight bow.

We three turned and rejoined the nervous courtiers, walking back past pagoda, gate, and courtyard to the large temple where prayers were about to begin. Nittaya, taking up position behind us, by precedent from the Valley, knelt on an exquisite rug that had quickly appeared, the courtiers arranging themselves behind her. I heard her clear treble voice in the singing of the prayers, not even one word misplaced. I might have known, with all she had said, was she an adherent of the Buddhist faith, along with everything else?

I slept like a baby that day, waking in the evening thoroughly refreshed. This night, the play and lesson are summations of ideas in the three previous plays/lessons and announcement of the founding of our monastery. It is not heaven-storming like the previous three, but it has its moments. If this, and the last, were the only evenings Nittaya was going to take in, she would have a poor idea of the effect of the five. That is not a real concern since she will be seeing all five in the city at the beautiful old pagoda there. I must say, I was surprised when I received an invitation to join Nittaya at breakfast out in the grassy field by the five circularies. I expected to see Life there, too, but was startled to discover I was to be her sole guest. Of course, it quickly became obvious why. First, there were messages from colleagues to be relayed. Second, there was general gossip on which to catch me up. Third, there was a general report on all building and refurbishing that was happening. Fourth, there was a 'to do' list on what needed to be done pending the funds to do them. And finally, fifth, general plans for the next week or so and how I was expected to play various roles. To top it all off she then launched into a general history of her family on Earth, stretching back some six thousand years. It seems Earth was known to the Nāga hundreds of years before they actually ventured here. They arrived with expectations, searched the whole planet, and decided on the powerful kingdom to the north of us in which to settle. Apparently, they had a rough go of it at first, before they learned how to shape shift to human form. There was one king, however, brave enough to approach the Nāga-as-dragons. He enlisted their help in a war that was currently afoot which they won, brilliantly. After the war, the king invited the Nāga into his court as guardians to the royal family. They pleased the king greatly and became fixtures of the court for several generations.

Nittaya interrupted her narration to say, "Keep in mind our species live five hundred years, or more. For us, humans are for a moment brilliant, and then they die. It's heartbreaking."

Historic flow had the Nāga either flourishing or having to go into hiding. It was while they were out of favor they discovered the ability to shape shift into human form. It made everything ever so much easier. Soon, they appeared again in court, in many different functions, always seeking the most enlightened person for whom they gave their support, intending to improve the human lot. Some of the more adventurous traveled extensively, eventually throughout the world. They would mostly observe, but sometimes join in, usually in human form adjusted to the local ethnic characteristics, rarely in their dragon form. As time passed whole family lines were being born on Earth, the feeling of being of the Earth strengthening with each generation. While their kind took up home throughout the planet, Nittaya's family stayed in the East. Her branch of the family came to my country two millennia ago, making themselves indispensable to the kings of the times. Several, even, became close friends of the contemporary monarch, were given titles and land. Nittaya here relates how her grandfather posed for dragon images at the monastery in the city where we shall next go, but also for several things in the royal compound. I'm hoping to see those, although it looks unlikely.

Nittaya was born here in the old royal city, but she would not say how long ago. She has been on the home planet, Nāgaland, twice, for her higher education and to receive diplomatic certification so that she would qualify for the appointment of Ambassador to Earth. She says she is only truly happy on Earth, that her home planet is depressing. I found that statement surprising in that she does not find the current state of Earth depressing, too, seeing as how she knew Earth in its pristine days. "This condition," she says, "is temporary. We're all going to work and fix it."

I tell her of the audience reactions that we've been having as we move down the coast, how they are surprisingly strong and favorable, how few negative reactions we've had, even to the idea of monks having children. Of course, we did have one place where there was a strong negative reaction and another of studied indifference. She didn't seem surprised.

We ended our far-roaming discussion with some thoughts on the current possible threat. Nittaya assuaged my concerns with tidbits like, "There are enough Nāga guards for every two of you," and, "The guards have been instructed to change to dragon-form if matters get out of control." Also, "My intelligence is not to expect anything here at this monastery, but rather in the city where they believe they have greater control."

Lest we get diverted from the main reason she has come, I tell her I shall look forward to her reaction to the performances tonight, and she apologizes for not being able to invite me to join her court, but security being such, *et cetera, et cetera*. I assured her I understood. We made our farewells with the promise to meet as soon as we could after the plays. Off we went our separate ways, I in the warm glow my friend always engenders.

Before the performance begins I only have time to ask Life how he is doing. He answers, "Well," and looks supremely confident. This night I shall watch the performance from the audience. I sit, as the custom seems, cross-legged on my mat. I stealthily look around at the audience and am surprised to see a large contingent of lay people. I scold myself for being surprised for we were told an invitation had gone out to the community surrounding the little hill. Why shouldn't they come. As I give it more thought I began to suspect the usurper king would have sent out scouts to take in what we were doing and report back. Yes. That one over there looks suspicious, too rough looking to be a simple villager. And that one over there? Humm. Him, too. Then I remembered what Nittaya had said about her guards. I glance to my right – a quite pleasant looking young woman. I smile at her. She smiles back and bows. I glance to my left – an equally pleasant looking young man. I smile at him. He immediately takes on a deferential mein and bows even more deeply than she. I glance behind me – a frail elderly gentleman, surrounded by obvious family. And to the front – a broad back. I could not tell much else. That one's got to be a guard. Who else would have such broad shoulders? Yes, he's one, for sure. I relax, not that they're expecting anything to happen here. But you never know. I tense up again.

A single spot up on Fame. He does his usual barkering, now honed down over the nights to a sharp focus. He says just as much as needs to be said and vanishes into the dark. Up three spots on the boys, and they are off and running. Pleasantly surprised, they, too, had honed their performances. Things that I had never noticed before had come to the fore and made such sense. Even Little Lord had toned his performances, not so much down as sideways, into a realm that actually had pathos. I was quite proud of them. The play was over, with cheers and whistles as the boys came back for bows, beaming from ear to ear. They deserved every decibel. Then, silence. Up one spot on Life, not as the ghost of before, but in his elegant brown habit, his face in a rosy glow. Now, he had committed this lesson to memory, too, and delivered warm, encompassing words of promise and hope. He carries the audience with him, as fits a seasoned trouper. At the end there were shouts, affirmative shouts, the audience on their feet, already surging forward. The boys came out and joined hands with Life for bows to stomping and applause. Without knowing how it happened, there were suddenly guards beside the performers; not looking like guards, they seemed to be of those anonymous folk required to mount anything theatrical. Now, that was impressive. Very few of us, I am sure, knew what really happened there. I hoped our attendant thugs were too dull to grasp the significance of that bit of theatre. The real dance began as the audience moved forward to meet our actors. The supposed crew stood in front, doing quick screens of the people pressing forward. Their selection was swift and precise, letting through a select few, adroitly blocking the rest, looking like people were moving up naturally. Only a schooled onlooker could have taken in what was really happening, it being done with such amazing finesse.

As I was standing aside observing the press of people around Life a Nāga courtier came up with an invitation from the Princess to join her in half-an-hour at one of the rooms in the monks' quarters. I did not happen to notice a similar invitation going to Life. After the crowds had dispersed, leaving the grounds of the monastery to regain their serenity, I went to the designated place and was pleasantly surprised to see Nittaya and Life, along with a host of liveried servants, waiting for me. It was a pleasant room with a round table and matching chairs now occupied with those in livery. There were several such standing outside the door bowing to me as I approached. Guards, I thought. I was announced, to my great amusement, as "His Holiness," causing both Nittaya and Life to look up startled, perhaps expecting to see the abbot of this place rather than me. The introduction, however, sparked a brief conversation that proved prophetic.

"Dear Palace," began Nittaya, "your introduction just now raises a point worth discussing, don't you think, Life."

"Yes, I do," replied Life. "Palace, take seriously what the Princess is about to say."

Before I could say a work, Nittaya launched right in. "Palace, you must seriously consider your own ordination as abbot."

"But, my dear friend, we already have our abbot," I retorted.

"Mark my word, yours shall be a large monastery with several major arms. There will be a need for even more than two abbots before all is said and done."

"I'm sure you are right, but now is not the time to act. Besides, I don't think I am 'abbot' material."

"Oh, shush. You don't know a thing about it. Why can't you just listen to me and do as I say?"

"Alright, I'll think about it."

"But you mustn't tarry. You don't have a great deal of time to think about it."

How prophetic were her words in the wee hours of that night. I think back often on this conversation and how perceptive she was. Nay! Clairvoyant. Yet I wouldn't have done anything any differently than I did.

Actually, the Princess had brought us together to discuss growing pains in the Valley and to make decisions on immediate directions of growth for both the monastery and university. Before proceeding very far, Life suggested Fame join us. A liveried one went scurrying off to bring him. The Princess was introduced to him, and I observed, through our discussion that night, her respect for him growing. Excellent! Of course, Nittaya was brimming with all kinds of wonderful ideas, and Fame was able to fill her in on our financial state—the fuel that was to run the machinery of expansion. And, it seems, we were doing amazingly well, financially speaking. Fame had already sent off another courier with gold and silver for the treasury in the Valley, and we were only half through our pilgrimage. Much more was anticipated.

Nittaya advised us on what we might expect in the southern part of our country. She predicted our fame should have proceeded us, that we should see this as early as the resort city that is our next destination. We should have bigger audiences, and they would be more … she hesitated, looking for the right word. "Enthusiastic," but she was not happy with it. "Raucous" came next, then "disruptive" floated forward. Interesting words to use. Later, we came to see what she meant. She predicted, too, the South would be more generous than the North, since the South had been wealthier, that there would have been more gold and silver lying around to be scavenged. But, she warned, we were also to be on the lookout for scams, for these were a happy pastime in the South. I looked over at Fame as he briefly blanched. In spite of these negatives, the Princess said, these people were warm-hearted and would become fanatical followers of us. Literally. They would join the caravan and follow with us from place to place as we performed. Our audiences in the metropolis to the south, she predicted, would be in the thousands. We should expect it and plan ahead.

"At your very last performance," she said, "you shall have to sneak off in the cover of darkness, for your fans will not want you to return north. In their adoration of you they will stop you and hold you virtual prisoners."

Heavens! Such things could hardly be imagined.

When it came time for morning prayer and sleep, my poor head was filled with such fantastic thoughts I could hardly settle down. Giant crowds, fanatics, scam artists, potential danger, becoming an abbot to top it off. How can one possibly deal with all that? I arose that evening feeling very shaky. At prayer, my gaze fell on Nittaya looking placid as ever, and felt no end of irritation. I didn't need all this baggage right now. I needed for my head to be clear to concentrate on just surviving this city, let alone what was in store in the south.

Tonight, the final play/lesson and the announcement of the aliens among us. Since it was all good news, I expected all to go smoothly, to go well. The boys ended the play with a real flourish. I had never witnessed better. The audience response was immediate and loud. They were called back again and again. Little Lord, bless his little heart, took his bows more deeply than I had ever seen another human execute. He was rewarded with shouts of approbation all around. Then it was Life's turn. He appeared wearing a garland of leaves on his head! I'd never seen that before. As it turned out, a follower in the audience had been up in the mountains, returning with laurel branches. He had woven the tender shoots into a garland and given it to Life while the boys were performing. On impulse Life had worn it onstage, and it was perfect. Just the right triumphal touch.

The fragrance was wonderful, too. The real *coup de theatre*, though, was a Nāga appearing in the light behind Life as he was listing the aliens of the Interstellar League. At the mention of the Nāgas, in a flash he transformed himself into a dragon and, in a flash, transformed himself back to human. There was such a scream as you could hardly imagine, but not everyone was aware of what happened. Afterwards, I could not find anyone in our group who would admit to knowing beforehand these transformations were to happen. Even Life seemed innocent of any knowledge, and he was my most likely suspect. Nittaya was second, yet I believed her denial of any knowledge. In fact, she seemed genuinely irritated that one of her people would make such a bridge of protocol. In light of everything that happened later, however, I came to advocate incorporating the event into all our subsequent performances.

Well, I thought I'd seen post-performance audience reactions, but this evening topped everything that had gone before. A sizeable part of the audience that came forward were truly angry. They were convinced we had perpetrated some kind of theatrical slight-of-hand they considered in the poorest imaginable taste and unethical behavior. Another sizable group missed the event and wondered what had happened. But the greater share by far had seen the event, had loved it, and wanted to know who all were aliens. They made themselves real nuisances going around poking their finger into everyone. What could that possibly tell them, I wonder? The boys absolutely loved it and went around yelling, "I'm the alien! I'm the alien!" And imagine, they were believed! It was all I could do to look serious and not break out in laughter. The Nāgas I knew of were pulling straight faces, looking as bewildered as the rest of us.

The elderly abbot of the monastery, poor fellow, had planned a reception for us in their large community room. We were deluged by our audience, and it took some time to extricate ourselves from them. By the time we got to the reception it had wilted and lost most of its grand gesture. He said a little speech that did not go as I'm sure he had memorized it, but we all applauded heartily anyway. Since it was mid-summer, the table was loaded with fruit, all kinds of fruit, which was special for us since we don't usually have access to much fruit outside the Valley. We asked where it was grown and were told of monastery farmlands high in the nearby mountains. It had been brought in fresh the night before and the kitchen people had been working nonstop to prepare it in time. I asked where they were so that

I could personally thank them and was told they were not invited to the reception. I conveyed my thanks to several members of the abbot's staff and hoped that would be enough to get back to the kitchen people. In my machinations I noticed Nittaya and the abbot, off in a corner, their heads almost touching, in intense conversation. Now, what was that about? Would it be something she would relay to us? Only time would tell.

I had the opportunity to talk with a number of my colleagues in this monastery and had a chance to tell them how much I admired their temple, the extensive use of wood, *et cetera*. They seemed appreciative of my thoughts, while on the other hand I was asked many questions about our monastery and university, especially. More than one brother expressed hope we might establish exchanges between the two establishments with which I strongly agreed, promising I would follow through once our pilgrimage was over.

A stroke on the temple bell brought to a close our reception and issued a call to prayer. Again, in the large temple, we congregated to sing prayers in honor of the Buddha and of things far bigger than any one of us. Afterwards, Nittaya met Life and me outside with an invitation to join her the coming evening boating downriver to the monastery in the city. We accepted without hesitation while wondering how she would manage to arrange boating and maintain security. After all, a boat on this river would be a sitting duck to cannon on the shore.

All in all, I felt our residence here at this beautiful monastery had been successful, in spite of the Nāga-flasher. Come the day, I slept the sleep of death, the entire day vanishing into nothingness. I awoke early evening, ready for another adventure. It took no time at all to pack up my meager possessions and head out the door of my little cell. There, to my great surprise, stood Life, looking much distressed. "Palace," he said, "I've been given a letter from Dragon which you need to read." He held out an envelope to me. Immediately, I sensed the heavy portent such a missive would surely carry and drew back. His hand remained thrust at me, not the least withdrawing, as I would hope. Reluctantly, I reached forward and took it from his hand. I turned it over and over, quickly taking in the slim information on its cover, simply "His Holiness, the Abbot Full-of-Life." My sense of foreboding now reached unbounded heights. "He's died, hasn't he," I said to Life.

"Yes," was his terse reply.

"Then must I read this?" I asked, hoping Life would withdraw his directive and permit my ignorance to continue.

"Dear friend, I would not withhold from you the closure you deserve, you who have been present at every step in the unfolding of this man's fate. Read it! For it is not as doleful as your imaginings would make of it."

And, so, with his command, I turned back the envelope's flap and drew forth the paper within. It read:

> His Holiness, the Abbot Full-of-Life,
>
> You, perhaps better than most people, can appreciate when an idea has come full circle and achieved its zenith. So I tell you the idea of my life has thus evolved and, in the fullness of its inherent logic, has come to its forgone conclusion. I rejoice that it has done so and hope that you and my other friends in your company will find it in your hearts to join with me in the rejoicing.
>
> About a month ago we had located the band of marauders that had attacked us last year at the monastery. We infiltrated their ranks, they not knowing who, precisely, we were beyond our being skilled warriors wanting to join their ranks. My companions and I carefully plotted our strategy and when the time ripened we launched a surprise attack. We cut them all down, every last one, even the warlord and the villain who had boasted of felling our beloved Brother Morning Star. It was I who thrust the blade into his heart and I that relished his final gasps. The toll on our little band was also high, five of us fallen with the foe. Others of us brought back to our base deep wounds that are felling us, too. I am such, with cuts that have worsened and infected, now beyond healing. My fate is set. I shall live three more days with increasing pain, into delirium when I, also, will follow my fallen friends into the great shadow of Death.
>
> Do not mourn my passing, my beloved friend, for I have achieved my very heart's desire in revenging our brethren. I pass on full of joy, as few in this life are

fated to do. I ask you, rejoice along with me that I have achieved all my treasured wishes, my spirit fulfilled.

In the name of that bright star, I remain yours,

Brother Dragon

I let fall to the floor the slender page on which such dreadful news was written, my heart unable to follow that poignant joy of our stricken brother. Instead, I wept for his passing, now another spirit added to that long list of the dear departed. I, fully aware of Dragon's many fateful choices, nevertheless went against his wishes, finding it all a hopeless loss of yet another precious life. And thus I mourned for him.

"I'm sorry to be the bearer of such bad news," said Life. "I'd hoped I would have changed the temper of the times enough by now that Dragon would no longer have had to carry through his revenge. The time has come for me to redouble my efforts and bring all this senseless killing to an end. Each of us is too valuable for such waste."

Following the letter I now, too, slumped to the ground, unaware of Life's proffered hand. "You cannot remain here, beloved Brother," he gently reminded. "There are people waiting for you. We are leaving here, now, for another venue; and you must rally, be alert." Gently lifting me up, Life kept his arm over my shoulder, we walking down the hill to Nittaya's circulary. "Are you thinking Brother Dragon's immortal spirit has fallen into Hell, where he never shall escape?"

"Yes," I responded, "that's exactly what I'm thinking."

"It seems it would be so, but one can never be certain. There may be a larger plan for Brother Dragon, the direction for which he is acting. We, you and I and all his friends, are not sufficiently informed to make a final judgement on what his spirit shall endure."

"You're right, of course. I do not know Dragon's karma. I'm the last one who should judge anyway. These are troubled times, without a doubt; and nothing seems to be following the accepted working out of things."

"All the more reason for you not to trouble over much for the passing of Brother Dragon. Rather, we might do as he asks and feel joy for him that he has avenged our departed brethren. What do you think?"

"I think that will be hard for me. I so strongly believe we must not take life, even of the most vile and deserving. I, myself, shall never raise a hand against anyone," I attested emphatically.

"And the more that reflects to your credit. But for now I suggest we follow Brother Dragon's request to share his joy. Time, in its unfolding, will surely show us the greater will here."

By now we had reached the field of parked vehicles where we were to meet Nittaya. There we waited some time for her to appear. While we waited Life told me of visiting the elderly abbot and conveying our collective thanks for hosting us, the abbot in turn thanking him for the provocative ideas we had brought, ideas the abbot was sure they would be discussing into the future. Good, I thought as I began to rally.

CHAPTER 8

At last! Nittaya appeared, looking fresh and ready for a busy night. "Where is the boat?" I asked. "I don't see any boats around."

"Here. Right here," she answered. "You're standing right beside it," as she pointed to her car.

"Oh, we're going by car," I said, disappointed.

"This vehicle is amphibious," she announced. "It can go on either land or water," smiling at my surprised reaction. "Come on," she urged. "Let's get aboard."

The interior was amazingly roomy. We made ourselves comfortable and settled down for the trip. Our liveried driver now arrived, started the engine, turned, and drove to the road, turning in the direction ahead where the road becomes submerged at the base of the hill, the pagoda looming above. Into the water we went, and soon we were floating in the middle of the river. This river had once been famous for its scenic splendor—kilometers of wooded shores with grand buildings displaying their upper stories over the treetops, broad bridges spanning the surge, welcoming travelers to pass beneath their underbellies, vessels of all shapes and sizes either traveling side by side or passing by and moving on. Now, sadly, the banks sported only broken and charred tree trunks blending into the night sky. Here and there one could see green as hybrid shrubs struggled against the fiery sun. Beyond were half collapsed towers and domes, cement and reinforced steel showing vulnerability. All spoke of humanity's folly. But rather than being a depressing sight, a kind of grandeur still existed and lifted the heart.

Nittaya was eager to discuss the eventualities of an attack. She had this strategy, and that. Life had a plan of his own but said little about it. I was simply terrified at the prospect and consequently contributed nothing to the conversation. I sat there listening to them discuss numbers of guards, firearms, maneuvers, strategies, not believing my ears, thinking on the passing of our beloved Brother Dragon. Life continued to amaze me what he seemed to know, how fearless he appeared, since, after all, he would surely be the principal target.

Eventually, I left the discussion to them and gazed out the window, soothed in no small part by the scrolling cyclorama.

We entered the city. Here was a different story. Most of the city existed on higher ground, avoiding the seaward inundation. The buildings, already old at the time of collapse, had long since been rendered into rubble. Here and there a nondescript hovel rose up, signifying the presence of a brave spirit, battling the elements. Round a bend in the river we saw them up ahead—on the left side the fortress and Forbidden City within, on the right side the low-lying hill with the ancient monastery on its back. The two, like crouching lions facing off across the river, in ancient alliance now stand in opposition, the one seeming to obliterate the other; but not. We hope to form a bond of friendship with the one, pass by the other unnoticed. Is that too much to hope for?

The driver maneuvered us to the right edge of the river, soon onto the road that led to the base of the hill, pulling to a stop at the foot of a majestic flight of stairs. There we were met by a good-sized group of Nittaya's courtiers who were awaiting our arrival. Festively, we ascended the stairs in a commotion, arriving at the top where stood a grand and ancient three-portal gate. The doors of the central portal, wider and higher than the sides, were suddenly thrown open by young monks and nuns, welcoming us in. Numerous torches were lit around an expansive courtyard outlining the gnarled and twisted trunks of ancient pines, struggling but still alive. At the far end were balustrades setting off a terrace on which rested one of the most serene edifices I have ever beheld, floating before our eyes above its own foundation. Long, one story with clerestory windows above, four pillars decorated with entwining dragons helping support the roof, the entrance calling softly for one to enter. Drawn as though magnetically to its overhung portal, we drift like petals in a gentle breeze across the terrace, past the pillars, into the sanctuary where peace holds sway. I pray for Brother Dragon's spirit. After that, there is nothing to be done but say a prayer of gratitude to the three Buddhas resting tranquilly on their altar.

That done, we turn our attention to our hosts. The monastery supports a sizable population of both nuns and monks, perhaps as many as fifty, nuns in the majority. What makes them akin to us is that they also support children, in the number of fourteen. Also like us, there are few elders in their ranks. Above all, I envy them their habits. Wearing a long simple white garment underneath, they then don an outer garment something like a lengthy coat with long sleeves, gray for nuns, dark brown for monks. In movement, the white undergarment is stirred up around the ankles, flashing its brightness from beneath the outer coat, elegant to behold. Children wear only the white undergarment. On our return to the Valley I'm inclined to suggest to Lucky Bird such a revision in our habits.

I found them as a group easy to talk with, but with an accent that was at times a bit hard to understand. This characteristic proved prophetic for, as we moved south, accents grew even stronger and equally harder to understand. Amid cascades of laughter we were shown our quarters and then to midnight meal in their dining hall, in the same color scheme as the monks' habit—white plastered walls, brown rafters and beams. By now, the night already half over, there was much to prepare for the coming evening's performance. Besides, Hero and Bright were off to the south to finalize our itinerary, I needing to warn them to be on the look-out for any trouble coming their way. They seemed unconcerned, which troubled me no end. I also fretted over security during performances, to be reassured by Farmer and Soldier it was all ironclad. Thus, having nothing more to do, I sought out places on the monastery campus where I might enjoy the solitude, there to mull over my friend's fateful departure of this life.

In my rambles I came upon a courtyard featuring a fountain with an ethereal Guanyin standing on stylized lotus flower. Here I decided to linger and take in the spot's serenity. None too soon, the site's calming effect wore in, giving me fortitude to face the coming nights. Or so I thought.

There were morning prayers and then sleep in my tiny cell. I expected some turgid drama to take over my head and render me exhausted by evening time; but instead, I slept like a child. And then evening arrived, prayer and breakfast. Nittaya came for me to take under her wing, she dressed splendidly in embroidered long coat over what appeared to be flared pants, a takeoff on the monks' habit here. Then into the courtyard he came, like a ghostly apparition, a child/novice, meandering through the convoluted space, dressed as the novices here in white-flowing habit, stopping finally beside the fountain to dangle fingers of one hand in the water, looking at us sidewise, as though he had been sent to speak with us but was too shy to go first. Nittaya broke the ice by calling the child over. He came readily enough, eyes cast down, moving more sideways than straight on. She asked, "What is your name, child?"

He answered, "Stalwart," a contradiction with reality now, room in which he could grow in future.

"You are a novice here?"

"Yes, ma'am."

"Do you not have studies you should be attending?"

"Yes, ma'am." Then, in afterthought, "They sent me here."

"Oh? Who sent you here?"

"They did, ma'am. I'm supposed to …"

"Supposed to what, child?"

"Ah … Take you around …"

"Oh! How delightful. Take us around. Palace, this youngster is to take us around, show us things. Can you think of anything better?"

"No," I said, "I can't."

"Then, take us," she said to the child/novice in the most gentle tone possible. "What is there to show us?"

And so he led us from place to place, telling us tiny things about the place in the most cryptic manner imaginable. Eventually we arrived at a wall, mid-level, where he paused saying nothing, gazing over the river to the monumental structures on the other side.

"What are you looking at, child," asked Nittaya.

"I'm looking at …" then suddenly pointing with finger and arm shoulder-height, straight as a ramrod, "that place. Where the Emperor lives."

"The 'Emperor' is he?" asked Nittaya, her voice picking up shadows.

"Yes. The Emperor." He answered, in some small degree of awe.

"And what do they tell you about 'The Emperor'?" asked Nittaya.

"Not to look over there, that he's just a story people have made up."

"But what do you believe? What do you really believe?"

"I've seen him. They ride around on horses in the open fields over there."

"You've seen him! Imagine that. How do you know it's 'The Emperor' you see?"

"Because they all bow to him. Because he wears fancy clothes."

"My goodness! That's certainly sharp of you to see that. And what do you think about 'The Emperor'?"

"Nothing. I'm not supposed to think about him."

"Not supposed to think about him? But still you do, right?"

"Yes. I'm not supposed to."

"It's a secret, right?" He nods. "I promise to keep your secret." She turns to me, in a hushed voice, "Emperor! He calls himself Emperor. Can you imagine?"

"No," I answered. "I can't hardly imagine."

"Back you go. Back to your classes," she said to the child. He made a cursory bow and drifted off as he had come.

"Emperor! Unbelievable!" she said to me, giving me a look of scandal. And then, "We shall see about that!" her jaw firmly set.

Off, in the near distance, spots flared up into the sky. The play was about to begin. "Come," said Nittaya, moving off in the direction of the spots. I run to catch up.

The play area is set up on the inside of the great three-portal gate, the main play area in front of the center doors, now firmly closed, entrances and exits to be from the two side doors. The audience seems to be drifting in from all directions, sitting in a large semi-circle in front of the gate. Nittaya is met by her courtiers, several of whom place rugs on the ground for us. They cluster around us. Suddenly, I realize all these 'pretty people' are security guards. They aren't courtiers at all! So I relax. It's unlikely I'll be a target anyway. Again, I look around at the faces of the people, trying to see if I can identify any of the thugs sent to attack us. Nearly everyone looks tough, like the Walkers. They all look like they're living a hard life. Is the hard life the thing that drives the young men to join the marauders? Probably so. I think of Loyal and of Soldier and Farmer, how they looked that night they rushed into the bus with their knives flashing. How their looks changed over the weeks they've been with us. Loyal especially. I thought of the lines of desperation in his face relaxing into caring and kindness. How sweet he is now. With a quick mind, eager to learn. With ...

Spots up onto Fame and his announcements, and the evening's entertainment begins. I don't think they were expecting an attack on the first night, but I think they were prepared anyway. The audience reaction was typical – cries, wailing, tearing the clothing. And finally euphoria followed, they rushing forward to meet the boys and Life. But Security got there first.

I jump forward to the second night, the subject the formation of communities. Nittaya and I arrive together and sit surrounded by 'courtiers', practically in the same place as the previous night, the audience with faces like the Walkers all around us. It ends, applause and whistling. The audience rush forward. Again, Security.

Now, on to the third night, the taking of the vows, pronouncing the end of war. Nittaya and I arrive, but the audience is considerably larger. The rugs are spread farther back from the playing area. I feel a different tension in the air this evening, but the only difference I can see is there are more of the people with Walker faces. That is all. The play proceeds as usual, declaring war obsolete, renouncing the negative emotions. It's over. Enthusiastic stomping and applause. Life appears in the spots and carries us from our calamity through war renunciation and our negative emotions to saying the Vow. Then he asks the audience to stand, for them to take the Vow, too. And we get up on our feet.

That's when it starts! A handful of men rush forward, toward Life, with knives flashing metallic in the light. Life steps back and Security rush forward. Screaming from the audience. Nittaya grabs my elbow in a vice-like grip as the 'courtiers' press in and move us toward the back. I glimpse a similar movement around our monastery people, but my sight is blocked by the press close up. With surprising speed we are beside a remarkable looking vehicle, I being pressed to put on a heavy vest-like garment, Nittaya taking off her coat and becoming male! Then we pile into the vehicle, pressed shoulder to shoulder with Security, the vehicle careening off in a wild trajectory. Nittaya-as-male is shouting in bass directions at me, something about a showdown in the Forbidden City and the big marauder boss, 'The Emperor'. We are crossing the river, not on any of the decrepit bridges but on the water, up the embankment, through one of the great gates, along the avenue toward a large, multi-storied building. There are two other vehicles just like ours in front of the grand entrance to the building, people emerging from them, weapons flaring, guards rushing from the entry suddenly collapsing to the pavement. I am compelled out of the car, running now toward the entrance, stumbling on those struck down, weapons flaring all around, up flights of stairs, pushing into a very grand room. And there we stop. Ahead, an old man in street dress, sitting on an oversize gold chair on a raised dais, many guards on either side. There is silence. No one moves. Then Life steps forward.

"Are you the man they call 'Emperor?'" Life begins, in a huge voice.

"I am that man," answers the tired old man.

"I come to tell you your warfare is at an end."

"What? What are you telling me?"

"You will stop the killing. No more sending men out to attack and kill people."

"What?!" The old man is enraged. "You are telling me to stop sending out my army?"

"Yes! You must stop fighting in any form and disband your armies."

"How dare you tell me what I can do! I can lift one finger and you all will be mowed down in a rain of bullets."

"My men are faster and can eliminate yours before they have even thought to move. My army is the Guardian Spirits of the Temples! They are not even human."

At these words numerous of the Security shift into their Nāga form, opening their mouths wide to show their teeth.

The effect is immediate. The Emperor and his men shrink back, all to a man.

"You are to stop sending out your armies to kill people and destroy property. If you stop your warfare I will permit you to remain here without your armies and live out the rest of your life. If you bring to an end any life, I shall send out the Defenders of the Temple to destroy your armies and bring your life to an end. Do you understand?"

"I ..., I ...," the Emperor stammered.

"Before dawn of this day, I shall send to you an emissary with documents that you will sign, declaring peace. You shall disband your armies and renounce war forever. Do you understand?"

Silence. While the old man stalls to contemplate his choices, what seems like a battalion of Garudas carrying impressive weapons burst through the doors and into the room. Towering over all of us humans, with wings spread high, these magnificent, manly creatures are commanded by their lieutenant, "Ready!" A dreadful silence as weapons are raised. Then, "Aim!" And the tension through the room is visceral.

"I ..., I understand," the old man agreed, resigned.

"You agree to sign the Articles of Peace and abide by their statutes?"

"I agree."

"Then I leave you in peace," said Life, raising his arm in signal. The Garuda battalion back from the great room, keeping the Emperor and his guard under watch, while we few others turn our backs to the old man and stride from the place to our waiting vehicles where we return as we had come from the monastery, albeit more slowly.

In the vehicle, I said to Nittaya, "Please don't change back into your feminine form just yet. I'd like to have a good look at you as a man."

He laughed, causing no little embarrassment, then said, "Okay." And that's how he remained through the last evenings of the plays.

Meanwhile, the documents for the Emperor had been prepared ahead and were sent with a heavily guarded delegation for his signature.

The swiftness of the whole affair left me dazed. It was Life's idea to use an attack on his person as an excuse to retaliate against the Emperor and, in keeping with his lesson, demand that he give up warfare and seal it in an official document.

Of course, there was no way news of this magnitude could be kept under wraps and, when it went out, Life overnight became a national hero. The significance of this was more apparent as we were to move south. Here, in the old royal city, our audience at the plays had not strayed far, wanting to hear what had happened. When we arrived back we were greeted with cheers. When word got out what exactly had happened, that Life had forced the Emperor to make peace, people just sort of lost all control. When people began to realize the old boss-man would no longer be sending out marauders to maim and kill, their gratitude to Life came to be boundless. He had become their hero.

The fourth night of the plays were upon us. Nittak, the masculine variant for Nittaya, and I took up our places on the rugs, but now considerably farther from the grand old gates, the playing area. The audience, twice the size it was the previous night, awaited the arrival of the actors with great impatience. I stole glimpses of their faces, still hard faces, Walkers' faces, faces I could no longer be ambiguous about, were all around us. Were there faces here I might have seen the previous night in another place? I think maybe him, there. And maybe him, over there. And, oh, I'm almost positive, him, far off to the left. To the right. Suddenly, they all looked suspicious. What I must keep in mind now with the armies disbanded is there are many violent men made idle, all potential sources of some mischief or other.

Fame is seen spotted in the light. He tries to give his usual speech but is interrupted by the clamorous audience. They insist on taking the vow which they were unable to take the previous night. Life leads the vow-taking, such a confusion arising from the audience. My instincts scream, "Danger!" There were no rules that said Life was now safe from attack, but might even be in more risk of such. Better minds than mine had already taken this into consideration, and security was all around him, our precious Life. Yet he stood there bravely, his arms raised to silence the crowd. And he began the Vow, saying each line for them. I looked at the faces I suspected; and I saw Hope, not Hatred. I looked afield and saw Hope everywhere, on every face, mouths believing every word they shaped and sounded, eyes seeing before them a new Truth. And my heart lept for joy. I believed these faces and the words issuing from them. And I felt at last I was witnessing the coming of The New Age; witnessed it as never before. These people who knew hardship, pain, death, were sick of it all and wanted something different, something more, for their lives. And had found what they were seeking. At the end of the vow-taking such jubilation went up. Arms high in the air. Jumping up and down. Light radiating from those faces, those hard faces, those Walkers' faces. And then, people hugging each other. Strangers hugging. Hugging for the death of War, the birth of universal Peace. The death of Hatred, the birth of universal Love. We all were swept up, swept up in the grand emotions. Tears streamed down my cheeks, tears of Joy. I looked at Nittaya, I mean Nittak, and tears were streaming from his eyes, too. We hugged each other and he shouted in my ear, "Ah! This is why I love human beings."

I'm sorry to say the fourth play and lesson were anticlimactic after such catharsis. The announcement of the founding of yet another monastery and university is not that earth-shaking. Yet there were such lines as, "What we must do is decide to live, to pursue our greatest dreams." That got people cheering again. This night, people went off, not thinking of a new monastery in the northern mountains but of the dawn of the New Age of Peace where Hope was reborn.

The fifth night, the announcement of the Interstellar League, was equally unexciting, except for the handful of Nāganese guards who shifted to their dragon form and put on a show for the screaming audience, screaming not in fear but in delight. They slithered around onstage, lashing their ornate tails, rearing up on their hind legs, opening their mouths and showing off their sharp teeth and claws. The audience, far from reacting in fear of the unknown, I think, saw them as familiar, as the source for all those images in the Temples. A perfectly natural thing. Afterwards, when Life had finished the final lesson and the audience surged forward, those Nāga guards got at least as much attention as he did.

Yet one more drama was to unfold before the end of the night. The wizened elderly abbot came forward on the helpful arms of obliging young monks and spoke with Life on the five plays and his assault on the Forbidden City.

"I am joyous my monastery has been the site for such revolutionary events. You know, there will be many retellings of the story, and I shall look forward to hearing every one." With unusual vigor for a man his age he embraces Life, returning to a now formal stance. "I extend regrets that I personally cannot visit your new monastery but expect this to be the first in a long series of exchanges between the two monasteries." Raising his right hand high, his fingers taking on the "Blessing" *mudrā* and his voice the resonance of youth, "Blessings to you, oh Abbot Full-of-Life. May your journey to the South be triumphal and bring to humankind the longed-for New Era of Peace."

He again embraces Life but this time in the decrepitude of age, all virility seeming to have been used up in the blessing. Monks come forward to his aid. The abbot places trembly hands together before his face and attempts a deep bow before Life. He is rescued from near-collapse by the handy monks and is led away.

I cannot read Life's reaction. He seems almost nonchalant in the wake of such a weighty blessing. He waves for me to join him and throws an arm over my shoulder. My knees still atremble from the dramatic event, his knees seem to be doing just fine. We continue to the Dining Hall where food is being served to the troupe.

I am much compelled to say, "Life, I ..."

"Shush! We'll discuss it tomorrow." But we never did.

The next evening we consulted with Fame on how long we would be welcomed at this monastery. He confirmed our 'donation' to them extended for ten days. Nittaya, now shifted back to her feminine form, had received permission from the former emperor to visit the Forbidden City where her family had at one time been established. I begged to accompany her. For prudence' sake, she insisted I take on a disguise to hide my being a monk. She got me all dolled up in flowing robes and a great tall hat to cover my shaved head, and instructed everyone to address me as "Your Excellency." What fun!

We went off after the midnight meal, accompanied by a sizable entourage. We entered by the East Gate and were met with several knowledgeable women who would be our guides. It was a splendid time well spent, one of many highlights being seeing the sculpture for which her grandfather was said to have modeled, and a remarkable mosaic made of seashells. There were other of his images around the buildings including decorations on the roofs of one of the royal residences. Also, we were taken to the multi-story building where we had confronted the old emperor and were informed then it was the "Coronation Hall." But it was in essence a throne room. It really was quite splendid with intricate construction of the beams holding up the roof, high overhead. Nittaya showed me where she had played as a child, pointing out a pond where she swam. Time had not been kind to the environs, in spite of feeble efforts at restoration here and there. I could see Nittaya was distressed about this, rendering her nostalgic visit a bittersweet experience.

The next evening, after prayers and breakfast, we were guests of the school where the young novices were educated. I was glad both Loyal and the five boys were present to observe what others were doing. I noted in particular the reaction of Mischief who is disruptive in class. Such behavior was totally absent in this school. They had a good library here, too. Not as extensive as the one upriver, but still substantial.

Time came to make our farewells and to go to the city's station where we would connect up with our next caravan going south. Nittaya insisted we take one of the amphibious vehicles with us along with more Security guards. We all insisted Life ride in that vehicle along with Farmer and Soldier. After much discussion, it was decided to have the five boys and Loyal in that vehicle, too. That helped with the overcrowding in our old bus.

Nittaya and I stood beside the entrance to her circulary making our farewells. "You were completely brilliant," I said.

"Hardly," she said. "My plan was rejected early on. What you saw unfold was totally the work of your leader and friend."

"What?! That was Life's idea?"

"Yes. Entirely."

"Amazing," I replied, pondering the unfathomable implications of that revelation. "Life continually amazes me."

"Oh, and by the way, my people were not using real trajectories in their firearms on the imperial guards," she related. "Their weapons were set on 'stun'. The felled guards were back to normal within twelve hours."

"I hadn't given it a thought," I confessed, "but it's good to know they were not being killed. I think the old boss-man believed they had been killed. It's hard to justify peace if you've just killed a bunch of people."

"Indeed, yes," she agreed. "That is the very reason why our weapons were set thus." Changing the subject, "Did you know Fame had given me a pouch of donations to give to Lily?"

"No, I didn't," I replied, not really surprised. "I hope it's good and heavy."

"It is indeed. It shall speed along several building projects, primarily for the university."

"Now you, personally," I asked, "have you had a good time? Did you do the things you wanted to do?"

"Me?" she asked, raising her eyebrows. "Beating down that arrogant would-be emperor was jolly good. One doesn't get to do that every day. Yes, I had a great time."

"No, I meant you personally," I gently corrected. "I mean you revisiting your childhood haunts, going to the Forbidden City."

"Ah, well," she said, a wistful look crossing her face. "You as a Buddhist should know change is everything. Nothing is static."

Now it's my turn to be wistful. "Yes, you're right. That is very Buddhist. But how do you feel about revisiting places of your childhood?"

"Frankly, it was sweet. But I would far rather have the place neglected, in disrepair, than fully restored, perfect. For one implies weakness, uncertain power, while the other implies entrenched tyranny."

"Yes, that is true," I replied, shaking my head. Then, in a complete change of mood, "Nittaya, it's been wonderful having you here. I missed you terribly."

"And I missed you, too," she replied, giving me a tiny hug.

"I wish I were going with you now," I said in some degree of despair. "I want to be back in the Valley so much. That's where I belong."

"You will be, sooner than you think," she said comforting. "You've accomplished a great deal, and you're almost through. You have grown from this experience, I can tell," she observed. "But there is more to be done, and it looks like this final part will be the most interesting, the most challenging."

"Oh!" I cried, "I don't want it to be interesting. I want it to be dull as anything. 'Interesting' is too dangerous."

"It is, isn't it," agreed Nittaya. "But you'll do fine with 'interesting'." With that she gave me a quick peck of a kiss on my forehead, turned, and was off. I didn't even have a chance to say "Good-bye" to her. I stepped back a few paces as the outer surface of the circulary began to rotate. Quickly it accelerated, rose into the air and was gone. Now standing alone, I am overcome with missing my friend already, and with terrible homesickness for the Valley. It seems I am doomed to never return there, the place where I must be to reunite with my heart, because I have absolutely left it there. My chin sinks to my chest. I feel inconsolable. Gloom settles over all.

Suddenly, I feel an arm thrown over my shoulder. I turn to behold Life, smiling at me. "Come on," he says. "It's time to go."

CHAPTER 9

Our country is at its narrowest point here, at the old royal city. The coastal range of mountains run north/south, parallel to the coast. Yet forty kilometers south of the city is a mountain orientated east/west that divides the country north/south, of enormous histori- cal significance. This mountain presents a substantial barrier to crossing. Formerly, there was a rail line not as high in elevation as the roadway and, therefore, easier to navigate, especially if you are a Walker, having to travel its length on foot. Consequently, the caravan provides service for the Walkers along the old rail line. The rest of us in vehicles of some sort take to the higher, more difficult, route. It is also more beautiful, vistas opening up all along the way. Yet it is sub- ject to violent storms, high winds, torrential rains. This time of year is the dry season, so we probably won't have rain, but we likely will have winds.

One sees this contrary mountain range off in the distance, to the south, as one leaves the city of the old royal court. It seems to emerge from the range to the west and extend across to the east, out into the ocean. As one travels south it approaches, ominously. And then one arrives at the bottom of the formidable incline. With fool- hardy daring one heads up, thinking, "Why, this shouldn't be such a bad thing at all." But it is. Oh my, it is. One must climb up for a very long time, and then one must come back down for a really long time, none of it easy. Plus, it takes three nights in the crossing, the only re- ward being cooler daytimes.

So, up we start, our old bus wheezing and grinding away. Up ahead the road is a constant twist and turn as it follows the contours of the ever-changing mountainside, on more than one occasion hav- ing to deal with serious washes. Behind, the broadening vista of land- and seascape, a few twinkling lights to be seen scattered here and there. Soon, to our right, we approach a dry riverbed snaking upward. We wed its contours until, in the wee hours of the morning, it peters out and we are on our own, the pass still high above, a frightful way off. Our companion vehicle, that which we have christened the Nāgamobile, is beside us, the occupants watching out their windows, looks of concern on their faces. Forests on either side of the road, no longer dead, now sport a courageous mist of green needles. As dawn begins to light the eastern sky, the caravan pulls off the road where tents under the trees await us, our little bus relieved of the constant upward haul. We all look up into the trees and bless them for their valiant show of life, then down at the disappointing ragtag of tents. We think of taking down our own tents atop the bus but, fatigued by the anxieties of the ascent, we decide it's not worth the effort, the tents under the trees looking better and better by the minute. Besides, a huge group of fellow-travelers have collected in front of Life, demanding he speak to them. Making an interesting choice, he delivers the first night's lesson, the one professing his faith. What a picture they all make under these troubled pines—sitting on the needled ground, backs against their choice of pine trunks, or standing leaning shoulder to them, rapt faces, starving faces, desperate for something to hold on to. They are silent. Then the soughing sound. Is it rising wind in the top-most branches? Is it Life's breath blowing through the emptiness of beleaguered spirits? Who can say? Then came the tears, tears from eyes that have beheld such pain, switch-backing down these cheeks, not hollowed and baked as the Walkers', but unwritten, blank, anonymous, now—finally!—being inscribed, incised, gaining character with knowledge. They understand, awed into silence. No applause at the end, no whistling or stomping, just these souls with hunched shoulders turning, going to assigned tents in silence. Not silence! For there is that soughing softly in the air, that poignant sound. They disappear inside the tattered flaps, the sound still floating in the air, weaving around the gnarled and crusty bark, it raises up, setting the needles to vibrating. They take it up and slowly amplify it over the daylight hours.

A stirring returns under the trees. In ones and twos, they come, beseeching Life to bestow his blessing on them. In the heavens, the intensity of the sun's rays sets the very air on fire. In the mountain's shadow, Life, seated, the palm of his hand raised in benediction, grants blessing on all who ask. Then he, too, retires into the semi-darkness of the tent for sleep.

As we sleep, across the crest of the mountain a wind rises up, protests, then rages against the obstruction, its fury mounting into the setting of the sun. Now, treetops above the tents are astir, currents of air hurrying down the mountain side. Folds and straps of the tents slap against themselves, adding their ruckus to the noise. We are stirred awake in the hubbub of the air. What is happening? What trial must we face this night?

Campfires refuse to light. Thoughts of hot food turn cold. We chosen few say our prayers, forego our standard fare and fast instead. We all pile into our vehicles and valiantly head out toward the pass, that notch in the rim of the mountain, that place right up there. Overhead, winds shriek their fury, portentously, causing one to fear for the night, speculating on the nature of the pass itself. Is it a particular high point to which one ascends, and having achieved, immediately begin the descent. Or, heaven forbid, is it a long undulating passage in the heights toward some far distant downward turn? The object of speculation here being how long we shall be in thrall to that ferocious gale. Those in the know tell us the bad news. We look upward, toward that tell-tale notch, hope for easy passage dying within.

And so, we take to the road again. Relentlessly upward the pavement projects us. At first, our old bus justifies our dependence on it, but soon its malady returns, its gasps for breath revealing a sickness at heart. It slows. It stops. We all pile out, thinking the less weight will get it moving again. But it doesn't. So, putting shoulder to its backside, we push. The vehicle behind us, knowing full well who we are, and feeling sorry for us, the menfolk pour out and join us in our labors. The old carcass moves! And we all push and push. It millimeters forward, and then needs pushing again. We are all exhausted and sit on the pavement by the side of the road, out of the downward rush of the raging wind. It tousles our hair in passing, as though in fondness, but that is a terrible deception. As yet another obstacle to its path, we are hated, to be thrust asunder. It pushes us, pushes us back down the slope; and it pushes the bus, backwards, too, contrary to our aspirations. We get up and put our backs to it, millimeters forward. The Nāgamobile stopped with us. They look out the windows at us, concerned. At last, when Life emerges to put his shoulder to the task, they join us, the Nāganese coming to our side, putting human-form shoulders to the bus's metallic backside. Suddenly, the vehicle leaps forward with their exertion, and forward, and forward again, leaving us behind. They are running uphill, the weight of a Sisyphus light as a feather on their backs. A cheer escapes our throats as we all, inwardly, admire the strength of these marvelous beings. We do not expect them to do so, but they continue pushing the bus the kilometers it takes to reach the pass where a semblance of levelness permits the bus to continue under its own power. We all rush to thank these titans, thanks which they accept with true modesty.

But, here, we cannot linger out of doors for the air is raging furious, picking up branches and pebbles to fling at the unawares as though we are to blame for its troubles. We and the Nāganese take to shelter in our respective vehicles and forge forward, marking our passage over this high mountain pass. We look out the bus windows as the winds whistle past. A loose bit of the bus's skin breaks free, comes flying by, sending us into paroxysms of worry the whole construction will come apart, fly away, and leave us stranded and exposed. A slapping sound is heard above, on the roof, and sudden concern mounts for the security of our tents and camping gear. Like a wrestler pinned to the mat slaps the canvas to alert his opponent he is giving up, the loose tent flap slaps the bus-roof to signal its defeat and desire for the pain to stop. But we are in no position to come to the tent's rescue nor fend off the opponent. It slaps on, hour after hour, we unable to answer its frantic call.

Toward dawn, we descend again, not on the far side of this obstacle range, but in a middling valley, its mouth opening to the sea far off to our left, where dawn etches a line of light on the horizon. We come to our campsite where we debark, turning our ear to the sky where, far off is heard the tyrant's ragings. Here, all is in peace. Our driver, our poor beleaguered bus driver, opens the hood of the bus, thrusting head and shoulders inside. He does not emerge for hours. We monks come together to say our prayers, led by Life. I amaze to see many fellow travelers on their knees doing the triplet bows, their hands pressed palm to palm, same as we. Afterwards, in ones and twos, they come again for Life's blessings which he bestows unstintingly, retiring to our tent only when the sun's rays penetrate our side of the valley.

That evening, prayers, and then cups of hot herbal, brewed from plants I found here, *regani*, under the pines. It is a great restorer, used for little ailments and disorders. It shall assist in keeping us healthy.

The caravan moves out, our bus taking up its assigned position. The driver had worked miracles, the motor chugging along happily. But two elements were in its favor. The highway did not ascend directly, precipitously, but by a series of switchbacks, at a gentle degree, and the windstorm was not blowing violent headwinds in its direction. That was to come later.

River and Autumn came back to join me, making a tight fit on a two-person seat. Of course, I was curious what they had to say. Autumn began. "Did you know I had my twentieth birthday several months ago? No? Well, I've been thinking I should begin planning for my ordination. I liked the monastery in the old royal city. It's famous for its educational programs and Zen teachings. Anyway, I thought I should like to go there. What do you think?"

Before I could answer, River spoke up. "And I, too. I'm going to have my twentieth birthday next month and feel I should begin planning my ordination, too. I liked the monastery where Abbot Life was ordained, the one in the far north, along the coast. But that's so far away now. Maybe the one Autumn likes would be good, too. What would you advise?"

"Oh, I'm so happy to know you both are thinking about such important things in life. Both monasteries are outstanding institutions, and I would recommend them both highly. Perhaps the one in the old royal city offers a slight advantage in that by the time we are returning you will have completed your studies and been ordained. You can rejoin us as we pass through on our way back to the Valley. But the final choice is entirely yours."

"Good," said River. "Then I should like to return to the old royal city with Autumn."

"When do you suggest we leave?" asked Autumn.

"You both will need to train someone to take over your jobs with our productions before you leave," I pointed out. "What you might do is train your replacements at our destination coming up, and then leave after that. How is that?"

"Good," they both agree.

"Then it's decided. I'll let Life know of your plans. I'm sure he'll be pleased. As for a replacement, the best I could think of is Loyal. Ask him if he would take over for you."

When the caravan stopped for the midnight break, I caught out Life. "Autumn and River want to return to the old royal city to study for their ordination," I said, putting everything out in front.

"That's wonderful!" exclaimed Life. "I'm so glad to know they are thinking about such important matters."

"What should I tell them?" I queried.

"Tell them I give them my full support, that they have made a wise decision."

"Anything else I should tell them?"

"Yes. Tell them to study Zen teachings as long as they are there."

"They have already told me they intend to do that very thing."

"Excellent! Are they intending to rejoin us on our return, or do they have other plans?" he asked.

"There's no question. They intend to rejoin us. They are most loyal to us."

"That makes me very happy to hear," he said, breaking into a broad smile.

And, so, it was decided. I must say, I liked very much the way our little monastery was growing. With each decision such as Autumn's and River's I saw a strong institution emerging. With their inspiration, I hoped Loyal would soon make a similar decision. Soon, too, we would start a program for the ordination of our own monks once we returned to the Valley.

Another broad plateau faced us as we reached the second tempestuous summit. Winds blew in our faces, throwing all kinds of trash at us. Much more optimistic was our mood now as we had but to transverse this place and then we would descend the far side of the mountain into tranquility. The worst was over. We could relax. Not so, I'm afraid. These winds had been generating across the coastal plain to the south and were hitting the lower slopes, sweeping up and over. There was much yet to be endured. Our little bus moved forward in spite of the headwinds, vibrating against the hard push of the rushing air. Slowly we made progress and, in the wee hours of the night, began our descent into the southland. Dawn brought to an end our descent, all the caravan pulling into another grove of pines, them, too, sporting a mist of green in their tops. We brought out our portable Buddha, spread out mats and bent knees to pray. Behind us, in this natural temple, green-ceiling, pillared pines, the entire congregation of the caravan knelt on the carpet of needles, to join in prayer. Afterwards, pilgrims came, those aware this was likely their last chance for blessing from the Heroic Master. Life yet still raised his hand in benediction until the sun's rays, raised up from the sea, brought to an end such activity. As we bent to enter our tents we caught our first glimpse of the lands spreading southward, promise all about. Happy sleep with happy thoughts of that grand vision, and of the crescent city on the ocean, our destination.

This city had once been the playground of the international wealthy. They had patronized luxurious resorts, strung along the long crescent-shaped beach, wide with billows of white sand and azure waters, the real wealth of the city. Resort vied with resort to offer up the most refined of pleasures, plush dining halls serving food and drink from the culinary capitols of the world, spas offering service to the corporeality of their guests, specialists catering to the most refined wishes of their pampered patrons. Every taste with its price, and a price on every taste. The wealth the city had accumulated was impressive. Come the fall, and many a covetous eye turned on this place, desirous of harvesting the fat for themselves. Chief of these was the king of the marauders, the one who called himself 'Emperor'. He came from the north with his men, over the contrary range, sweeping down upon the fattened goose, plucking its golden feathers, smashing the bones of that which could not be carried off. Time after time they came, until the carcass of the city lay with its skeleton exposed to the sky, its mirrors and marble rendered into shards discarded in the dusty corners of the broken edifices. Gone, too, were all the beautiful people, the very wealth they wore snatched from their person, replaced with thrusts of the knife slicing away the fat. Some they took in ransom to exchange for gold. All now gone.

At the farther reach of the crescent sand is to be found an ovate tiny mountain, its crest once a splendid backward glance at a splendid city. There, centuries ago, humble fishermen discovered a sculpture floating out of the unknown. It was of the gender-shifter Guanyin, feminine counterpart to the masculine spiritual teacher. The drifted sculpture, brought ashore, was given a new home here in a hallowed spot. Some thought the high ground above this beach should also make a fine home for scholars of the faith, monks, and nuns; and so dedicated the land. No stranger to the ebb and flow of wars raged across this place, each time the sculpture was smashed it was resurrected larger and more glorious than before until in its final form, the white lady stood on her gigantic lotus blossom, this base several stories high, she herself rivaling the height of the tallest of the skyscrapers along the nearby beach. Around her feet were built splendid temples, gold lavished on other of the faith's icons. When came the marauder hoards, their greed was not sated in the city, close by, but spilled out here, too, bringing down the giants all about. Their abbot was gone, all their teachers, just like us, mown down. Of the survivors were a few of the very old, all the rest novices, just as we had been. They did as we had done, buried the ashes of their beloved fallen, sought the way of survival in all its bitter humility.

We were asked to visit this desolation in the hope a new spirit would be enkindled to awaken sleeping ardor. We felt, at least, we could offer succor to our fallen brethren and perhaps awaken faith and hope in their hearts, enough to begin the heavy task of rebuilding. And so we arrived, casting our eye on an altogether familiar dolor, promising that, indeed, the tyrant of the north had been corralled. He would not return. It was we, in a reversal of roles, the visitors, who spread a banquet for our fallen hosts. They came in their hunger, those ragged few, and found the nourishment they needed at our table. And it was we, too, who made our own brooms to sweep away the shards and dust in the cracked and broken corners, pulling back the rubble into heaps out of the way, repairing the little there was worth saving. Glad indeed were we that we could give.

Life called a meeting on our arrival. "We all know in our hearts," he began, "the sorrow these, our brethren, are feeling. We, little more than a year ago, were in exactly the same crisis as these embattled spirits are now. I urge each of you to seek out one of the survivors to befriend while we are here. Spend time with them, talk with them, and share your good fortune. Help them find Hope hiding in their core. Help them bring it forward so that they have the courage to press onward. It is not just for these spirits alone you must aspire but for the poor lay spirits round about that have no core of faith to buoy them up, who need leadership. If you can ignite the fire in the spirit of your brethren, then they can hold aloft their light that others may be led out of the darkness in which they have been plunged."

There was silence all around as we thought on our assignment and how we should go about fulfilling it, not a simple task.

Time was rapidly approaching for the first evening's play and lesson. The chosen site was the courtyard at the inside of the three-portal great gates, entryway to the site. People arriving from the city-side would ascend a long flight of stairs, through the portal and on to the courtyard where they would sit. Autumn placed one of our spots where it would illuminate the city side of the ruined sculpture. The Guanyin grand sculpture had survived intact until recently when marauders had placed explosives halfway up inside the edifice, upon detonation severing the figure at the level of the left arm positioned at her waist. The upper part of the superstructure came crashing down onto the lotus flower pedestal, the lower part of the figure left intact as testament to its downfall. Seeing even the ruin of this beloved landmark flooded in light would instantly catch the attention of any of the city's survivors and alert them something out of the ordinary was happening at the Monastery. Perhaps they would come out of curiosity and stay to take in the play. At least, that was the intension.

A group of us had fashioned brooms out of materials collected in the environs and were sweeping clean the play area and courtyard where the audience was expected to sit. The courtyard was quite grand, paved with tile. On its edges left and right were rows of marble sculpture, the eighteen Arhat, ferocious protectors and gentle, prayerful monks alike. These were mostly intact, but a few had been attacked and left in broken disarray. There were many large cement planters left haphazard about the courtyard. I was told they were planters for some kind of Japanese tree, but these were long dead and disappeared. At the end of the courtyard opposite the gate were the burnt out remains of the main temple. There wasn't much to see there but heaps of green roof tiles piled up. To the right of this temple was a simple outdoor altar with a reclining Buddha directly in back. These were intact and the site where they observed prayer. Directly behind this altar was a short flight of stairs leading to another tri-portal gate and pagoda beyond. Attempts had been made to topple the pagoda but were unsuccessful. Still, large scars remained from the efforts.

Several of the monks and nuns of the monastery here had joined us in helping to sweep the area. It was explained to us a kind of inertia had settled over the survivors, they feeling it was hopeless to do anything to reverse the effects of the marauders. Seeing us out sweeping their home was freeing to some of them, causing them to question their lethargy enough to get them up and moving again. Often it is the little things like this that make the difference. In an inspiration, I invited these handful of people to sit with me for the play and lesson. They all accepted my invitation, a few happily so. I had not intended to attend this evening's performances but felt the cause justified my change in plans.

Nothing could have been more felicitous. My guests were excited by the mere novelty of having something to attend that night. Remember, too, these people are young orphans, in their teens; all but one who is twenty. None of them had ever so much as attended a play before, and had only the most cursory idea what a play was.

I was given, then, the opportunity to school these individuals in what drama was, what its refinements were. I was in my element. There we were, our group now swollen to eight, sitting on the tiles of the courtyard with our heads together, my extolling on what Drama and Acting were all about, they trying to grasp it all. Suddenly a spot goes up on the main gates, catching the filigree on the rooftops in stark contrast against the night sky. Smiley and Little Lord make their entrance. I hear several quick intakes of breath around me and know a spark has been lit. Without moving my head, I look at those young people within eyeshot, watching their reactions. It is an unexplainable miracle how Art, even in its most elementary form, speaks to the spirit. The simple act of putting on Art's mantle seems to set in motion machinery that grinds away—touching, touching, touching—and we burst out laughing, or we weep; wherever that machine touches, we react. And so this night, the play grinding away like clockwork, the emotions played. From the Boys' entrance to the affirmation of Faith at the end of Life's lesson, my poor little group went through paroxysms of feeling; and, after all the applause and stomping were ended, they were left as though wrung out, like a wet cloth. Their knees gave way as they tried to stand. They had to lean on each other to remain upright. They could hardly move. Now, Life's plays are not the greatest works for the theatre ever created. But, for these people in these times, the machinery works. All the pieces put in place, it was the emergence of Life's affirmation of Faith that stayed with them. They went instantly to talking about it, marveling over it, picking it up and taking on its mantle. And that was the playwright's intention, especially for ones like these. I had to smile, though, when one of the boys enthused, "I can hardly wait until tomorrow night!"

The clockwork does other, bigger things, too. Life's fame is fed, especially now since he has stood up to the Emperor singlehandedly and is a hero in everyone's eyes. And Fame, like clockwork, collects up the gold and silver donations for the Valley. These are built into the drama as well. There are also instructions to the audience, built into the drama, too. "This is my faith. You can believe thus, too." Or "Form into communities, live this vow to abolish war and the destructive feelings." And people go out and take up these causes, hopefully thereby improving their lives many times over. All this is part of the machinery, as well.

And, too, a new tradition is started here, this night, the people wanting to be blessed by the Great Hero Abbot, he who has freed them from the wicked marauders. Life raises his right hand in benediction and says the prayer over the heads of the humble faithful. They in return come to adore him and carry away the growing myth of this youthful savior monk telling all how to reform their lives and live in a new spirit. His fame spreads like wildfire.

After the surprising number of people from the nearby ruins depart, we all collect for prayer before the reclining Buddha altar, under the night sky. Then we with gladness in our hearts serve our desolate brethren the midnight meal, and we sit at makeshift tables and talk on whatever subjects happen to be brought up. Most were curious to hear how Life had stood up against the Emperor and forced him to renounce war. I, being the sole other witness present, was happy to tell them all about it, they taking in every detail. I chose my words carefully, knowing full well this tale would be told over again endlessly. I edited out my fears of the hordes of unemployed thugs out there that might self-employ in ways with which they were familiar, re-employing themselves in a bit of unlawful wealth-seeking. It was sure to happen, I felt.

Later, after we left our various tables and went our separate ways, the thought dawned on me I may not be the sole observer here of the events at the Forbidden City. I sought out our two assigned Nāga guards. I asked them, "Did you go with Abbot Full-of-Life to the Forbitten City?"

"I cannot discuss that with you," said the one; and, "Yes," said the other, in full octave glory.

With that knowledge, I then went to Farmer and Soldier and asked the same question. "Yes," they both answered. Well, I thought, it seems I am way out of line in assuming I was the only one of our little troupe present at that big event.

"Where were you standing?" I asked.

"Second row, near the middle," replied Soldier very straight forwardly.

"Both of you together?" I had to know.

"Yes," confirmed Farmer.

"Then you two were much closer to the Emperor than I was," I had to admit. "Do you think the Emperor and the guards around him thought we had killed those guards at the outer gate and the entrance to that building?"

"You could see it on their faces. They were terrified," said Farmer, Soldier nodding in agreement.

"Yeah, the Emperor was trying to bluff his way through at first," Soldier said.

"They all knew the trick was up, that their little game was over," added Farmer. "But we didn't expect Life to be calling the shots. We expected the Princess – uh, I mean her as a man, a prince? – he would be the person speaking up."

"Yeah, that was a big surprise for everybody, the Nāgas included, I think," observed Soldier.

"Well, then, were you surprised when the Emperor accepted Life's terms?" I needed to know.

"Oh, yes," confirmed Soldier. "We were expecting a shootout at any minute. I had my finger on the trigger. I'd turned the stun setting off and was going to shoot live ammo at them if even one of them shot at us."

"Me, too," Farmer agreed.

"Wow. We were that close, were we?" I asked, chilled at the thought.

"Yeah," confirmed Soldier.

"I knew we had them, though, when Life mentioned the Guardians of the Temples," quipped Farmer.

"Ha, ha," laughed Soldier. "When the Garudas came in and when the Nāgas shifted into their true shapes I knew then we really had 'em."

"Ha, ha," Farmer joined in the laughter. "The way they all jumped back when they saw the Nāgas; and the looks they had on their faces!"

"Now be serious and tell me your thoughts," I admonished. "Now that all these thugs are out of business—the warlords, all their henchmen, the marauders, the whole lot of them—do you think they are all going to go out and start tilling the land? You know what I mean. Do you think there are going to be groups of them reorganize and start stealing and killing people again?"

"Yes!" they both said at once. Then Farmer carried on, "I think it's going to be the Emperor that will shut them down, though. Otherwise, he'll be the one to get it in the neck."

Soldier added, "The Nāgas may have to be the first to chase down the thugs, but the Emperor will be right behind them. They will listen to him, maybe not the Nāgas. I'm not sure about that, though. The Nāgas and Garudas look so much like all those paintings and sculpture in the temples, you know those thugs have gotta believe they really are this holy army backing up our little Abbot." He laughs again, Farmer joining in.

Farmer picks up the thread. "Can't you just imagine all those tough guys thinking this little abbot has managed to get this whole supernatural world on his side, and he's gonna turn the monsters loose on them if they don't behave."

"Yeah, but a few of them are going to have to try it just to be sure," said Soldier, expanding on the idea.

"It's going to be interesting to watch what happens," confirmed Farmer.

Well, there you have it. I was far from being the only one of us there that night, and perhaps we had not yet heard the end to the story. My feeling was if there were those foolish enough to try moving out on their own, the Nāgas would have their say in the matter. It would remain to be seen if our 'Emperor' would survive the event, or not. I, for one, am not willing to place my bet with him.

As the evenings and series of plays/lessons progressed, I shepherded my little flock through the unfolding of the meanings and metaphors. On the second evening they were confused by the call to form communities, yet they failed to see they, here at the Monastery, were a community in the full sense of the term. Several admitted they had thought, or were thinking, about leaving the Monastery because of personal callings. Once they began thinking of the Monastery as a community, that changed everything, they said. They saw themselves as being able to specialize and bring personal talents to the benefit of all at the Monastery. High on everybody's list was food, and the cultivation of food products. There were several stubbed toes over the controversy of going out and collecting alms, now extremely difficult because of the general lack in the environs, and the alternative of raising one's own food. When to start cultivating a garden was of prime importance as this was now high summer. Crops should have been started months earlier. Yet numerous things could be planted even still that would be ready for harvest within weeks. They were amazed when I told them about the food fellowship in progress in the Valley. Several of the novices volunteered to go there to study. I sent off a message, via our helpful Nāga guard, a request for an immediate internship and the very next day had it confirmed. We were still at the Monastery a few days later when a really brave eighteen-year-old set out for the Valley, we all wishing him our best 'farewell'.

In the interim, I shared some of my precious seeds with them to get them started. We picked out a sheltered bed in which to locate a garden and set up a search for organic material with which to enrich the sandy soil. Such enthusiasm! It gladdened my heart to see. Meanwhile, we became a search party going all over the little mountain where the Monastery was located, looking for herbals and edible plants. When it was not possible to transplant specimens we marked the spot so that gatherers would know where to return. And, where needed, I gave instruction on how to maintain the sites so that the chosen plant would flourish. Some few we collected cuttings to root or, where available, dug up specimens for transplant. They were all such avid students, having much motivation to learn. Within a few nights we had collected enough for them to start a more than modest garden and being sufficiently trained, I felt, in its maintenance. I came to feel inside I had done my duty in igniting fires in the souls of all my young gardeners, as Life had instructed.

But to return to the evenings of plays. The third night was a major occasion for my novices, in that they all took vow-taking most seriously. At the end of Life's lesson they jumped to their feet without hesitation, wholeheartedly taking the vow to end war and the destructive feelings. It was only afterwards they began to have second thoughts.

"Should I, as a vow-holding Buddhist novice, have taken on these other vows, even though they come from the Hero Abbot?"

"Yes, it's perfectly all right."

"How do I control negative feelings?" or even more pointedly, "Negative feelings can be revealing of the struggle to do the right thing. Should I negate these feelings, too?"

"The point is to know your feelings, the whole range of them, and to transform the negative into positive. You will find ways to recognize the negative in yourself and make them positive. With this vow, you take on the responsibility for making that transformation."

"But isn't that included in the two-hundred-ninety-six vows we take as novices and monks?"

"Yes, indeed it is."

"Oh!"

The fourth night was not a great surprise to them as they heard us from the Valley constantly talking about it. They were eager, however, to set up and maintain a strong bond between the two monasteries. We were most happy to do so. The fifth night announcing the Interstellar League was not that big a thing, either, since we had talked a good deal about the Nāga guards and Garuda militia. They were exquisitely thrilled when the two traveling with us shifted from human to Nāga when Life mentioned them in his listing of the League members. Afterwards, the novices went up to them and persuaded them to shift again so they could get a good closeup look at them. The guards complied, and there was much deafening screaming and carrying on. The two guards simply loved it and put on quite a show. Many years later the Nāganese set up a major facility here on this little mountain to study Earth's oceans. I always felt this site was chosen because the monks were early on unusually accepting of them. Of course, with the site jutting out into the ocean and in the middle of two spectacular crescent beaches, it was a logical place for such a facility.

Our residence here came to an end, except for one more major event. Life, inspired by the poignant state of these religious here, wrote a story that he read to us all the last night we were here. What inspired him cannot be said, I guess; but it was a divine inspiration. Life based his story on the historical event of fishermen discovering an effigy of Guanyin floating in the water, fishing it ashore. A mound was chosen on which to set it up. People then came to pray. One thing leading to another, the monastery was founded with Guanyin images being always the most important. The difference in Life's story was that it was set at this time, and he used the names of the novices for the fishermen and others in the story. It was as though the whole cycle was beginning all over again in the here and now. You could see the young people took it very much to heart. They took up the proffered mantle, no mistaking it.

With the reading, I felt it time for us to move on.

CHAPTER 10

At the monastery on the little mountain peninsula we received word our caravan was forming in the resort city ruins, that we should join them. We climb into our respective vehicles and, amid fond farewells, are off.

In the ruins of the city where we meet up with our 'van, River and Autumn join their group going back north. They have chosen to take up with the Walkers as a kind of pilgrimage, a penance if you will, to cleanse their spirits before beginning their studies for ordination. Besides, they say, they know what the highway passage is like; now they want to know the lower passage, the Walkers' Way. We share special prayers and farewells, and send them on their way.

We have been traveling along the coast for months now. At this point our itinerary will change. We are in the Dog Days of high summer with heat along the southern coastal plain too great for mortals to bear, with little or no shelter from the scorching sun along the road. Consequently, we'll be turning inland on the Central Highlands highway in order to avoid the worst of the heat. It's not as though we'll be missing many wonderful Buddhist monasteries, though. Over two hundred years ago the country was in one of its phases of division into North and South. The southern government was controlled by converted Christians, Catholics, and while they were in power they closed many of the Buddhist temples and monasteries. A few of these managed to reopen after this government fell and the South was once again reunited with the North. For us, that means we shall be traveling long distances between performances until we reach the great city of the South where, once again, there are more Buddhist temples and monasteries. Along the way, I am told, we shall see many lasting marks from that turbulent period of my country's past. I await them with a certain degree of foreboding.

"Palace. I've just gotten a letter from Brother Lân renewing his invitation for us to come to his holy little mount in the vast southern seas. Hero and Bright have not scheduled for us to go there. What do you think? Should I make a point of our doing this?"

"Humm. Very interesting. Does he know about the Valley and our high commitment there?"

"Yes, I think he does. He emphasizes in this latest letter how he would like for us all to have a little stress-free vacation in a fascinating place, while he and his people extend much hospitality to a troupe of weary travelers."

"Sounds marvelous."

"So should I write back accepting his invitation? Hero and Bright, you know, would still need to go there and work out the details with Brother Lân."

"To my mind, a visit there is like fulfilling a grand plan to travel our country its fullest extent. One can go no further south than that little island located at the very edge of what was once the great river delta on the border with our neighboring country to the west. Yes, I think we should do it."

"Good! Thank you, Palace. That's my thought, too."

Our pilgrimage now enters a new phase as we head out from the crescent resort city, arriving shortly at the junction where the caravan turns to the right onto the Highland's road. It's not as though this area is that much higher in elevation than the coastal plain, but it is closer to the high mountains that form the country's western boundary where cooler air descends into the valley, cooling it significantly. Yet even at night the heat can be oppressive, and we keep the bus's windows wide open to catch every breath of air. As we bump along Fame reports to me another large sum of gold and silver pieces donated to us at our last performances. These he sent off to the Valley by the usual courier service, he retaining just enough to cover immediate expenses. It means financing for another building boom in the Valley. I can't imagine what we shall see when we finally return home.

He said to me, "I never think to ask you if you understand the dynamics of why we are given gold and silver and why we take it. Do you understand what is at work here?"

I reply, "I have some thoughts on the matter, but they probably are all wrong. Maybe you should explain it to me."

"Very well. Under current circumstances, a barter system would be the normal way of carrying on trade. Take us, your staff, for instance. The reason why we would prefer to be paid in room and board, and occasional clothing, is these are our real needs. Having gold or silver doesn't help us because neither food nor a place to live can be bought with it. You feed and shelter us, and we work for you. Simple! Now, when you take big institutions and big things like land and buildings, that's different. When you deal in those things, they are complex. Food can be grown on land, but you need gold to buy land. I bet you didn't know the food we've been eating for several months now is all grown in the fields just outside the Valley, beside the landing field."

"What?! No, I didn't know. That's ... that's marvelous!"

"Yes. You see, these poor people that make donations to us after performances have collected up here and there a few pieces of gold or silver which they have saved for maybe a long time, long enough to realize it's never going to be of much help to them. They exist by bartering. They think, 'Maybe these guys from the monastery could probably be able to put this gold or silver to good use, better use than I can.' So they give it to us. And we can put it to good use, and do. Do you understand now?"

"Yes. No. I understand that we needed gold to buy the Valley from Lord X, but I don't understand why we need gold and silver to build the new buildings on our campus. It's not like we're buying some building somewhere and miraculously flying it into the Valley. It's being created out of an idea. How does gold and silver help us there?"

"The contractor probably is a self-contained building unit with all aspects supplied by one business. The owner of the company is probably also the architect and the engineer. He undoubtedly owns a manufacturing company that supplies all the building materials for the project. He probably pays his workers with food and shelter, but he would have to buy the food from some supplier who could provide the quantity that he would need. He probably owns facilities where his workers can live since that's his business.

"Did you know the Valley Foundation has acquired the land directly outside our Valley and is in the process of having it cleared and terraced where needed in order to go into food production in a major way? We're going to end up a big food producer for probably the whole northern part of our country. We're way ahead of any competition, and it's one of those guaranteed industries that everyone needs.

People are now moving back into the outside valley to work in food production. It's going to be really big."

"Wait! Don't go on. This is more than my poor little brain can handle. I was just beginning to understand barter and currency before you brought up food production."

"Oh. Now, that surprises me. You were the one that started the whole 'Food Production' concept."

"I was? I don't recall starting anything like ... Ooooh, that. The kitchen gardens. Experimental food sources. Nettaya's chef. Food preparation. Yes, that is one of my interests. But I had no idea ..."

"You see? It was an idea whose time has come. I would advise you to wear the mantle of 'Founder of the Industry' with humility and modesty, and above all not protest your role in its start, like you are doing now."

"I have no trouble acknowledging my interest in plants, preparing them, and eating or drinking the results. Honestly, I have a lot of trouble seeing myself as the father of an industry. That mantle fits more deservedly on others' shoulders."

"Don't you see? It was your enthusiasm, your fire, which inspired others and got them working. They are the first to acknowledge their debt to you, and it's an affront to them if you do not accept their crediting."

"Well, then, I shall take your advice and think on what you are saying. Please know that I am excited at the news food production in the Valley is advancing so speedily, that we are giving people reason to return there to work the land. That is indeed exciting news. Oh, and thank you for clarifying bartering and dealing in gold and silver. This understanding will be helpful, I am sure."

Fame gave a smile and tiny bow as he turned and walked away. I was pleased beyond words at the news of the Valley being the source of the food we were eating. Such news was enormously gratifying. The other bit of news, about my being the founder of an industry, I could have done without. Whatever I did was to be of help to others, to briefly lighten their burden, to give them a moment's pleasure in this world of tears. I was thinking of little herbal gardens next to the kitchen door; these others are conceiving of huge fields of crops with which to employ hundreds in order to feed thousands. Is this not two

completely separate things? Well, however one construes such obscure points, it shall not deter me from continuing my search for new
edible plants to send back to the Valley. If we are to move ourselves
out of our current quagmire we must first learn anew how to feed ourselves. If we are to fly again, we will do so on a full stomach.

I look through the bus windows at the forest we are passing. I
begin to feel the itch. With trees as a superstructure, underneath their
spreading branches is a sub-structure of plants, some of which are
awaiting my discovery. I know any chance I get I shall go exploring in
the Highlands forests. I know discoveries await, promising, exciting
discoveries. I know there will be little packages to be sent back to the
Valley containing living samples of those discoveries. I know others
on the receiving end of those packages will get excited too as they see
the contents. And they will take those little snips of life and nurture
them, and fill whole fields with their descendants. In the doing, life
becomes a little easier for all of us. That is what it's all about.

We are following alongside a placid river where up ahead, two
mountains on either side make of it the central feature of a picturesque valley floor collecting in tributaries from streams and creeks on
either side, waters draining from the upper slopes. Even though we
here are hardly more than five hundred meters above the elevation of
the coastal plain, airs from the high mountains on either side do a remarkable job of cooling down the valley floor. There is green vegetation all over, from the peaks to the floor where we meander along.

The mere presence of Life in the caravan has attracted many
people to us. They have clamored for their own performances of the
plays/lessons as we travel to our next destination. As luck would have
it, the trip will take us six nights, enough for a performance a night
and one to rest. Of course, we have agreed to do this. We will pass
three small villages along the way rumored to be the home of ethnic
minorities, prelude to the Central Highlands ahead where even more
ethnic minorities have made their home.

The first night we came to a lovely campsite beside the river,
the mouth of the valley looming just ahead. It is decided to have the
setting for performances as similar each night as possible. The choice
falls to doing it in-the-round, the carbide spots low, next to the
ground, shooting up at a sharp angle so as not to shine in anyone's
eyes. We've done it this way before, so there should be no trouble doing it this way again.

Except for security for Life. But even that can be worked out. There is an intense discussion with Security, and the decision comes down to perform in ¾-round with a portable backdrop behind the action. Us creative types are assembled to make the backdrop. We come up with a highly portable frame and attachable painted cloth that fits brilliantly with every play/lesson in the sequence. I was so proud of us. So, keeping in mind a clear escape route from the rear, we set up a safe distance from the vehicles yet close enough to the river to hear its murmurings. Loyal set up his lighting in the trees around the site, and we were in business. I think every person in the entire 'van was there. It was a formidable crowd. Their reaction reminded me of performances we had given last year in the 'van—impressive, and also a bit scary I thought. Invitations came flooding in from potential hosts for individuals to travel with them in the lap of luxury, especially invitations to Life. Naturally, the boys would have an adult in attendance since they could not travel alone with strangers. Soldier and I investigated the potential hosts and felt safe with enough to permit all five boys, with caretaker, travel with hosts. After that, there weren't many of us adults left. Life asked that I be company to him to which I happily agreed. Whereas before there were people in the tens asking for blessing, now there were in the hundreds. Poor Life! He strove to bestow his blessing on each and every one who asked. I saw as his fatigue advanced, but was not permitted to intervene. Rather than be his companion I had become the crutch on whom he leaned to make it to his bed every morning. Too spent to talk, he needed hands to massage his cramping legs or just hold his hand until sleep overtook him, all services I was more than happy to provide. Behind the scenes, I was the sole witness to the light of passion go out each morning, the vulnerable human beneath emerge. I witnessed the face of a youth of twenty-two advance in age beyond reckoning. And yet, whenever asked, he gave.

I attended him while we were with this caravan. I'm not clear which day it happened, the plays I've seen so often by now run together in my mind. Travel was rigorous, having to make up for time spent watching the plays/lessons. Then morning prayers with multitudinous blessings afterwards, daylight advancing. I remember Life sinking onto his cot, trembling with exhaustion. Kneeling on the ground by his side, I remember holding his hand while the trembling subsided and the tension lines in his face slowly crept away. I remember there was no transition. The fabric of the tent beyond Life just became streaks of mist flying by with great velocity, shrieking like distressed souls as it flew past. The mists were illuminated from beyond, a soft white light; I could not make out its source. Then I saw, vaguely, a figure kneeling on white marble in the near distance, just beyond the hurtling mists. Through the sonic disturbance I heard this person speaking to me, not nearly all the words distinctly crossing over.

"Palace. Pal... speak with you. ... listen! ... reaching over to you ... hard from here. ... I've wanted you to ... shall return, but it is very difficult ... The forces to ... souls with the next born ... strong. ... resist them ... all one's might. But I am waiting ... perfect ... place, perfect parents, perfect ... time will come ... I will return ... promise you ... watch for me ... I will return."

And then the light was gone, the shrieks silenced, and the tent fabric became immobile. I was thunderstruck. Waves of violent emotion engulfing me. Longing! Sadness! A wrenching despair! I collapsed, fell into nothingness!

There were sounds outside the tent, people stirring, up and about, preparing for the new night. These modest noises roused me from my lethargy, half sprawled on the ground, half on Life and the cot. I remembered nothing of the day, only Life and his great fatigue. I arose, all my muscles aching, to prepare the way for Life to meet the new night. Like the incident under the bridge, the voice in the whirlwind lay dormant inside, I convinced it was no more than a dream.

Our portable Buddha was brought out, placed in a makeshift altar, and evening prayer began. In our natural temple of majestic trees overhead, rugs of thick pine needles on the ground, the souls spread out to partake in the timeless ritual of singing bowls and smoke from joss sticks floating in the air, deep bows, and repose. Somehow, for me, these prayer sessions seemed to partake of more spirituality than when enclosed indoors within four consecrated walls. I came to love these special sessions in the trees, twice nightly.

Prayers over, breakfast too, we ecclesiastics began a hurried setup for the performances, keeping in mind the possibility of having to make a hasty retreat for safety's sake, the Nāgamobile parked close by. The play and lesson over, and the meeting with the audience afterwards, the set was quickly struck, and we all were on the road again to the next morning's rest camp. So we progressed through this long mountain valley to our destination city, days later. That final night, we passed over a low mountain closing the southern end of the long valley, and descended into the first city since leaving the coast a week earlier.

One could hardly call it a city. Walk twenty minutes in any direction and one would be in the surrounding forests. Still it had its charms. Spared the many disasters that plagued other areas, the one that struck the people here was dwindling productivity of the land, a slow starvation. In this manner the population was inexorably reduced, the very young and the very old being the first to feel the sting. It was the heavy rainfall of the area that proved the downfall of the little city's buildings, rotting them outward from their core. But, with diligence, the buildings were salvageable, with monuments to the effort outstanding around the town. Notable of these were two large Christian churches and a Catholic bishop's mansion. So, too, was a modest Buddhist temple, in a neighborhood of small homes. The feeling one had in approaching the temple site was the cluster of homes around were protecting it, crouching down to better spring at invaders.

At the monastery's outer walls the road on which we were traveling made a sharp left turn, traveling parallel to its stucco wall. We paused at the gate, half expecting to be met there, but made our entry without such greeting. The place was modest in every respect. There was no grand plaza with marble tile paving. There was sculpture, however, scattered along the periphery, raising out of the ordinary what would have been otherwise modest gardens. We parked our vehicles on the bare ground, the obvious place on which to place them, and walked toward the first building in the compound, its doors wide open in anticipation of any such visitors. A friendly interior illumined with a gentle light awaited us, yet no person appeared on the scene to greet us. Then we heard, softly but not far off, the sound of chanting, in ritual prayer. Following it through several open doors we come to a larger room with higher ceilings, supported with two rows of small columns down either side. There, in the center of the far wall is seen an altar with small Buddhas arranged on tiers, two large pyramids of boxes stacked on either side in front. And there, on the floor a number of prostrate worshipers kneeling, their foreheads touching the floor, upturned palms on either side, a disembodied chanting voice floating above them. Knowing exactly what to do, we kneel down and join the others. Prayers come to an end, all of us rise, and we are now greeted with warm smiling faces. Greeted like newly arrived family, we are given warm hugs and cool cups of tea. We soon are feeling as though we have known these people all our lives, have been coming here years on end. But yet, we still need a tour of the premises which is conducted as though we are being reminded and not introduced. We, from our side, are thoroughly charmed and follow the charade, acting out our part. Soon we have seen everything and have accepted their suggestion for a performance area, an exquisite private garden open on one side to a grassy yard. The actors will enter from the surrounding building where several potential escape routes offer themselves, heaven forbid, not that we shall have to avail ourselves of them. Our potential audience shall be the residents at the monastery and members of the neighborhood, an exact count uncertain.

At midnight meal we are suddenly expected to know nothing of the environs and the general history of the area and are plied with helpful information from all around. The broad plateau of the Central Highlands is cool enough to support extensive agriculture, being an abode for humans for eons. Now, it is a patchwork of small fields intersected by forests, traditional crops still being cultivated. My ears prick up at this, I wondering what seeds I might collect of plants imagined extinct. Rice?! Rice is still being grown here? Wonderful! And wheat and corn, too? My avarice wells up, I rushing to conceal it. How exciting! I must tell Life to allow me the freedom to go around collecting seeds and specimens to send back to the Valley.

On a darker, sadder side, there is much talk of the violent war raged by foreigners over the Highlands two hundred years ago, how they spread chemicals on the land to strip away the foliage, still noticeable where the land has eroded into strange formations. How the ethnic minorities were pitted against each other, their numbers significantly reduced so that, coming of the time of starvation, none survived, now only a few tribes where once there were many. Where once was rolling fields feeding millions, now are jungles of tangled vegetation yielding up little. My imagination fairly shouted with glee at the thought of what treasures might be found under such conditions. I saw myself making a preliminary foray into this jungle, determining where and what a more extensive team from the Valley should come and explore. I imagined world-shaking discoveries of lost species and new specimens yielding up miraculous possibilities. It took a strong jolt to bring me back to reality, my beaming features in discord with the otherwise long faces of everyone else, the result of the tragic discourse.

I ask Life if I will be needed for the performances, or if he will give me permission to go scouting out into the surrounding forests. "Yes, of course, you may go. But go with a local person who knows the area. I don't want you out there by yourself." Thank you. I will be sensible and do as you say.

I ask one of the brothers, explaining the reasoning behind the request. He knows just who to recommend, gives me directions to his house and a hurriedly scratched note introducing me. Off I go, note in hand, to this person's house where I'm greeted like family, what else. And that was even before the man read the note. He explained, normally he would be honored to accompany me, but his family and he were eagerly anticipating taking in our performances. Therefore, he would recommend his nephew, a sturdy young fellow who knew the environs like the back of his hand. He could take me wherever I would want. Wonderful! And so it was arranged.

The following night, as my brothers were rushing to prepare for performances, I was strolling out the slender gates and down the road to the prearranged meeting place. There he was, and with his two boys, ages ten-ish to twelve-ish. The boys immediately relieved me of the little bags and boxes I was carrying and would have gladly carried my trowel, too, if I had allowed it out of hand. Off we went into the first available forest on the outskirts of the town. I had thought to bring my wonderful pocket light, carbide like the spotlights for the plays. My companions were in awe of it, the nephew taking over its use on the excuse he needed it as our guide. I willingly turned it over to him, but first with the stern promise that he would return it when its need was over. I told him "I understand what a wonderful thing this pocket light is and to what practical uses you could put it. I promise you, in the not-too-distant future, this handy little devise shall be available to everyone. Nothing would please me more than to be in a position to gift you the light. First, it doesn't belong to me but to the Monastery. Second, it is what's called a 'prototype' with problems in design they are working to correct. How would you feel if after using it for a week or two it just went dark and refused to work? You would be upset, wouldn't you?" He had to admit he would and apologized for asking. "No, no," I said. "It's a human thing, I understand. Look at it this way: here you are with this thing in your hand, in on its little secret. That puts you way ahead of everybody else." And then we came upon some specimens right there, under that tree, that distracted us. The subject was not brought up again. Yet, at the end of our explorations for the night, standing in front of his house, the time came for him to return the light to me. To his credit, he paused only a brief moment when returning it. "Tomorrow night? We shall go out again tomorrow night?" he asked. "Yes, of course, we shall. Thank you."

I trudged home, back to the friendly neighborhood monastery, happy as could be. I could hardly wait to open up all the little boxes and check out again all the treasures we had found, especially one. Yes, there it was, no mistaking a wheat plant, its immature seed head just emerging from the top of its stalk. From this little thing, generations later, would come ground flour, bread, and cakes. I could practically taste them even now, smell them in the oven baking. Of all the things I've collected over the years, this thing here, this modest little green thing with its white roots looking vulnerable, may be the greatest discovery yet. I shall not tag it with its name, but leave it to the persons in the Valley receiving it to name it. What fun.

The next evening, I mention 'vegetarian' to my guide. He smiles and motions me to follow him out back of his house. There, we come upon a small garden fair to brimming with thriving little plants. He reaches down and pulls up a specimen, healthy roots, a stalk and leaves about ten centimeters high, handing it to me, saying, "soybean—meat substitute, very nutritious." I couldn't believe my eyes. So this is soybean! Food for billions. He pulls up two more plants and hands them to me. My heart leaps for joy at the prospect for humankind's future, these simple things in my hand. They must go to the Valley as quickly as possible. I say my thanks, cancel the night's outing and turn to go. My guide, confused at my imminent departure, tries to stop me. I explain, "My friend, these," I hold up the three soybean plants, "are the most precious gift to humanity anyone could hope to give. I must see to it they get safely to the Valley in the far north, that they should arrive there as healthy as they are here. There is nothing, nothing, we could do the whole night as important as that." And, so, I turn and depart as quickly as possible without actually running, not giving him time to say anything that might delay my departure.

Back at the monastery, I am startled by all the people at the gate and doors to the main temple. The little courtyard was too small to hold everyone, so the troupe is moving to a larger space. I look for Fame, but he proves to be a major force in the moving process and can't be reached. Next, I look for my Nāga guard friend only to discover him glued to Life's side, unavailable, too. There is nothing to be done but to bide my time, getting the soybean plants safely packed up, being careful particularly for the roots, that they remain moist for the journey. Wait a minute, I should send the wheat, too. If I have the time, I should pack up everything collected thus far and send it all. So I get busy.

Startled at how long it's taken me to get everything packed up, I go out of my room to look for our Executive Director. Following the sounds of the noisy crowd, I soon come upon Fame. Drawing him aside, I tell him of the soybean specimens I have to send to the Valley as quickly as possible. He is startled at the news, thinking, as many of us have, such varieties have long since passed from this earth. He jumps to the task and runs off. Deciding, so as to be easy to find, I should not move far from this spot. Curiosity over this large audience swiftly overtakes me, and I go to peek at it from around a corner. There they are, the compulsive young audience that has become fanatical over the Hero Abbot. They have sought him out and have found him. They don't listen to what he has to say, they just scream at the top of their lungs. Life stops trying to deliver his lesson, standing in silence, hoping the noise will stop. Eventually he gives up, turns, and leaves the playing area. Only slowly does the commotion subside. If Life returns the screaming takes up again, and nothing is to be done. Fame comes back into the spotlights holding his arms aloft, trying to silence them. Screams turn to jeers and Fame, too, is driven offstage. I've not seen anything like it. We shall have to call a meeting to work out a resolution to this problem.

Fame, in a state of fluster like I've not seen before, takes me by the arm, asks, "Quick! Where do you have the soybeans?" I motion for him to follow, we going off to my room. On the way, I explain I've packed up everything I have to go to the Valley, that I might as well send everything, rather than one little package. Taking several cloth specimen bags, he fills them with the little boxes, giving several bags for me to carry and several for himself. Out the door, through a now angry crowd in the entry court, out the main gate and down the street at a near run, to the edge of town where a circulary is parked in an empty field. We are met at its door by a handful of Nāganese crew who take our precious cargo, assuring us they shall be in the hands of responsible people within two hours. We stand aside as the circulary begins its revolutions, lifting up into the sky, then gone.

Fame and I turn and walk back toward the monastery, now at a leisurely pace. 'Thank you," I say, "for arranging this hasty pickup."

"Yes, anything I could do to be of help," Fame replied.

I ask, "What are we going to do about this unruly group of people that's latched themselves to us?"

"Yes, what," Fame replied. "I'm really concerned there's going to be a fight tonight between them and the locals. They've got to be made to disburse."

A showdown between locals and the new fanatics was avoided by the practical-thinking brothers who diverted the local attendees through a back entrance, rather than out the front way, which would have put them in direct confrontation with the angry fanatics. Near this back exit we met with the familial monks in hopes of hammering out a solution to our problem. After much discussion, it was decided the next evening's performance would be given in the same place as the first evening's, closing entrance to the fanatics. The locals would enter by the back way, in that manner avoiding any direct confrontation. Meanwhile, Fame would attempt to talk reason to the disrupters and get them calmed down. I was advised not to go out foraging the next evening but to stay in the monastery where I could count on a degree of safety.

Early the next evening, Fame was out front with his megaphone, several of the local monks backing him up. He talked with small groups of the fanatics as they arrived, walking down the street to the locked gates. He talked reason with them, and it began to have its effect. He persuaded them to forego attendance at the plays in this town but, instead, to meet up with us a week hence in the city just a few kilometers down the road where our host facility would be better able to handle the large numbers. He also asked that they be a more considerate audience, restraining their noise so that performances could proceed. Remarkably, they agreed to these conditions with one stipulation, that Life come out to them this very evening and deliver one of his lessons for their particular edification. Fame agreed, strongly urging the suppression of screaming in His Holiness' presence. Agreement to everything was reached all around.

That evening Loyal brought out one of the spots and set it up in the entry court. Seemingly from out of nowhere a dais materialized in front of the spot. The gates would remain closed, the fanatics on the street side and Life within the front of the monastery. We discreetly parked our Nāgamobile nearby, just in case, and placed security by the dais. We were not going to take any chances. Before Life's appearance Fame with his megaphone reminded everyone of the agreement for them to be well-behaved and was met with little resistance.

It was the third evening of performances, the Vow evening. While the boys delivered their performance to the locals within, Life emerged from the Temple's entrance, making his way to the dais flooded with light. A hushed silence fell upon all. Life stepped onto the dais, shimmering in his all-white habit, and raised his arms to these people. There was a gasp and stirring, quickly hushed. He began, recalling the terrible times we all have been living through, in its artfulness touching, touching. Soon, this unruly crowd was reacting as all our audiences have reacted, as written into the script. Now, the Vow-taking has arrived, and they leap to their feet as audiences have done before, reciting the words as Life gives them. At the end they are jubilant, now giving vent to all they had pent up. They press up to the gates stretching bare arms through the metalwork toward the Hero Abbot. For us, it is a scary moment, but the gates hold and Life is safe. He holds up his right hand and delivers a blessing in the sudden hush. He quickly turns and disappears into the dark temple as screams now finally emerge from this crowd. In thanks that all went well, we all follow Life into the temple where he delivers the same lesson to the local audience. They, too, jump to their feet and recite the Vow after him, shouting and stamping their approval afterwards. They are but a pale version of the previous doings outside, but just as heart-felt, I think. They rush forward as the boys join Life in taking bows.

Soon, the public evening comes to a close and the private, fatigued, begins. I assist Life to his cell, lie him down, massage his leg-cramps away, allowing him to sleep. His double performance has taken its toll, stress lining his face. I stand watch as sleep comes to him, relaxing my vigil only when I see he will not be easily aroused. Only then do I allow myself to entertain slumber and follow him into the mists.

There he is, up ahead. I see his back as he moves onward into the ether. I follow, as I so often have done in the past. I would not travel this way on my own, but do so because I follow him, my friend, my savior. The air all about is astir, as though something powerful is agitating it. It moves more so as I follow after him, the air-movement becoming alarming as it increases in violence. Up ahead I hear a howling, not that of humans, but perhaps a force of nature. I cannot be certain. Up ahead, he has stopped, stopped before some vast object vibrating so fast I am not able to make out what it is. He raises his arms before it, his hands making strange gestures, he tiny in proportion to this other. I cannot make out what he is doing. What was that? That object that flew past with such speed, caught in the unknown force. Wait! There is another. And another. I recognize the shapes: they are spirits, flying by, caught in that terrible blast. And now I recognize that horrible power, that irresistible might which, once taking you over, never releases you. It is the Whirlwind, that of the Ages, once in its thrall never released. He is in horrible danger! I shout out to him, "Stop, Life! Don't enter that force. It will never release you. Stop! Stop! For Love's sake, stop!" He turns his head and looks at me over his shoulder, smiling. He gives a jaunty wave with an upturned hand, turns, and enters the violent vortex, disappearing quickly from sight. Immediately, a thunder-blast knocks me off my feet and onto the rocky ground, rendering me immobile. I scream at the outrage, but my voice is lost in the greater din. Forever there, I am caught, screaming my outrage into the gale, unheard, of no consequence.

I awake with a jolt. I am again half slumped on the floor, half slumped over Life's sleeping form. I hear in the middle distance, cheerful voices, blissful discussion on some trivial subject. I, however, am shaken to the core over the vision from which I have just awakened, its grip on my heart still strong. I gingerly touch Life's sleeping form, beloved friend, firm and warm, very much here and not at all caught in the other's dire straits. Reassuring, real. I command my racing heart to slow its frightful pace, return to normal. What could this vision possibly mean? The whirlwind, the second vision in only a short time. I think back on that earlier one, the whirlwind between my visitor and me. Perhaps it is so violent this time because I have failed to unlock the metaphor of the first? The white crouching figure, a messenger from the other side? His message failed in the deciphering, my deciphering. So the condition has become more ominous in the interim. And still I fail in the understanding.

There is the sound of the singing bowl announcing morning prayers and meditation. I rouse Life, not as easy to do these days, and we go together to the nearby temple where all are congregating. I am thankful we are here, in this place, in this most ordinary of places, at this time. A blessing the peacefulness of the neighborhood, the casual friendliness of the people, their easy acceptance of us. How discordant the fanatics following our caravan to this place of easy calm. Will they really leave us, wait for us in the next town? I suspect our troubles with them here are not at an end. With a start, I realize prayers are almost over and my mind has missed focusing on them rather than those senseless worries over which I have little control. I should not be so easily distracted. Better the distractions put off than prayers! How undisciplined I've become. Another warning in the several already floating around. There. Prayers are over. Time for meditation, my challenge clear. Focus, focus, focus. And, so, I start meditation. Everything is disposed of, everything, that is, except the image of Life entering into the whirlwind, I can not dislodge it. So I decide to meditate on that image, solely. Whirlwind / Life. Life / Whirlwind. Whirlwind and Life, the thought-image the central focus. And, thankfully, it holds. For this night, alas, that image remains opaque, holding its secrets. I am disappointed in my lack of results and am quiet at supper, not my usual chatterbox. No one seems to notice. Not needing to attend to Life, I retire to my own cell for the day.

Fame knocked at my door early in the evening, while it is still light out, to confirm the safe arrival of the soybeans, wheat, and other specimens in the Valley. The people there have asked that I be on the alert for other specimens of soybeans so as to assure its genetic robustness. I'd already decided to do that anyway, and for that very reason, now striving not to be irritated at their request. As a distraction, I ask Fame whether or not any fanatics had showed up at the gates this evening. His reply, "Let's go look." Sure enough, there were a few of the fanatics there looking hopeful. "I'm sorry," said Fame to these people, "there is not enough room in the little hall inside for you to take in the evening's performance. The Abbot will not be able to come out this evening since responsibilities will keep him inside."

"Yes, we understand. We just wanted to be near His Holiness' presence," some replied.

"You do understand," Fame plied, "you will be able to actually be in his presence next week in the next city over."

"Yes, we understand," their repeated reply, yet still looking hopeful.

While Fame was thus speaking with them I used the opportunity to look at them closely. They were thoroughly unremarkable. Yet, I swear, just at that moment, I had one of those creepy feelings I was in the presence of the Nnnnmr. It was most disconcerting. Not strong enough to put any faith in it, I made a mental note with a vow to watch out for future such alerts.

As we were walking back into the monastery I said to Fame, "I'll bet you those same people will be back in the same place tomorrow evening."

"Oh, do you think so?" he responded. "Why do you think that?"

"Because they're watching us, making sure we don't steal away in the dark of the night," I retorted.

"Why would they ever think that?" he asked, looking startled.

"Because they aren't who they appear to be," I shot back, not intending to be obscure.

"Oh?! Who are they, then?"

"I'm not certain; but I intend to watch them as carefully as they are watching us," I remarked.

"Please," asked Fame, "be sure to keep me in the loop. Whatever you find out."

"Of course; I shall."

By now, we had entered the small hall where we were giving performances. All was astir in preparation for the evening. We were at the fourth play/lesson, the one announcing the formation of the Monastery and University; so it should not be supercharged, emotional, like the previous ones. The boys are not being sufficiently attended to and are causing a ruckus. I call them together and remind them they should be sitting quietly and envisioning their performance that evening. Much deep sighing all round. With persistence, they are soon enough all sitting quietly, eyes closed, expressions playing over their faces. I stay with them, my little angels, knowing full well they are going to open their eyes from time to time to see if I've left them and they can get back to their foolery.

Soon, people are filing in—nuns and monks, people from the neighborhood—taking places on the floor. Soon, all are assembled, ready for us to begin the performance. Fame steps forward and delivers his usual speech, at the end signaling for the lights to lower. The boys are given their cue, lights come up, the excitement of another performance kicks in and we are off and running. On my part, I sit there regretting having to go through another performance in which I can anticipate everything—the boys hitting their cues, the audience reaction. It is all so predictable. I feel my mind turn to lead, though soon it flies back to my concerns over the whirlwind—unpredictable, unresolved, opaque, resisting my analysis. I am startled with applause and cheering as the play comes to its end. Then Life is in the light. He begins with such gentleness, a new feature of his performance. That's exciting; and, before you know it, I'm caught up in his narration, carried along, and only at the end am I startled. The whole sweep and arch of it is new, different, as though Life has seen a new vision for the benefit of these people. Or maybe it is they that are different, deserving of the redefined interpretation. Who is to say. But I'm glad to have witnessed it, register the change. The boys come out for the final bows, amid renewed cheering and stomping. Such a racket in this little room. Then they come forward, the audience, and Security's chance now to show their acting chops. It all winding down, happily. Soon it is just the resident monks and nuns, and us. We go off to have supper, meditation, and morning prayer. Over a hot bowl of soup and cup of passable tea, they continue our education on the history of the environs. It seems, in the war that raged two hundred years ago, the foreign forces had used a strong chemical on the dense forests, stripping everything of their leaves, the combatants now visible on the ground. The problem was the chemical killed the trees and the undergrowth, poisoning the ground, becoming intolerant of all life. The years passed. Nothing would grow on the land. It eroded without plant covering, water cutting deeper and deeper into the surface. Now these cuts are perhaps fifty meters deep, encroaching on good, fertile land, threatening to reduce all to a bizarre kind of desert. How strange, this once happy, fruitful land, verdant across the entire plateau, should now be sliding into vertical cliffs unsupportive of life. So sad. Can it not be stopped? "Not with any technique we are aware of." And, so, the conversation ground to a halt.

Then, it was off to morning prayers and meditation. I cherished the feeling of tranquility that would descend during prayers, to be carried over, and intensified, during meditation. This particular morning, for what reason I know not, my mind seemed to pick up on past events unfortunate to dwell upon, specifically how my instruction in ways of meditation was so brutally ended with my teachers meeting their deaths at the hands of the marauders. Thus was my instruction interrupted. So I can blame the marauders for my being so poor at meditation techniques? No, I can't blame them, as horrible as they were. My shortcomings can't fit on their shoulders along with all that truly belongs there. My shortcomings are all of my own making. This morning, my meditation of the whirlwind went no better than yesterday morning, and I came away not a whit wiser.

Again, Life was in fine fettle, renewed in the presence of the simple souls here, and was able to wrap up his night without assistance. I went off to my cell, and my slim cot, and was asleep in no time at all. I dreamed of fantastical forests in which I found fantastical herbals and spices, flora and fauna, most delicious looking little feathered or furry creatures, destined to be spitted and roasted over glowing embers, unctuous and tasty. When I awoke in the evening, tinged with guilt, I thought, "So much for vegan vows!" I am an atavist and dream of eating meat! Am I even worth saving? Even if it is I who am trying to save myself? No! You are hopelessly lost. To even dream of eating meat! I had to chuckle at the thought.

There was a kind of excitement floating about this evening— the last of the plays/lessons, our eminent departure on the morrow. I had clandestinely arranged with my local guide to go foraging in the forest again and slipped out just as the play was starting. Soon I was walking with my guide and his two sons back into the forest, the pocket light switched on as we entered into its deep sheltering bower. There is a kind of quiet hush to be found in forests. Our ancestors said it was the cause of many leaves absorbing waves of sound, destroying echo of any kind. Thank you, my little green friends, if that is what you do. I love that sacred hush, now all too rare in our modern world. The four of us, in natural reaction, move closer together and speak in whispers. It would be a sacrilege to speak any louder. And whispering makes conspirers of us, kidnappers who have come to snatch away the offspring of the unsuspecting to hold in slavery by uncertain masters. It's true the parent shall not see the child again in its lifetime. But the fate of the children shall be most glorious indeed, this making all the difference. The particular evening our fate seems to be to come upon plants bearing berries: ruby red, royal purple, lemony yellow. We do have berry-bearing plants in the Valley, but none like these. Don't you think, there's always room for more berries? We found eleven different species all told. I was beside myself with joy. Not only did we take rooted specimens, but we also filled our caps and hats with sweet, juicy fruit that we picked from parent plants. In total, we felt quite good about ourselves, bringing our treasure back to civilization. I was touched when my three guides insisted I take their berries, too, to share with the good brothers at the neighborhood monastery. I pictured a sprinkling of berries on top of each bowl of porridge served up with the evening's breakfast. What a nice gift to leave for our kind hosts. I thanked them and took every last one of their sweet little orbs for the brothers and sisters.

I arrived back at the monastery with my treasures. The hangers-on were not at the gate, nor were any of the sacred to be seen inside, either. Then I heard them, all at their supper; and, if I didn't hurry, I would miss out on mine. The cooks had put most things away by the time I got to the dining room. Yet, once they saw the little jewels I had brought them, they managed to put together a respectable meal for me. They were so pleased with the fruit and immediately launched into a discussion on how they could be utilized. There were some grand plans put forward, and bless them for thinking thus. On the morrow it was as I foresaw—fruits sprinkled on each serving of porridge. The diners could hardly have been more appreciative. Often, the simplest way is the best. I felt a great gift had been given me to share with this simple folk who had in turn given us this blessed period of peace.

As we left this place the following evening, I felt good about the whole experience, we humans giving of our best to each other. In a just world, this is the way it should be.

CHAPTER 11

It was a short four-hour drive to the next city where we were to perform. We did not wait for the caravan since the distance was not great. What could happen in such a brief span? Well, nothing happened, and we arrived at our destination in good shape. Whereas the former place we were in was really a town, this was indeed a city, even sporting [I guess] what goes nowadays for a 'Downtown.' It was a beautiful moon-lit night, giving one a feeling for how the plateau was really a giant bowl with a ring of mountains all around, the coastal range to the east and the border range to the west.

The plateau itself gently undulates in little valleys and hills in all directions, not obtrusive in any way but always quite pleasant. I am told it used to be a patchwork of terraces and fields with occasional forests widely scattered about. Now, it is just the opposite with forest everywhere and the occasional clearing under cultivation. There also used to be numerous villages sprinkled about, most of them of distinct ethnic orientation, now many of these ethnics gone extinct, only a few tribes surviving. It is widely believed the forests hide from view many botanical treasures waiting to be rediscovered. My limited forays indicate this is probably true. Before leaving the Highlands, I felt I must now explore further. I have enough reason already to recommend an expedition from the Valley come here for extended study. But I maybe a little selfishly would like to poke around just a bit more, perhaps to uncover a few more priceless gems before relinquishing the field to others. Toward that end, I've already arranged for a guide in this city to take me out and about. I shall simply disappear each evening in the bustle of getting the plays underway, to return in time for supper, no one the wiser. Except for Fame whose job it will be to send specimens off to the Valley.

Our designated hosts are in the city's center, slightly to the southwest along one of the major north / south thoroughfares, making it easy to find. It is further distinguished by being on a hill that can be seen from nearly every point in the city. It was one of those Buddhist temples closed by the Christians two hundred years ago, its reopening a struggle to accomplish. Even now, as we are told, the city dwellers take much pride in the place and help with its maintenance.

The main entrance is more charming than the customary three portal gate issuing onto a square. It is as though the designers took a temple edifice, with highly decorated doorways and rooftops, and shrunk it down to but a doll house, with all the delights presumed. Yet still were us adults able to pass through and be like children again for an instant. From there a modest flight of stairs led to the main temple, a thoroughly grand edifice with elongated corners of the roof that turn back into dragon heads – mouths open, showing teeth – looking down upon phoenix birds, two roofs, one directly above the other, giving a wonderful rhythmic effect. On either side of the main doors to the temple's interior are large, round windows giving a bold stroke to the strongly horizontal *façade*. Beyond the temple, and to the left, is a wonderful nine-story rectangular pagoda with sweeping views of the city. There are other extraordinary but lesser elements to the monastery situated in surrounding gardens. Unfortunately, the foliage in the gardens has obviously suffered much over the years and now only hints at a former glory. The effect is to leave smaller buildings, statuary, ponds, and other water features, showing awkward edges and arbitrary placements. I would not want to harp over much on this element since nothing can be done now to fix it. Just enjoy the intimacies of the grounds for what they are and not dwell on the disappointments. Those dragon heads on the roof make up for much. I can imagine what Nittaya would have to say about them and smile at the thought.

In looking around the grounds for the place for our performances there really was only one place—in front of the flight of stairs leading up to the main temple. The stairs might be incorporated into the movement for the action, adding significantly to the drama. Smiley might stumble and fall up and down the stairs, but Little Lord would throw himself upon them, writhing in all kinds of fabricated pain. I can just imagine.

Around the grounds were to be discovered numerous wonders including, as one looks back toward the city from the first court, a white Buddha also looking back over the city, too. Rows of the Arhat, life-size, the vanguard of our faith, all around the first courtyard; bright red, two-story tall guardians, hidden on either side, to take one by surprise as one enters the temple; a mustachioed giant Buddha at the altar there; a five-meter Guanyin quietly reigning over an inner courtyard; a large pond with real live colorful carp swimming within. The real wonder of the area made its appearance just moments after a passing shower when, to us visitors' great delight, mists suddenly appeared all around. With amazing speed they crept in everywhere, softening edges, playing hide and seek with architectural detail, vanishing vistas.

Our individual quarters are actually almost luxurious, some of our finest yet. They are all in rich dark wood, featuring intricately carved screens, the thing that raises them beyond the ordinary. I shall sleep here like a baby.

They have held the midnight meal for our arrival. As we all are washing up before entering the dining hall the gong sounds to announce serving time. The walls are rather plain, but decorative elements for the ceiling above add into the thousands, demanding one to wonder over its detailed skill and assembly. A creditable tea is served along with a respectable vegetable in spicy sauce over rice, better fare than most. There is a bit of an awkward confusion as we visitors ask over the history of the monastery and the residents ask for details on the plays they soon are to see. We work out an agreeable agenda for the conversation and are soon chatting away to each other. I am relieved to hear a peace treaty had been adopted by both sides of the Catholic/Buddhist community with no rancor remaining. "It was the thing to do," observed one of the older resident monks. "We needed each other if we were to survive."

Another group were discussing our potential audience. "There will be us monks and nuns, that's about forty people. We've invited the people in the neighborhood to come, and we usually get a good turnout. With your famous Abbot, there's a lot of interest. I think we'll draw them for that reason, too."

I ask, "Have you noticed a large group of strangers coming into the area?"

"No. Not particularly. People passing through usually stay on that side of town," she said, pointing toward the downtown area.

"We have had a large number of people following us," I observed. "We're a bit concerned they might become unruly and cause trouble. I would not want that to happen here."

"Oh, no! Me neither," she agreed. "What kind of trouble do they cause?"

"They scream whenever our Abbot appears and don't stop."

"We mustn't have that here. That would ruin it for everyone else."

"Exactly, our thoughts, too."

She asked, most concerned, "How can we prevent it from happening?"

"Yes, I wonder," I replied. "They shall not be kept out of the Square, no matter how strong the effort. Besides, resisting them I fear will only make them worse. Do you think your locals might be inclined to fight with them?"

"No, I don't. Our people here are peace-loving, caring people. If anything, they will try kindly persuasion on them. Perhaps that might work."

"'Kindly persuasion.' Now that's a novel tactic I should like to see applied," I responded with keen expectation.

As time neared for performances to begin, I found myself torn between departing for a serene stroll through the forest encircling the city, or staying to witness the unfolding drama between factions of our audience. The beckoning forest won out, my guide and I walking briskly toward its darkness ahead. As we were encircled in silvan shadow I quickly lost any curiosity over factious audiences. I switched on the carbide pocket light, purposely handing it to my guide to carry, he reacting mightily at the wonder. In no time at all we were deep into uprooting wild onion and sweet potato, and other savory discoveries, the height of the night reached when coming upon a family of slumbering water buffalo. We startled the poor gentle creatures and upset them no end, I'm afraid. I'd never seen their kind before and was curious to observe them as much as possible. So odd they were, hulking huge bodies, big dangerous-looking horns, yet shy, fearful of puny us. I immediately developed an inordinate love for them and would have put them in my pocket, carried them away with me, if I could have.

In no time we had collected our quota of specimens and headed back to the city, my guide helping to the door of my cell. There we parted, agreeing to go out again next evening. As I organized and stacked boxes, I noted the general tranquility of the night here at the monastery. So, nothing of very great moment transpired here this evening? Good! I looked forward to hearing all about it during midnight supper. Not having long to wait, I heard the gong sound out in the night. I went off to the dining hall eager with expectations. "How did it go this evening?"

"Well. It went well," was the consensus.

"We had a really big audience. The Square was packed full," the mental image beginning to flesh out.

"It was exciting. The audience was really responsive," they agreed.

"Was there any trouble? Unruly factions? Undue screaming?"

"No, just a lot of applause, stomping, whistling," the answer.

"Oh! Then a good night, everybody excited at the play and sermon?"

"Yes! It was great fun!"

"I am so glad to hear that," I said to them while looking for Fame out of the corner of my eye. I made my way over to him soon as I could and asked, "How did our camp followers do this evening?"

"They behaved themselves. There were a lot of them, but they behaved."

"That's really interesting. I half expected a riot this evening."

"Come with me and help count the evening's donations. I don't like to stand here carrying a lot of coin."

"You know I can't help you count money."

"Well, then, come and talk with me while I count it out," Fame asked, a bit beseechingly. So I went with him, to his cell.

Once inside the room, a bulging canvas bag materialized, he dumping the contents onto his cot. The coinage caught the light from his lamp and flashed it back as it tumbled and rolled about. "So, we had no trouble from the camp followers?" twisting the statement into a question.

"I wasn't expecting trouble from them, you know," he replied. "They aren't in a position where they can cause much trouble. If they would, they'd just get booted out, and that's the last thing they want to happen."

"You're right, I guess. But, sooner or later, there's going to be trouble," I proclaimed, believing it to my very core. "For every one of them that venerates our Abbot there's another that hates him beyond enduring."

"As the camp followers grow, our Security has been promised more support from the Valley. You know, those Nāga guards are pretty formidable, and our Abbot is a favorite of their princess. Nothing is going to be allowed to happen," he said in a calming voice.

"Wow, look at that!" he exclaimed, nodding toward neat stacks of coin lined up on his cot according to coinage: gold or silver.

"How much is it?" I ask out of curiosity. He states a sum: so many pieces of gold, so many of silver. "Is that a lot?" I ask, not having any sense of its value.

"It's a lot," he answers with some degree of awe. "The second highest single night since I've been collecting. I'll be sending the courier to the Valley before we leave here."

"And I'll have botanical samples to send back, too," I add with equal enthusiasm. Suddenly, a feeling of sadness washes over me and I exclaim, "Ah! I wish we all were going back to the Valley, too, and not continuing south!" The feeling escaped from me before I could tamp it down. Fame looked up, startled. Then his expression softened, and he reached out for my hand.

Gently patting it, he replied, "You are our official chief worrier, my friend. You see these disasters looming ahead and feel none of us takes you seriously. But we all do. We all take you very seriously. We all are here to see that nothing happens, that your worse fears will never happen. We stand between you and them. Worry, if you must. But believe. Believe. We see your fears and stand here, between you and them."

Stupid me! How do I react to such a strong declaration? I start crying. I can't stop it. I end up on his shoulder, he patting me on the back. "I … I know," I stammer, "I know you have my back. Please forgive me. I seem to cry at everything."

"I understand," he said in a deep, soothing voice. "I wish I could cry like you, but my tears seem to be buried so deep inside I'll never reach them."

And then we hug each other, knowing how kindred we are, one to the other.

"Bless you, Fame. Bless you for this moment."

"I believe in you. I believe in the good that you, and Life, and the boys are doing. I believe in this quest we all are on, in the importance that it be completed. I give my whole life that you all finish what you have started, that you bring The Word to the suffering, that we all can begin living in a new way. Lean on me when you must. I am here for you."

I am struck by the exquisite beauty of what he has said and again erupt in a torrent of tears. His shoulder, pats on my back. Now, there is nothing more that needs being said. We, each, know the other to be truly kindred.

Time moves on. "Do you want me to walk with you to your room?" he asks.

"No, that's not necessary. I'm going on to meditation. They've already started, so I don't want my entrance to be too disruptive." And off I go.

With my emotional upheaval I expected most of my time to be spent in calming down. Instead, I felt amazingly calm. I focus on the whirlwind and have at it. I discover I can visualize it, and there it is before me. So I look at it, and look at it. Then meditation time is over, on to our little meal and prayer before sleep. And so, came to an end this momentous night.

Breakfast at sunset, with another cup of respectable tea. I down the porridge fast so I can linger over the tea. And then my comrades are in commotion over getting set up for the plays. I sneak away to my guide's house, where he and I strike out for the forest. We go in a different direction so that we might meet up with different treasures. We have hardly gone into the undergrowth when I hear it, some kind of bird fussing at us for entering its territory. "What's that?" I ask.

"Those are chickens," my guide replies.

"Chickens!? We must catch a pair. Where are they?" I spit out with much excitement.

"No, no. They are too much trouble to catch. There's a better way," he whispers, eyebrows raised. Then he starts looking at the ground, left and right, pushing back undergrowth with a stick.

"What are you doing? They're going to get away. Hurry!" and I start out following the sound. He grabs my arm, holding me back.

"Watch your step," he hisses back. "You're going to step on their nest if you're not careful."

"Nest? What kind of nest?" I ask, greatly interested.

"A nest on the ground that's hard to see, so you've got to be careful and mind your step." Pushing back a leafy branch, and there it was – the nest, much bigger than I thought it would be, full of tan-colored eggs. I was in awe. Yes, the eggs would be much easier to deal with, but so many: six, eight, ten, twelve, fourteen, fifteen. Fifteen eggs! What a great start to the Valley's chicken farm. "How are we going to carry all those eggs? Without breaking any?"

"We are not going to take all the eggs," he said. "We are going to take a few and leave the rest for the chickens. It would be a disaster for them if they lost all their eggs."

"Oh, you're right. Darn it! How many do you think we should take?"

"Six."

"Ten?"

"No, six."

"How about eight?"

"Six. Think about the chickens. Nine chicks would be a good number for them to raise. Not all the eggs may hatch. One or two may die or get eaten."

"The same could happen to our eggs. We need at least eight."

"Six is a good number. As long as you keep them warm they should do fine. You'll have them in a place free of predators and free of other hazards. They all should hatch."

"Oh, alright. You're probably right. How are we going to carry them?"

"We can put them in my cap. Put some dry grass around them to help keep them warm."

We collected six of the eggs, put them in his cap with dry grass all around them and took turns carrying them back to the monastery, arriving without incident. I found a nice box for them, putting the grass in first and then arranging the eggs in the center. "Now, please, stay here and guard them while I go make arrangements to send them to the Valley." I was out the door before he had a chance to respond.

Fame was right where I thought he would be. "I've found fertile chicken eggs which need to go to the Valley as quickly as possible."

"Chicken eggs? How do you know they're fertile?" He was about to say more, but I interrupted.

"Are you able to help, or should I go to the Nāga guard?"

He held up his hand. "No. Don't go to the guard. He should not be distracted. I'll help. If there is a delay, can you tend to the eggs yourself?"

"Delay? Yes. I suppose so. Why? What's up?"

"We have received an alert to expect an incident tonight."

"Incident? What kind of incident?" I asked, suddenly distressed.

"Our intel was sketchy, but we are on high alert."

"Oh, no! Just forget about the eggs. Do what you have to do. I'll mind the eggs and stay out of the way."

"Thanks."

Shaken, I walked slowly back to my cell, looking around to see if there was anything out of the ordinary. I saw nothing.

The guide was seated at the little round table beside my cot, staring intently at the eggs. I sent him on his way, with thanks, and settled down in the chair he had vacated. I, too, found myself staring at the eggs, but my mind was on the prospect of a threatening event. I was confused. What kind of an event? An attack? Directed at Life, no doubt. But not necessarily. Am I safer here by myself or safer out with the company, with everybody else? Then I thought Fame would not have let me come back here if it were dangerous. While these thoughts were muddling in my head an all too familiar, happy sound wafted through the night air—applause, stamping, whistling, shouting, from what must be a big audience. That would be at the end of Life's sermon. The sound intensified. The boys have come out to join Life. If something's going to happen it will be any moment, now.

And then I feel it, the presence of the Whisps [Nnnnmr]! But not in the room. Like it's outside, but moving past, the feeling coming and going quickly. I jump to the cell door and throw it open. I see figures off in the distance, running away from the Monastery buildings toward the periphery. No one seems to be pursuing them. How strange. Even more odd that there has been no interruption in the applause for our performers. I go back to the square looking for Fame. I don't see him anywhere. What I do see is a large security contingent around Life and the boys and a lot of familiar looking people scattered throughout the audience. I suspect they are Nāgas, like that time at the old royal city. It's a big crowd. And they're really boisterous. But they all seem happy, not the least menacing.

I see Loyal manning the spots and make my way over to him. "How's the evening going?" I ask.

"Great," he says, flashing a big smile. "They gave a good performance tonight, and the audience is really charged. Look at them." I look and see a happy throng, most jumping up and down, arms high in the air, blissful expressions on their faces. I could hardly imagine a less threatening crowd. They surge forward now toward Life and the boys, security around them strong and tight. No immediate danger there. It is only slowly that I notice several large cubes standing on the pavement off in the twilight to the side of the play area. The cubes seem alien, strange to our environment, not made of earth elements. Each large enough to hold twenty-five people packed in shoulder to shoulder. But I see no opening in the surface of the cubes, no door or window. I think, "The doors must be on the sides facing away. There's got to be doors of some kind." I ask Loyal, "Where did those big boxes come from? What are they?"

Loyal turns and looks at them. "I don't know. They brought them this evening when they arrived just before performance started. I was busy and couldn't give them any attention."

"'They?' Who are 'they?'" I asked, bewildered.

"Oh, a bunch of security people from the Valley. They had a tip-off there was going to be trouble tonight and came to help. They brought those boxes with them and put them there. But we didn't have any trouble. Everything went fine."

My mind flashed on those shadowy figures I saw running into the dark and the fleeting feeling of the Whisps presence. They must have been part of the threat. Well, I shall have to get to the bottom of this before the night has long progressed. I look around to see who might be available to speak with, note a press of people around Life and the boys and also notice Fame, Farmer, and Soldier there in the thick of the press. No one is giving any signs of departing soon, a party atmosphere dominating. That's ominous, I thought. Why should the audience be hanging on if the show were over? Obviously, the show was not over. There was more to come! Over my dead body, I thought, bristling. Instinctively I looked around for a weapon to take up. There were none at hand. I began to panic. Loyal, seeing my alarm, put a soothing hand on my arm.

"Don't get all upset. Security has a good hold on everything. They're not going to let anything happen." He was right, of course. So I tried to relax, as best I could.

It seemed to take forever, the audience in twos and threes departing into the night, eventually enough to set a trend. And then all were gone. Just us monastics and our security remained. I saw Farmer and Soldier standing together and went to them, hoping for a satisfying report.

"What is going on?" I ask. "What are those strange boxes over there?"

"Hadn't you heard?" replied a surprised Farmer. "A delegation from the Valley arrived just before the play was to begin, with more security. They had gotten a report there was to be trouble tonight."

"But nothing happened, right?" I asked.

"So far as I know," confirmed Farmer. "Trouble may have been scared off with the arrival of reinforcements. They were pretty up-front."

"Yeah," seconded Soldier. "Not only were they noisy but they came into the light carrying obvious weapons."

"So that was what happened," my mind finally able to piece events together. "I was in my cell watching my eggs, when ... My eggs! Oh, no. I forgot about my eggs." Suddenly torn in two directions.

"Eggs!" asked Farmer. "What eggs."

"Forget the eggs. I'll explain later," I said, finely able to assemble priorities. "Just a while ago, I guess when the security arrived, I was in my cell and heard people running past. I opened my door and saw these dark figures running over there in the opposite direction from the square. They seemed panicked, eager to get away from here."

"Really?" said Soldier. "Then there really were people going to attack us."

"You must report this to the head of security from the Valley," added Farmer. "They need to know the report they got was right."

"Yeah," confirmed Soldier.

"Can you take me to this person?" I asked.

"Sure," they both said together as they started craning their necks looking for the Security head.

"There he is," pointed out Soldier. I looked in the direction he was pointing but saw no obvious person. "Come on, let's go." He took me by the arm and started out.

"Wait!" said Farmer. "Wouldn't it be better if we put Palace in a room where it would be private and bring the Security Head to him there?"

"Yeah, you're right," Soldier confirmed. Without releasing my arm he turned in an opposite direction and headed toward the building with the monastics' common rooms. We went into a comfortable-looking room with table and chairs. Soldier motioned me to sit and then was gone. I waited only a few minutes when Farmer and Soldier returned with two imposing looking persons wearing uniforms familiar from the Valley. They looked at me with the kind of intensity only Nāgas can achieve. I bowed with hands pressed together at chin level. The Nāgaese bowed in response.

Farmer made the introductions. "This is Brother of-the-Palace, ordained, and assistant to our Abbot. He was in his cell over on that side of the monastery campus earlier this evening when the incident occurred that he shall tell you about."

I opened by saying, "May I begin by telling you I am in acquaintance with Princess Nittaya and have exchanged with her the several episodes with the Nnnnmr I have had. She has alerted me to the possible unscrupulous activities they may be undertaking. I tell you this so that you will have background on what I've experienced this evening." The two Nāgas nod their understanding.

"I was involved with specimens collected here in the local forests when I had the chilling sensation I have when an Nnnnmr is nearby. Only this time the sensation was fleeting as though the Nnnnmr were rapidly approaching, passing close by my door, and going on. I also heard footsteps of several persons running by, too. I got up, looked out the door, and saw a number of dark figures running toward the periphery of the monastery campus. They gave the clear impression they were fleeing from something. I did not count them, but there were at least five. The persons I saw I presume were humans. They looked human, although I have no reason to be certain on this point."

"This chilling feeling you said you had, Your Holiness," asked one of the Nāgas, "how do you know it was caused by Nnnnmrs?"

"I've been in their presence enough times to recognize the effect they have on me," I replied.

"And you are certain this time?" asked the other Nāga.

"I am certain," I replied.

"Thank you for this information," said the first Nāga as he pushed back his chair preparatory to standing.

"Wait! Please wait," I ask. "I would be most grateful, since I'm privy to the unfolding situation, if you could explain just a bit the situation this evening. Security in the Valley had found out there was a planned action for here, this evening, an action with Nnnnmrs and humans in collusion. Is that correct?"

"That is correct."

"Is this the first incident planned by the Nnnnmrs and humans?"

"No."

"Is this the first incident directed at us of this alliance?"

"No."

"Can we expect more such incidents?"

"Yes."

"Is not an alliance of this kind illegal in Federation law?"

"Yes."

"Is there anything on our side we can do to protect ourselves?"

"Yes. We in the Valley are in close contact with your Security and can move with considerable speed."

"Does that mean we here do not have to be alert?"

"No, Your Holiness. It is imperative a high level of security be maintained."

"Then it seems reasonable to ask for more personnel to be supplied to us, does it not."

"Yes, but a wide surveillance is already in place following more than one line of incidence."

"Then why can't a legal action be taken to stop the Nnnnmr in pursuing this alliance with the particular human faction."

"I presume such legal actions are underway. Your testimony this evening will be a part of such action."

"I don't understand why the Nnnnmr can't be stopped now, why we continue in some degree of danger. Also, if the former Emperor's men are at all involved, why that treaty can't be invoked and a stop to this business be made."

"May I suggest Your Holiness be in communication with Her Royal Highness, the Princess Nittaya for more detail than I can provide."

"Thank you, then. And thank you for coming to meet with me. I hope I have been of some assistance to you."

"Yes, you have been of substantial assistance." With that, the two Nāganese got up and left the room. Soldier went with them, but Farmer remained behind.

"Farmer, what are those strange cubes that are by the play area? Do you know?"

"I'm told they are used to lock up those invisible people you were talking about."

"Hummm. Interesting. Maybe they had something to do with them running off. I imagine they would not like to be locked up and isolated from their group."

"I don't know. I've never seen them, so I have a hard time imagining what they look like."

"Well, I've seen them, and they are strange, let me tell you. They are creatures of pure energy. They take on human shape when they need to talk with us, but they don't know how to use facial expressions. They get them all wrong. They also give creepy feelings to humans when they are present because they usually are in their energy state and invisible. A delegation tried to recruit me to form an alliance with them, but I wouldn't have anything to do with them. One of my worries is that they will form an alliance with members of the Emperor's former army and start attacking places again."

"But that would void the Emperor's peace treaty and maybe even get him killed. Wouldn't he put a stop to this kind of messing around?"

"He may not know of it. The better thing to have happen is for the Interstellar League to take action against the Whisps. That is where the heart of the problem lies."

"And while we're tightening things up, maybe we should ask for another one of those Nāgamobiles," suggested Farmer. "I don't think that old bus has much more steam left in it. All we need is for it to break down along one of these roads around this part of the country. We'd have to sit along the roadside and wait for help to come. It would put us all at risk."

"You're right. I'll write to Nittaya and ask her for a replacement."

"No, I'm not asking you to do that. If you'll approve the request I'll go through channels and make the requisition."

"You have my approval," I replied, not able to suppress a smile at how little time it takes for even simple spirits to learn bureaucracy. Suddenly stubbing my toe, "Hey, shouldn't the request originate with Fame, not me?"

"Yes, but now I can go to him and say it was all your idea. Coming from you, he won't be able to give me any guff. We'll have that new Nāgamobile in no time."

Now I had to laugh. Farmer was way ahead of me on bureaucracy. And then I remembered: "My eggs! I forgot all about my eggs. They'll die if they're not kept warm."

"Not knowing what kind of eggs you're talking about, I'd say you don't have much to worry about them getting cold in this climate. It's what? Maybe 40 degrees out right now?"

"Chicken. They're chicken eggs. Do you know what chickens are? They're meat, edible meat. Back in the days before we humans were forced to be vegans, we were carnivores. And that meant chickens. We ate lots of chickens. And we will again in the future if I can get these eggs to the people in the Valley. Oh, maybe you can help. I need the courier service to pick up the eggs and take them to the Valley. Do you know how to contact them?"

"Sure. I do," confirmed Farmer. "I'll get somebody out right away. Where are they?"

"They're in my cell, where I shall be, packing them up."

"Okay. I'm on it."

And so we parted company, with good projects to move forward.

I went directly to my cell. I felt each one of the eggs. They were as warm as eggs ever would want to be. But what if they were to hatch on the way? I had no way of knowing how far along in development they were. I thought to put the carbide pocket light to the side of each egg to try to get a look at the chicks inside. They all showed a dark shape within, but that was about all I could tell from the effort. They might even start hatching on their way to the Valley. Therefore I should plan the packing accordingly, just in case. I chose a bit larger box, poked air holes in the sides and top, then packed eggs and grass, separating each egg so it's little occupant might have room to work free of its shell and then have a bit of room to move around. Already, this was a big stretch of my imagination, having trouble picturing anything actually "hatching." I said a little prayer that these tiny spirits might fare well, and then I swiftly closed the lid and sealed it. The matter was now out of my hands and in those of fate.

Turning my thoughts back to the Whisps and the duplicity they were undertaking, I forced myself to rethink my path of logic concerning alliances they might try to form. Since an alliance with Life or me failed, where next could they try for a fruitful alliance with humans? It seemed to me there were any number of desperate humans around they might approach. Should they approach the starving they would find desperation enough but people too weak to do anything. Looking over the entire field of humanity as it exists now, the only group capable of bringing much to a bargaining table were members of the Emperor's ex-army, that is individual warlords and their squads of thugs. I could not help but feel the Whisps would come to this realization sooner than later and form an alliance with them. With such an alliance any warlord would jump at the chance, being fully cognizant of the advantage it would give him. What he wouldn't be able to determine would be the forces the Interstellar League would bring in opposition to this sordid alliance. The Whisps would undoubtedly gloss over any such opposition in dealings with the warlords, actually leading them to misjudge any potential resistance to their allied efforts. Something to consider too, the Whisps themselves may be misjudging the ability of the Interstellar League to launch an effective resistance. For that matter, I may be the one misjudging the ability of the Interstellar League to oppose the Whisps! Did you ever see such a group of lily-livered, effete, peace-at-any-price, incompetents as the Other Five? An emphatic NO! I am sure of my judgment. I know which side is the assured winner. Still, forcing myself to follow this train of thought did manage to shake me up a bit. It's always good, is it not, to rethink how the forces might stack up?

Absorbed in such thinking, a knock at my cell door brought me back to reality. Opening it, a person from the courier service asked for my parcel going to the Valley. I gave the precious container to him explaining what was inside and what safeguards needed to be taken. Hoping for even the briefest moment of repulsion to flash over his face, he took up the little parcel with total matter-of-factness, assuring me every effort would be taken in providing its successful delivery. And so it proved to be. I shall jump ahead with a quick history of this shipment of eggs. On arrival in the Valley, they were taken in hand by perhaps the greatest living expert on such things, this person fully cognizant of their significance. They were the beginning of brood stock that successfully reintroduced the chicken to humanity's table, accomplished in a mere ten years. Of course, said history did not proceed in a straight line. There were the usual ins and outs, ups and downs. I think another strain of chicken was discovered, used to expand the gene pool, resulting in a number of breeds off-shooting from this original. But I'm not sure on that point.

Back to our troubled night. Fame called a meeting for the wee hours. Life had been invited but declined. Present were Farmer and Soldier, two representatives of the Nāga guard, Fame, me, and a new liaison with the Valley, or rather with the Interstellar League, a Garuda and thoroughly impressive person. In our country Garudas were never well established in their role as temple guardians as were the Nāga, unlike our neighbor countries to the west where the Garuda were more widely acknowledged. Garudas are not shape shifters. Being perhaps two / two-and-a-half meters tall, having bird-like legs, a human-like torso, and a head disconcertingly a mixture of bird and human features, the whole being put together, not grotesquely as one might imagine, but truly magnificently with all the best possible aspects of flesh and feather. Our new Garuda, a thoroughly engaging person, agreed to our giving him a new nick name, one that we all can pronounce. It was clear he would be a stellar addition to our team. Decisions would have to be made whether he would appear in public, or not. I, for one, was all in favor of placing no restrictions on his movement. I felt the more he was seen the more quickly people would be accustomed to seeing aliens in their midst, a reality that should be widely embraced.

He brought some good news. Our new Nāgamobile would be arriving that evening, as would a new 'command center' installed with all the highest technology the Interstellar League could muster here on Earth. Both vehicles were designed to look not significantly different from the usual run of Jerry-rigged vehicles to be found in every caravan. We were told the energy source was Thorium and would not need refueling for the entire time they were in our service. We understood the one fact but not the other.

Farmer brought up an interesting issue. With three advanced vehicles at our disposal, did we really have to continue traveling with the caravan? It would be easier on us all if we were to travel at a higher speed, now being able to outrun everything else on the roads. Incidentally, this would mean leaving in the dust our problematical groupies and other looming unknowables out there we may not be aware of.

Fame countered by pointing out the potential loss of an income source in our fellow travelers, plus Life's fan club now growing exponentially. He mentioned the unusual distances between the next two cities, the potential for performing the plays and sermons helping to break up the tedium for our fellow-travelers, not to mention potential income from these people, too. He also suggested we rethink the issue as we head south once we have finished our residency in the great city there. Nearly all the river delta area from there on is inundated by the southern sea. We will need another mode of transportation and a rethinking of the security efforts. He mentioned Hero and Bright would be rejoining us in the next city and would be the ones to give the best advice on the issue since they will have just come from the area.

It was like the elephant in the room with no one mentioning those strange black cubes now prominently placed near the playing area at the bottom of the stairs in the square. Must I be the one to bring up the subject? Apparently so.

As the meeting was about to adjourn I stopped everyone in their tracks. "Why haven't any of you asked about those strange cubes out there in the square? Am I the only one who does not understand their function? Do I have to be the one who does the asking?" Apparently so, for no one picked up the hint. "Then, let me ask you, our new liaison," addressing the Garuda, "to explain their function."

"It would be my great pleasure to explain, Your Holiness," he began with a deep-bending bow. "These chambers, only just now being developed, are to trap and hold the Nnnnmr, in their manifestation as individual, before they have opportunity to return to the group. In observation, being prevented from rejoining the group causes the individual much distress, a state they would wish to avoid at all costs. The several individuals we have thus confined have yielded up much intelligence on strategies the Nnnnmr have set in motion. We are consequently confirmed on the intentions of the Nnnnmr—the conquest of Earth, the elimination of all human beings, and the establishment of the planet as colony of the Nnnnmr Empire. A motion to censure them has been introduced in the Interstellar League, but several member worlds think this too weak an action, not enough to deter them from their plans. Other proposals are currently under consideration by the League."

The Garuda's report could hardly have been more devastating. One never expects to hear of a plan to eradicate one's species from one's own planet, much less that it shall be taken over as a colony of another species' empire. I could hardly have imagined a more evil undertaking. No one else seemed the least bit troubled at the prospect, either. Once again, I was alone in being concerned over such a dire eventuality.

"All of you, wait a minute. Am I the only one disturbed at this news?" I almost shouted out to my fellow human beings.

Fame, the only person to show any concern, spoke up. "I'm sure I speak for all of us when I say we have faith in the League to come up with a solution to the problem, that there is no need to be unduly upset. They will not allow the Nnnnmr to accomplish any part of their plan, you can be sure."

"Well enough, indeed. This news fairly guarantees the Nnnnmr have set up an alliance with the warlords, and it is they who will give us the real problems. It is they that will actually do the attacking. And they will start with us." I feel tears welling up.

Fame, bless him, steps forward. "I understand your fear and think it is justified. I think we should suggest the League send an emissary to the Emperor explaining the situation, along with a reminder his life is in the balance. Should he not act, or act ineffectually, his life must be forfeit. The death of the Emperor, in turn, should be enough to cause the warlords to give a second thought to what they are doing. And the Nnnnmr, as well."

Now, the Garuda came forward. "My esteemed colleagues, I see the imperative of carrying your concerns to the League and shall do so before this night is ended," he pronounced, bowing to us all.

"Thank you," I said to him, placing my hands together before my face, bowing slightly. Feeling somewhat mollified, I announced, "I'm going now to the temple to say prayers. Anyone so inclined is welcome to join me." I turn and leave the meeting room.

Soon at the temple, I note no one has followed me. On my knees I bow to the three gilt Buddhas, chanting the appropriate prayers. Then I feel I am no longer alone. The final remnants of bitterness flee my being while beatitude takes up its sacred place in my spirit. Unsounded prayers of gratitude are sent heavenward along with those vocalized, and peace floats serenely above my head.

end
Book 3: The Questors

continue
Book 4: The Victors

Amazon Review

Dear Reader,

Thank you for choosing this book to read. I hope your reading experience was fulfilling. We all bring our own viewpoint to reading experiences. Would you consider writing a review of this book? Below is a link that will take you to the Amazon.com page where you can create your review.

Thank you, and Aloha. *author* Jerre Tanner

The Novices ~ Book 3, The Questors
Https:www.amazon.com/review/create-review/?ie=UTF8&channel=glance-detail&asin=B0B8RCFLPT

Character Sketches

THE NOVICES

the first 8 –

Full-of-Life ["Life"] – The eldest at 20 years; a natural-born leader whom others will get behind and follow; his desire to set mankind back on the path to the Stars sends the novices on their mission

Of-the-Palace ["Palace"] – The narrator; 19 years old; possessing numerous abilities but feeling inadequate to everything; he is plagued with recurrent visions of apparent significance that he cannot decipher

River – Next in age at 18; dependable, realistic; he has a firmer grasp of the workings and needs of the Novices than either Life or Palace

Dragon – Around the same age as River; his desire for revenge is so strong it drives him from the Monastery into a secret militant group

Autumn – At 17 years he feels sympathy for those younger that he and impatience with those older; he will find a dynamic place for his energies in the Valley

Dutiful –
At nearly 16 years he is still swept up in youthful emotions and fluctuates between child and adult

Peace – The youngest at 15 years he possesses the strong emotions of youth and a practical adult bent, making him useful at crucial times

Elder Lucky – Appearing out of the smoke of the funeral pyre he seems both folk demon and dotty grandfather; the young novices take him under their care where he is mostly placid, occasionally erupting into critical wisdom

THE ORPHANS

The second 8 –

Smiley – The eldest at 5 years he had been a fearful child but after the marauder attack he changed and now seems to smile perpetually

Mischief or *Rascal* – Next oldest, this child took on a *façade* of obedience while actually scheming trouble for his elders

Charming – At perhaps 4½ years this child knew he was not the most attractive of the group but took on characteristics that seemed to persuade others he was so

Little Lord – Acting beyond his age of 4, this child could memorize quickly and take on grand airs; it was discovered he had a talent for acting and was given roles of consequence in the plays that were to follow

Sweetheart – At 3 this child desperately needs to be loved and returns love in equal intensity; being light skinned, it was thought he might be the result of a mixed-race union

Baby or *Helpless* – At 1 year this child requires almost constant attention; later he becomes indulged and spoiled, making him singularly unattractive

Rose – The nun, teacher, protectress of the children, evolves into the leader of the female ecclesiastics

Faith – Widowed early, befriended by Rose, she finds a natural place in the monastic way of life

THE LAY GROUPS

The first 3 [from Brother River's extended family] –

Elder Brother – Descended from officials in the Royal Court he brings his small family to the Monastery seeking obscurity and to serve; he is of middle age, knowledgeable in practical things and of considerable help to the Novices

Lady Bird – Elder Brother's wife, a veritable powerhouse on domestic matters—cook, seamstress, you name it; becomes indispensable to the Novices

Jade – Daughter of Lady Bird's late sister, perhaps of 20 years; quiet, mousey, withdrawn, yet with several much-needed abilities

The second 3 [the hoodlums] –

Farmer – In early twenties, having fallen into a destitute life and brought into a marauder group, he was welcomed into the monastic circle, later to become security for the group and still later co-head of Security for the Monastery

Loyal – Not yet 20; orphaned at an early age and thrown on his own resources he has led a desperate life until taken into the monastic fold; there he learns mathematics and to read and write, becoming teacher to the orphan boys

Soldier – Also in early twenties, having been orphaned at an early age and finding no adult mentor to shelter him, he has suffered much and fallen into the hands of the marauders; he too is taken into the monastic group, asked to provide security for the group, later becoming co-head of Security with Farmer

THE EXECUTIVE STAFF OF THE VALLEY FOUNDATION

The Seven [all are in their late teens, early twenties] –

Fame – The Executive Director, he heads the Staff; electing to go on tour with the monastics he becomes a barker at performances, attracting audiences, conveying information on performers and performance; he handles donations and pays obligations
Angel – Fame's assistant, she is the executive in the Valley in Fame's absence; departing for the Valley she discovers she is pregnant
Lily – Chief Financial Officer, she is headquartered in the Valley where she oversees financial matters
Virtue – He is Lily's assistant and a workhorse
Hero – The head of the Department of Planning and Implementation [DPI]; his main preoccupation is the grand tour of the monastic troupe
Bright – Hero's capable assistant
Grace – The liaison between the Executive staff and the monastic staff

THE INTERSTELLAR LEAGUE

The Nāgas [Dragons, shape shifters]
Nittaya Charoënkul – Consulate head and a major force in the reclamation of Earth; her ancestors have lived here for 6,000 years
Asnee – Head of the Consulate guard
Long Dô – Chief planning executive at the Nāga Consulate; creator of the grand tour plan
Paitoon – One of the Nāga guards assigned to Palace
Saraman – A guard at the Valley; one of the Knights of the Stars

The Garudas [Half bird/ half human; major guardians of the temples]
Pen-Chān – Head of the Garuda Consulate; she and Nittaya are close friends
Captain – Name given to the Garuda head of Security on the southern part of the grand tour

The Nats [Giant human-like beings, purportedly the primordial source for human beings on Earth]

The Yaksha [Giant rotund bear-like beings both frightful to see but of high culture, specializing in epic poetry and dance]
Manjushri the XVI – Head of the Yaksha Consulate; gemstones from his ceremonial robe help in the purchase of the Valley

The Kubera [half the size of humans with big head and eyes; brilliant strategists possessing great wealth]
Good – Palace's steward onboard the luxury yacht in the inundated Delta Sea

The Nnnnmr [strange invisible beings with little personality outside the group]

OTHER CHARACTERS

Abbot Mountain – The novices' teacher; one of the marauders' victims at the start; appears to Palace in a vision pointing to the future
Abbot X – The child-like spiritual head of the monastery in the capitol city where Life and Palace are ordained
Abbot Y – The elderly abbot of the Central Highlands, warm host to the visiting troupe, bestowing manuscripts for the Valley library in appreciation of the performances at his monastery
Abbot Zed – The abbot of the Blue Guanyin, sole resident of the pagoda still standing in the midst of the shallow Delta Sea; prolific writer on many subjects; paragon for Palace to emulate in his old age
Abbot Å – The loquacious and scholarly abbot of the monastery at the far southwest, of the island/mount of some considerable historic weight; he explained at some length his knowledge of the ancient sites and artworks for his visitors
Arhat – Primarily seen in the form of sculpture, these are the early sages of Buddhism, helping to give shape to the beliefs and point the way for the followers; in modern times a movement was underway to discover and extoll what is called in these books "The Modern Arhat" to stand beside their ancient counterpart
Brother Lân – Life's friend from the monastery in the far southwest; invited the novices to come there to first join the monastery and then later to perform; he is ambiguous in portent
Brother Morning Star – Dies in Palace's arms at the beginning; later appears to Palace in a whirlwind; to be reincarnated as Palace's student and supremely inspired leader of the Valley Monastery

The Emperor – Leader of the various marauder groups and pretender to the old royal seat, himself little more than a thug

The Hermit – A wizened old monk, bringer of sage advice; appears in several guises

Lord X – Head of a much-diminished branch of the royal family; inheritor of the Valley and aspiring for it to have an elevated destiny; early supporter of the Novices

Man – Life's agent in business

Sister Fragrant – A novice nun at the devastated monastery at the city of the two crescent beaches; her spirits are revived by the visit of the novice troupe, she holding great promise as leader into the future

Acknowledgements

I am deeply indebted to the many videographers whose videos of people and places in Vietnam I watched on YouTube, especially those of the mountains in northwest Vietnam and numerous Buddhist temples throughout the country.

To Kyle Le whose many videos reuniting families, casualties of the American war, caused me to fall in love with the Vietnamese people and with Vietnam itself.

Also of great value were videos of His Holiness the XIV Dalai Lama, including documentaries of his 1959 flight from Tibet to India, and his eventual resettlement at Dharamsala.

Special thanks also to two beloved friends—my sister-in-spirit Linda Hess and Todd Farley—whose love and support through the creation of this work were a salvation.

Copyrights

For further information address: armupo@hawaii.rr.com

First paperback and eBook editions August 2022

Book design by Editions Art – Music – Poetry in consultation with Todd Farley. Cover art licensed through 123RF.

ISBN (paperback): 979-8-8440896-9-5

armupo@hawaii.rr.com *or* jtanner@hawaii.rr.com

please visit www.jerretanner.com

amazon.com/author/jerretanner

https://www.youtube.com/channel/UC1AwU1DWK0rN993-HXOO6Wg

dedicated in loving memory to

John Paul Thomas (1927 - *2001*)
and
Harvey Hess (1939 - 2012)

About the Author

Jerre Tanner has spent most of his adult life in Hawai'i composing music, contributing to the small but growing repertory of classical works based in Hawaiian culture. Several of these works have met with success including *Boy with Goldfish* recorded by the London Symphony Orchestra (1979, among the first digital recordings made), *The Kona Coffee Cantata* Prague Chamber Orchestra, Suite from *The Singing Snails* Slovak Radio Symphony Orchestra, and *Aukele (the Swimmer)* Polish Radio Symphony Orchestra.

But Tanner was also busy writing, his scenarios for operas from Hawaiian mythology being especially good preparation for the novels to come. In 2018 his first novel, *Boy with Goldfish*, emerged, the second volume in the series *Children of the Godlight* coming the next year. And then in 2019 he began the monumental *The Novices*, spreading over four books. Set in the ruins of 2170 Vietnam with death and extinction all around, the result of climate change, a handful of young Buddhist novice monks struggle to stay alive and keep faith. True to the author's musical roots, this work is like a grand opera in four acts: sweeping and lyrical, full of deep feeling. One leaves the 'opera house,' wending homeward, with soaring lyric flights still resounding in one's head.

About The Novices

In southeast Asia a hundred and fifty years in the future seven young Buddhist novice monks are survivors in a devastated world and yet another marauder attack on their monastery. In desperation they decide to abandon their ruined sanctuary and go to the far south of the country in search of asylum. Along the way they meet survivors—some doing well, others not—and temple guardians that are more than mere sculpture. We laugh with these brothers, and cry with them too. It seems they have the keys to the salvation of Mother Earth and humankind. Or do they?

Book 1 – The Dispossessed

Book 2 – The Seekers

Book 3 – The Questors

Book 4 – The Victors

Made in the USA
Columbia, SC
16 February 2023

12487221R00102